WHERE HOPE
Dwells

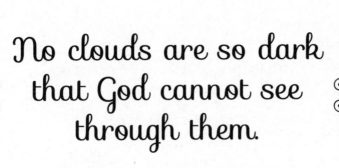

No clouds are so dark
that God cannot see
through them.

—An Amish Proverb

SUGARCREEK AMISH MYSTERIES

Blessings in Disguise
Where Hope Dwells

WHERE HOPE
Dwells

ELIZABETH LUDWIG

Guideposts

New York

To my beloved granddaughters. I am doubly blessed!

WHERE HOPE
Dwells

CHAPTER ONE

The bell above the door to the Swiss Miss chimed a greeting. Cheryl Cooper looked up from the basket she was stuffing and peeked around the long wooden counter that stretched across the back of her aunt Mitzi's gifts and sundries shop. Business had hit a lull in this awkward period between Halloween and Thanksgiving, but with Christmas around the corner, it wouldn't be long before customers once again packed the aisles.

Cheryl straightened and pasted on a bright smile for the flustered-looking woman hovering near the entrance. "Good morning. Can I help you find something?"

The woman flicked a glance in her direction then turned an almost desperate stare on the baby toys and crib mobiles on display near the window. "What can you tell me about these?"

Swiping her hands briskly against her jeans, Cheryl rounded the counter and went to stand next to her customer. "Those are all made by local craftsmen. Some of the designs have been handed down for generations. This one, for example,"—she tapped a small wooden horse on a handmade carousel mobile and sent it spinning—"was passed down by Jacob Hoffman's grandfather. Jacob owns the furniture store across the street..."

"How much?"

Cheryl blinked. "I'm sorry?"

The corner of the woman's mouth twitched. "How much for that one?"

"Well, I . . ."

Cheryl tore her gaze from the woman's thin lips and fumbled for the price tag, but the woman grasped it before Cheryl could, flipped it over, then pulled two twenty-dollar bills from her wallet.

"Keep the change."

Cheryl motioned toward the old cash register on the counter where she'd been working. "Are you sure? It'll only take a moment. I can get you a bag."

The bell tinkled again, and this time a slender woman in a brown cape dress stepped through the entrance. She carried a wooden lug crammed with jars of jam.

Cheryl spared a quick smile. "Hi, Naomi. I'll be with you in a moment."

Naomi Miller, Cheryl's friend and mystery-solving partner, shook her head. "No rush. Do you need me to get anything ready for you to take to the farm?"

"Nope. I've got it all together. It's over there on the counter." Cheryl returned her gaze to the woman. "As I was saying . . ."

But the woman was already slipping the mobile into a large pewter-colored purse with initials emblazoned across its front. "I don't need a bag. Thank you."

She hurried to the door before Cheryl could protest.

A frown bunched Naomi's brow as she too watched the woman scurry away. "What was that all about?"

A feeling of unease pressed on Cheryl's chest as she watched the woman scuttle down the sidewalk and out of sight. She shrugged and turned from the window. "Tourists. Who knows?"

Chuckling, Naomi followed her to the back of the store. "Sorry I'm so late." She lifted the lug. "A few of these jars looked dusty, so I decided to wash them before I put them on the shelves."

At the sound of Naomi's cheerful voice, Cheryl's Siamese cat, Beau, leaped from his spot on the counter to weave figure eights around her feet.

She set down the jams and bent to tickle his chin. "Looks like someone is happy to see me."

"He's always happy to see you. So am I." Cheryl smiled and turned the basket on the counter so that Naomi could see it. Festooned with blue bows and a card that read *Congratulations* in neat, curvy script, she said, "What do you think?"

Naomi fingered the slender strips of satin. "Is this ribbon new?"

"Just got it last week." Cheryl reached under the counter for two handmade baby rattles, one shaped like a fish, the other a bird, and tucked them into the raffia lining the bottom of the basket. "With all the babies being born around Sugarcreek, I had to set these aside." She stepped back and eyed the basket critically. "Well?"

"Very nice." Naomi nodded approvingly then lifted the strap of a floppy tote from around her neck and laid it on the counter. Folding open the flap, she removed two baby quilts. One featured a traditional log cabin pattern, and the other featured a playful figure embroidered in each of six blocks.

Cheryl gasped and smoothed her palm over the quilts. "Oh, Naomi."

"I thought you would like them.",

"I love them, and so will the Swartzentrubers. They're beautiful." Struck with a thought, she frowned. "You don't think this gift is too extravagant?"

Naomi's gentle smile warmed Cheryl's heart. "Not at all. The family will be blessed by your thoughtfulness."

Cheryl shook her head and tucked the blankets next to the rattles. "You did all the work. I just provided the cloth."

"Do not make light of your contribution, Cheryl. Generosity, in itself, is a gift. You administer yours faithfully."

Though Naomi was shorter by nearly four inches, Cheryl had learned to look up to her friend. Certain her cheeks were as red as her hair, she gave the basket a final pat. "Okay then, I guess it's ready. Sure you don't want to come with me?"

"*Ja*, I'm sure." A shadow flitted over Naomi's face, and she lowered her gaze. "When Esther gets here to tend the store, I thought I'd pay a visit to Rebecca Zook."

Silence descended at the mention of the grieving mother, so recently made childless.

"Besides," Naomi said, her tone brightening, "I need to get these jars on the shelves." She gestured toward a vacant spot. "I also brought a few more jars of apple butter and pumpkin butter."

Cheryl smiled mischievously. "Still no hope of wrangling the recipes from you, I suppose?"

Naomi wrinkled her nose and tugged on the strings dangling from her bonnet.

Cheryl laughed. Hooking one arm through the basket, she said, "All right, then. Thanks again for watching the shop. Please tell Esther I'll see her this afternoon."

Purring loudly, Beau rubbed against Naomi's stockinged leg.

"What about him?" Naomi bent to pick him up. Cradled in her arms, Beau peered at Cheryl through narrowed lids.

She sighed. "You're right. I'll have to run him home first." Fortunately, it was only four blocks and the mild fall weather made the trip pleasant.

"Or I could take him," Naomi offered, tickling Beau's chin and earning another loud purr.

"You don't mind?"

She clucked gently and shooed Cheryl with a wave of her hand. "Go on, now. Tell the Swartzentrubers hello and let them know I'll come around to check on them next week."

"Will do. I know they'll be very glad to see you."

Though no longer a stranger, Cheryl was still amazed by the closeness of the Amish community at Sugarcreek. Their concern and care for one another was a far cry from the harried lifestyle she'd left behind in Columbus.

She drew in a lungful of crisp country air as she left the store and hurried to the used Ford Focus she'd driven to work in lieu of her normal walk. She grimaced as she folded herself into the driver's seat, the top of her jeans pinching into her waist. So much for shedding a few pounds. Naomi's cooking had nipped that idea, but quick. She determined to get in some exercise after she left the Swartzentrubers'.

Pushing aside thoughts of a diet, Cheryl concentrated on the short drive. The dairy farm wasn't hard to find now that she'd acclimated to the landscape. The first couple of weeks had been a nightmare of new roads and obscure landmarks. Now she felt right at home among the lush hills and farms of Tuscarawas County in eastern Ohio.

A dog's bark greeted her as she pulled into the Swartzentrubers' driveway. Though gruff, she'd learned not to fear old Rufus's warning. A simple dog biscuit could quiet him in a hurry. Smiling, she withdrew a treat she'd tucked into a side pocket of her purse and tossed it over the fence to him before making her way up the stone path to the front door.

Rachel Swartzentruber welcomed her after the first knock. "*Guder mariye*, Cheryl. You are out and about early today."

Like herself, Rachel was an outsider to the Amish community, having only recently joined the church. But she was trying hard to adopt all of their ways, including a few of the Pennsylvania Dutch words and phrases her husband used.

"Good morning, Rachel."

Cheryl accepted a brief hug before being ushered inside. It was nice to have someone who could relate to all she was going through to gain acceptance in the Amish community. But sometime during the recent mystery of foreboding notes and strange additions to the Swiss Miss's inventory, she'd made friends. Many of the families had already dropped the formality with which they treated most

Englischers. A few others were still warming to her, but she felt like she was making Sugarcreek her home.

"The twins are sleeping," Rachel said, sighing wearily. "I just got them settled and was about to sit down for some coffee. Would you like some?"

Since she hadn't taken time for her ritual caffeine, a steaming cup of coffee sounded wonderful. Cheryl nodded and followed Rachel into the quaint farmhouse kitchen.

"The boys still having colic trouble?" she asked, pulling a chair out from the massive oak table that dominated the space.

Rachel nodded. "Well, Joseph is, anyway," she said as she poured two cups from a blue enamelware percolator then carried them to the table along with a sugar bowl and creamer filled with heavy cream. She passed a mug to Cheryl, who ignored the sugar but added a substantial amount of cream to her cup. She missed the morning frappe stops on her way to work back when she lived in Columbus, but she had to admit, fresh coffee brewed over a propane stove was a delicacy she was learning to enjoy just as much.

"I wish I knew what was causing the stomachaches," Rachel continued. Worried lines marred her brow. "Joseph especially suffers from cramps. He keeps us all awake at night."

Which explained the dark circles below her eyes. Cheryl nodded sympathetically and took a cautious sip.

Rachel sat then said, "Perhaps I should be thankful the boys are fraternal twins and not identical. Their personalities and constitutions seem to be totally different even at this early age, not to mention their looks. You'll see when they wake up, John favors me and Joseph looks more like my husband. I can't imagine, though, what I'd do if John were as fussy as Joseph." She gestured to the basket at Cheryl's feet. "So what is that you have brought with you?"

"Oh, I almost forgot. It's a gift." Cheryl set her cup aside and lifted the basket for her to see. "It's from me and Naomi. I hope you like it."

Rachel accepted the basket with a sincere thank-you. "These are beautiful," she said, fingering the stitched edges on the log cabin blanket. "That Naomi Miller is quite the seamstress. I only wish I could sew half as well. I simply haven't mastered the patience required."

Cheryl pointed to the dark blue curtains draped above the kitchen sink. "It appears you're learning. Those are new, aren't they?"

Happiness flushed Rachel's cheeks. "They are not so complicated as Naomi's blankets, but I am pleased with the way they have turned out."

"They're sweet," Cheryl said and patted her hand encouragingly. Rachel was a new wife and mother, and everything she did displayed how important it was to her that she make the farmhouse feel like home. Cheryl had felt the same way once... back when she'd almost been a bride.

She squelched the thought—and the bitter feelings that accompanied it—and turned her thoughts to Naomi's thirty-year-old stepson, Levi. Before coming to Sugarcreek, Cheryl would never have believed she'd entertain romantic notions again—and for an Amish man, no less! Could there be a more different way of life? Yet Rachel and Samuel had found a way to make it work.

Rufus's bark drifting from the front yard cut short her thoughts. Cheryl quirked an eyebrow. "Were you expecting someone else?"

Rachel shook her head. She started to rise, but the dog quickly fell silent. She grimaced and returned to her chair. "Must have been a squirrel. I just hope he doesn't wake the boys."

No sound carried from the nursery, so the two women resumed chatting. Before long, an hour had slipped by. The coffeepot was empty and so was Cheryl's cup. She smiled and rose to leave.

"I know you're busy. I won't keep you any longer, Rachel."

"Thank you for the visit," she replied, standing with her. "It was nice to enjoy some adult conversation."

Cheryl hesitated by the door. "Still no word from your family, I take it?"

A fleeting look of sorrow crossed Rachel's features, and she shook her head. Though they'd been born and raised in Tuscarawas County, her mother and father had not approved of her decision to join the Amish community, and they rarely visited. No doubt, choosing to leave the life she'd known had been difficult for Rachel. Heat warmed Cheryl's face. Was the right man incentive enough to try?

She squeezed Rachel's shoulder. "They'll come around, especially now that they have two fine grandsons."

Rachel ducked her head. "I pray you are right. Samuel doesn't say so, but it hurts him that my parents are so unaccepting."

A crimp gripped Cheryl's heart. She'd been wary of the Amish lifestyle herself, and not so long ago. Ignorance could be a crippling thing.

"Keep praying for them," she whispered. "God will speak to their hearts."

Tears filled Rachel's eyes, but she nodded and opened her mouth to speak. Her words were curtailed by an infant's angry wail. Using a corner of her apron to dab at her red eyes, she managed a watery smile.

"There's Joseph, right on cue. Will you excuse me, Cheryl? I'll get him for you if you'd like to take a peek before you go."

Cheryl laughed and motioned toward the hall leading off of the kitchen. "Better hurry or we'll have two squalling babies on our hands."

Rachel's head bobbed in agreement. "That is true. It doesn't take Joseph long to get John riled up. I'll be right back."

Her rubber-soled shoes made barely a sound against the hardwood floor. Cheryl waited patiently, the soft ticking of the mantel clock in the family room marking the seconds. It was certainly a quiet life the Amish lived, with no hum of electricity to fill the air, no squawking television to interrupt conversation or divert attention. A gust from the half-open window riffled the curtains, and Cheryl realized she had even learned to appreciate the whisper of a gentle breeze—something she'd never taken time to notice in Columbus.

"John?"

Rachel's voice carried from the nursery, a surprising note of urgency adding sharpness to her tone. In the background, Joseph continued to wail.

Cheryl furrowed her brow. "Rachel? Is everything all right?" When she received no answer, she took a hesitant step toward the hall. "Rachel?"

"John!"

A second later, the peace Cheryl had been appreciating was shattered by a mother's frantic scream.

Chapter Two

Cheryl pushed through the entrance to the Swiss Miss, closed the door behind her with a firm click and locked it, then flipped the sign. Closing time was still over an hour away, but this was no ordinary workday and she couldn't face customers. Though the trembling had left her limbs, the sick feeling in the pit of her stomach remained. Little John Swartzentruber was gone, and the only explanation was that someone had stolen him from his crib while she and Rachel sipped coffee and laughed.

Cheryl pushed away from the door. The Sugarcreek police had been contacted and an AMBER Alert™ issued. Neighbors were being questioned. Rachel's husband, Samuel, and several of the church elders had organized a local search. It was all anyone could do, but it didn't feel like nearly enough.

Naomi hurried around the counter toward her. "Anything?"

Anxiety pulled at her features just as her fingers pulled at the white cotton fabric of the apron tied around her waist. It was unnerving to see anything but steadfast peace on Naomi's face—on any of the faces of the members of the Amish community. Yet everyone Cheryl had seen since the discovery of the missing infant mirrored the same tense look.

Finally, Cheryl managed a slow shake of her head. "Nothing. Rachel is devastated, as is Samuel."

Sorrow soaked Naomi's gaze. She sighed then lowered her face while she smoothed the wrinkles from her apron. When she looked up, a small portion of peace had returned to ease the lines of worry around her lips and brow. "We will continue to seek *Gott*. His eye is on that child as surely as it is on the sparrow."

Seek God. Cheryl had done nothing else from the moment the empty crib was discovered. All during the police questioning, she had pleaded with the Lord for insight into John's whereabouts...more when she'd driven back to town and around Sugarcreek hoping for the smallest clue or sign. Unfortunately, God remained silent and the baby remained missing. Why, oh why, had Cheryl chosen today to visit? Perhaps if Rachel hadn't been distracted—

Naomi gestured toward the small table where the Vogel brothers played checkers four times a week. "Sit. I've made tea." Her warm hands closed around Cheryl's. "We could both use a cup."

What Cheryl needed couldn't be brewed in a teapot, but she trudged to sit at the table. Moments later, Naomi returned and set a wooden tray down with a clatter. She poured a cup and pressed it into Cheryl's hands.

"Now," she said firmly, pulling out the other chair, "what exactly happened at the Swartzentrubers' farm?"

Tension gripped Cheryl by the shoulders. "I wish I knew. One minute Rachel and I were enjoying a nice visit, and the next..." She trailed to misery-sodden silence.

Naomi rubbed her chin thoughtfully with her thumb. "Cheryl, did Rachel mention how long it had been since she'd laid the boys in their beds?"

Naomi's calm, practical approach revived Cheryl's sagging spirits. She pushed up in the chair to think.

"Well...I believe she said she had just gotten them settled when I arrived." She scratched her temple. "I remember thinking she must have been up all night because she looked so tired."

Naomi's fingers stroked the strings of her bonnet. "No doubt. With newborns in the house, twins especially, sleep is a rare thing." She leaned forward in the chair, braced both elbows on the table, and cupped her mug with both hands. "And how long was it before she went to check on them?"

"I was there a little over an hour."

Naomi's brow furrowed. "Not a lot of time for someone to get in and out again."

Cheryl's eyebrows rose. "They had to have been watching the house."

"And knew that Rachel would be preoccupied."

Dread squeezed Cheryl's heart. Naomi was thinking the same thing she feared. "You think this was premeditated?"

"Don't you?"

Cheryl blew out a breath, appalled that whoever had taken John Swartzentruber had used her presence as a diversion. "Who would do such a terrible thing? And why only take one of the boys? It's horrible to think about, but why would they snatch one from his crib and not the other?"

Naomi shook her head, her dark brown eyes troubled. "I assume the police questioned you?"

Cheryl shuddered. "Yes, though I don't think I was much help. And Rachel was too upset to recall much of anything."

"Perhaps that will change once she's had a chance to calm down. I think I will send Levi by their place later with a canister of my special medicinal tea. The chamomile in it is good for the calming of one's nerves."

"I know you work wonders with your home remedies, Naomi, but if it were me, I have a feeling it would take more than a cup of tea to calm down, no matter how good it was. I'd only get more upset as time passed."

Naomi's mention of Levi sparked a mental image of his face. How would he react to such news? Heat washed through her as she realized she already knew. He would look to God, find peace and strength in his faith, just like his father and stepmother—peace Cheryl feared she might never again know.

Afraid of where her thoughts had taken her, she cleared her throat and continued. "For now, we're just supposed to make a list of everything we can remember and turn it in to the police this afternoon."

"That's *goot*." Naomi rose and pulled some paper and a pencil from the drawer under the cash register. Crossing back to the table, she sat and wrote the date and time Cheryl had left the store in neat, careful script.

As she'd done when questioned by the police, Cheryl recited everything she could remember, from the time she'd arrived at the farm to the moment Rachel had gone to check on the boys. She even described in detail what she and Rachel had talked about.

"It was an ordinary visit, Naomi." She gripped the handle of her mug tightly. "I mean, shouldn't there have been some warning that something was wrong?"

Cheryl went still as a sliver of a memory flitted through her brain.

Naomi looked up from the paper. "What is it?" When Cheryl didn't respond, she reached to clasp her fingers. "Cheryl? Are you all right?"

Cheryl rose and paced the narrow space between the display cases. When she reached the end, she turned and motioned toward the door. "Naomi, I think we should go back out to the farm."

Her chin lifted and her eyes shone expectantly. "You have remembered something?"

"Maybe."

"What?"

It was such a small thing, but the officer who'd questioned her said every detail was important. She shrugged and raked her fingers through her spiky hair. "Rufus."

Naomi gave a puzzled frown. "Who?"

"The Swartzentrubers' dog. He barked."

Uncertainty mingled with doubt flashed across Naomi's face. "Dogs bark, Cheryl. What is unusual about that?"

Cheryl tugged her car keys from her jeans pocket and held them aloft. "Maybe he saw something we didn't."

"And that helps us, how?"

In all honesty, she didn't have a clue, but driving out to the farm beat loitering around the Swiss Miss.

She jangled the keys. "It's just a hunch, but I still think it's worth checking out. You coming?"

Naomi's brows crinkled as she deliberated, and then she rose from her chair with a determined nod. "Ja, I'm coming. Like you say, it is worth checking out."

The two left the store, and scant minutes later Cheryl pulled into the Swartzentrubers' driveway for the second time that day. Police cars no longer lined the road in front of the house, but several buggies were parked outside. In the gathering gloom of early evening, they hunkered like funeral home hearses in one long row. Naomi motioned toward the house.

"I will go inside, see if anyone has learned anything new. You check on Rufus. If you find anything, send one of the children for me."

Cheryl nodded and waited until Naomi had slipped inside before circling around to the fenced part of the yard. As before, Rufus greeted her with a happy bark, completely unaware of the turmoil affecting his owners.

"Sorry, boy," Cheryl said, giving the old hound a pat on the head. "No doggie biscuits this time."

It took some effort, but she managed to finagle through the gate without letting Rufus out. The dog stared up at her, his round, soulful eyes full of question. He watched while Cheryl snooped around the yard, and then he sniffed at her hands when she bent to peer into his doghouse.

"Nothing, eh, boy?" Cheryl said, pulling her head from the curved doorway.

In answer, Rufus snorted once and then bounded across the yard to dig at a spot near the fence. The distraction allowed Cheryl to finish her search of the yard in peace.

Not even a footprint.

Discouraged, she dusted off her hands and then braced them on her hips to stretch her back. The air had turned colder now that the sun had dipped behind a bank of gray clouds. Soon it would disappear out of sight. Cheryl blew out a sigh. Could she have been wrong about the bark being a signal?

At the fence, Rufus's hindquarters waggled furiously. At the very least, she could help him find whatever it was he was looking for.

She picked her way across the yard and then bent to give the dog's collar a tug. "Move, boy. Let me see what you're after."

The hole Rufus had dug had grown to the size of a football and stretched under the bottom of the fence, but aside from mud and roots, she saw nothing to claim a dog's interest.

She gave her leg a pat. "C'mon, Rufus, let's go see how Naomi is doing."

The dog refused to budge. After only a quick glance in her direction, he went back to sniffing at the ground—or more accurately, the fence. He let out a low whine then flopped on to his side and burrowed his nose in the hole.

"Rufus, c'mon." She gave her leg another pat. "I promise I'll bring you a treat next time I come."

At the word *treat*, his front paws clawed into overdrive.

"Rufus."

Exasperated, Cheryl nudged toward the fence and peered over. The cooler weather had turned the tall grass on the other side brittle and brown. She couldn't see anything, but obviously the dog was aware of something beyond her sight. Curious now, she let herself out of the gate and scurried to the section of the yard that Rufus seemed determined to claim. Using her boot, she swept aside the calf-high grass. After only a few steps, she spotted the prize Rufus's nose had told him lay just outside his domain. Cheryl's heart skipped as she crouched for closer examination.

It was a bone. Not the natural kind, but the store-bought doggie treat that Cheryl kept with her on occasion when she visited. When she wanted to keep the dog quiet.

Or when someone else did.

Chapter Three

Fortunately, the bag of carrot sticks Cheryl had tossed into her purse before leaving the house that morning still snuggled in the space between a pack of tissues and her wallet. After emptying the uneaten vegetables into the trash, she managed to scoop up the bone and fold it into the baggie without touching it—a precaution that was completely wasted if the Swartzentrubers had supplied the treat and it had somehow ended up outside the fence.

Rufus whined as she tucked the bag into a pocket of her purse.

"Sorry, boy. This one's not for you."

Cheryl signaled Naomi from the doorway and then settled onto the seat of her Ford Focus.

Naomi was slightly out of breath as she climbed in beside her. "You have found something?"

Cheryl nodded faster than a woodpecker on an oak tree as she held up the ziplock bag with trembling fingers. "I think so. Look."

Naomi examined it curiously. "Cheryl, this is a dog bone."

"I know. I found it outside the fence."

"So?"

"So what if the kidnapper used this bone, or one like it, to distract Rufus while they snuck inside?"

Apprehension clouded Naomi's face. "If this is so, should you have touched it?"

Cheryl shook her head. "I didn't touch it. I used the ziplock, but I doubt it matters. It's a textured surface, which means collecting fingerprints will be difficult if not impossible."

Naomi nodded. The two of them had learned a little about conducting investigations after someone began leaving mysterious messages inside the Swiss Miss a few weeks back.

"Ja, that is true. Shall we speak to the Swartzentrubers? See if they know how this bone came to be in their yard?"

Cheryl nodded, her hand already reaching for the door handle. When neither Rachel nor Samuel claimed to have seen the bone before, she and Naomi headed back into town to drop off the contents of the baggie at the police station. As they passed the Old Amish Store, a worried frown pulled at Naomi's lips.

"Cheryl, the woman who was in the Swiss Miss this morning...have you seen her before?"

She shook her head. "I didn't get a name either, and she paid with cash, so no chance of lifting her name off a credit card receipt."

"But she bought a baby toy, ja?"

She shrugged and turned off Main Street into the parking lot of the Sugarcreek police station. "Lots of people buy toys, Naomi," she said, but she understood what Naomi was hinting at, and a niggle of suspicion wormed into Cheryl's head.

Naomi pulled at her bottom lip. "I suppose. Still, something about the woman seemed strange to me. She was in such a hurry to leave."

Cheryl pondered that as she and Naomi strode up the sidewalk and went inside. The woman had seemed a bit harried. What if her urgency had been caused by the need to arrive at the Swartzentruber farm before Samuel returned home? Perhaps whoever took the baby believed Rachel would be there alone. Cheryl's presence had simply provided a welcome distraction.

Her steps faltered as she realized that the woman must have seen the basket on the counter when Cheryl had pointed it out to Naomi, or maybe she had overheard some of their conversation. It wasn't a far stretch to think the woman might have learned that it was for the Swartzentrubers.

Fresh anger and guilt warmed her cheeks as she and Naomi stopped by the desk of Delores Delgado, the police station receptionist and all around girl Friday.

Cheryl pointed toward the back of the station. "Good morning, Delores. The chief in?"

She peered up at them from behind a pair of black-rimmed glasses. "He is." She cast a warning look over her shoulder then dipped her head to whisper conspiratorially, "He's a bit grumpy though. Sure you need to visit with him right now?"

Cheryl stifled a groan. "Great. Do you know why?"

Delores shrugged and pushed a lock of frizzy dark hair behind her ear. "The Swartzentruber kidnapping has him worked up."

Hope flared in Cheryl's chest. "Actually, that's why we're here. Maybe we can help."

Delores look skeptical, but she buzzed the chief's office and then waved Cheryl and Naomi in.

Good luck, she mouthed as they passed.

Indeed Chief of Police Sam Twitchell looked to have storm clouds brewing over his head. He hunched over his desk, an entire atlas worth of maps and paper spread out before him. He glanced up as they entered and rose. "Mornin', ladies. What can I do for you today?"

"Thank you for seeing us, Chief," Cheryl said. "We know you're busy."

"That I am." He gestured to a couple of chairs opposite his desk and sat when they did. He wasted no time on pleasantries but cut immediately to the chase. "So? Delores says you think you may have something that could help with the Swartzentruber case?"

Cheryl reached into her purse and presented him with the ziplock bag and its contents. He quickly confirmed what she and Naomi feared—fingerprints would more than likely be undetectable.

Cheryl leaned forward to press both palms on the desk. "What about determining where the bone was purchased? Samuel and Rachel said they've never seen it before."

Naomi sat with her hands folded tightly in her lap, the white skin on her knuckles exposing her inner tension. "That's right. The kidnapper could have used it..."

Chief Twitchell held up a large hand in a move that Cheryl's father had done many times when staving arguments from his children. "Ladies, please. I appreciate your tryin' to help, but one dog treat isn't much to go on, especially a brand that can be purchased in any grocery or pet store. I buy these same treats for my own dog."

Cheryl blew out a disappointed sigh. She knew the bone wasn't much of a clue, but she'd hoped for a better response than the one they'd just received. The tension in her stomach returned full force.

Chief Twitchell straightened in his chair to direct a firm look at Cheryl. "Besides, you have more important things to worry about. Have you had a chance to work on that list I asked for?"

She plucked it from her purse and handed it to him. "It's everything I can remember. If I think of anything else, I'll call you."

His cheeks wobbled as he nodded. "Good. Now I suggest you two go on home. Especially you, Miss Cooper. A good night's rest might jog your memory."

Except she doubted she'd rest—not with Baby John still missing and no one any closer to discovering where his kidnapper had taken him.

A deep sigh did little to dispel the concern weighing heavily on Cheryl's chest as she and Naomi exited the police station. She let the glass door slip from her fingers and *whoosh* shut. "Well, I suppose the chief is right. We probably should get some rest."

"Probably." Instead of moving away, Naomi eyed Cheryl steadily, giving the distinct impression that she had more on her mind.

"Although…" Cheryl scratched her temple, perking up a bit as an idea struck. "It's still rather early and neither of us have eaten supper. We could always stop by Yoder's and grab a quick bite before we turn in for the night."

Naomi tipped her head as though considering. "Well, tonight is Elizabeth's night to prepare the meal and the family knows to go on without me if I'm not there…"

"And you know," Cheryl continued, faster, "the Village Inn is not too far off of Main Street. After we eat, we could pop in…just to see if anyone new has checked in recently—anyone with a baby."

"Or to see if the staff have noticed any strangers hanging around town."

Cheryl stuck out her hand. "Dinner?"

Naomi gave it a firm shake. "Dinner. And then we ask a few questions."

It beat going home to an empty house, where there was no happy chatter to dampen the echo of Cheryl's guilty conscience. "Agreed."

After gulping a hasty meal that did *not* include Yoder's famous cinnamon rolls, Cheryl and Naomi wound past the main street of Sugarcreek until they reached a large, two-story inn with brick and clapboard siding. Alongside it, two railroad cars had been converted into guest suites. Though she hadn't expected to stumble on to any major clues at the first place they visited, Cheryl was still disappointed when a conversation with the proprietors, Jeb and Molly Bakker, failed to reveal any new information.

"I'm not ready to give up," Cheryl said as they left the inn.

Naomi frowned, obviously as disappointed as Cheryl felt. "There are several more bed-and-breakfasts and inns and such in the area. We could check a couple and then finish up tomorrow if we don't find anything."

Urgency filtered up from Cheryl's midsection. She snapped her fingers. "Yes. If the woman is staying in Sugarcreek or close by, someone is bound to know...or knew," she corrected, realizing as she spoke that the woman could have already hightailed it out of Ohio.

Naomi gestured in the direction of the Swiss Miss. "Your aunt Mitzi used to keep a phone book at the store. Maybe if we look through the yellow pages..."

"For what?"

"A list of all the hotels in the area," Naomi said, frowning as if Cheryl had lost her mind.

Chuckling, Cheryl tugged her cell phone from her pocket. "We don't need to look through the phone book. That's what search engines are for."

"Search engines?"

"You type in your question, and the search engine 'searches' the Internet for the information."

"Like Google."

Cheryl's mouth dropped open. "How...?"

Naomi's lips twitched then turned in a smile.

"Never mind."

Naomi and her family managed without electricity. They didn't own computers, cell phones, or modern appliances, but that didn't mean they were ignorant of the world, even if they didn't take part in it. Not to mention that her children had gone, or were still going through, their *rumspringa*.

Cheryl typed in her query and soon had a list of possible locations. The first two places were within walking distance, but their elicited responses revealed nothing. They approached the third place—an older Victorian-style house—with a little less enthusiasm. A sign on the fence read Little Switzerland Bed-and-Breakfast.

"I know this place," Naomi said, pushing open the gate. "Laura and Frank Early opened it a couple of years ago. They bought it from some friends of your aunt Mitzi who moved away to take care of their elderly parents."

The place was well kept and inviting. A wheat wreath adorned a brightly colored door. A brick path led to cream-colored steps framed on both sides with potted mums. And in honor of fall, Indian corn spilled out from baskets carefully situated in the flowerbeds. It was exactly the kind of place Cheryl had dreamed of calling home before Lance broke off their engagement.

For the second time that day, Cheryl tamped a bitter twinge. Funny how he'd been surfacing in her thoughts lately, especially since she'd determined months ago to close the door on that part of life.

Lifting her chin, she shook free of thoughts of Lance and marched inside the bed-and-breakfast to the reception desk. Seeing no one, she turned to Naomi and motioned toward a brass bell on the counter. "Should we ring?"

Naomi nodded, and a few seconds later, a short woman with graying hair entered from a hall near the back.

"Naomi Miller? How good to see you."

She crossed to Naomi and offered a quick hug then turned to Cheryl questioningly. "Who is your friend?"

Naomi extended her hand. "Laura, this is my friend, Cheryl Cooper. She is Mitzi's niece."

The confusion cleared from the woman's brow, replaced with a sudden wash of warmth that Cheryl had grown to expect when introduced in this way. One thing was for certain, her aunt had been a well-known and loved figure of the community.

"It's a pleasure to meet you, Mrs. Early," Cheryl said.

She waved dismissively. "Call me Laura. How is your aunt Mitzi?" Laura asked after giving Cheryl's hand a hearty shake. "We sure do miss her around here."

"I just got a letter from her. She's loving it." Cheryl smiled. "Everything she writes exudes excitement. I definitely think she made the right choice leaving for the mission field after all these years. Except for when my uncle was alive, I don't think she's ever been happier."

Laura's face beamed with pleasure. "I'm so glad to hear that. Many times I heard your aunt Mitzi talk about what it would be like to become a missionary. I'm thrilled that she found the courage to follow that call."

Though she missed her aunt, running the store had been just the reprieve Cheryl needed. She nodded. "Thank you."

Laura turned to Naomi. "Now, what can I help you ladies with today? I know you're not inquiring about a room."

Naomi shook her head. "Not a room, exactly. More like a guest list."

Confusion returned to cloud Laura's gaze. "Guest list?"

Naomi nodded. "Have you had any new arrivals in the past couple of days?"

Laura shot an apologetic glance first at Naomi and then Cheryl. "I'm sorry, Naomi, but we don't share information regarding our guests."

Cheryl held up her hand. "No, no…nothing like that. Naomi and I were just wondering if you've had any out-of-towners check in recently. Maybe someone who has never visited before."

Laura still appeared reluctant. Cheryl gestured toward a sofa flanked by a set of overstuffed wingback chairs in the parlor. "If you'll give us a moment, we'll explain."

Laura only hesitated a second before proceeding toward the sofa. Once they were seated, she fixed her gaze on Naomi. "What is all this about?"

Naomi drew a deep breath, her clasped hands resting lightly in her lap. "You heard about the Swartzentruber boy?"

She nodded. "Terrible. I take it there's been no sign of him?"

Naomi shook her head. "None."

Laura's brows lifted. "And Cheryl was…?"

"Present when the baby was taken," Cheryl said, her chest tight.

Laura clucked her tongue sadly. "I'm so sorry."

Cheryl scooted to the edge of her chair. "We're sorry too, which is why we decided to do a little investigating. You see, a woman came into the Swiss Miss this morning."

Drawing a breath, she quickly explained the reason for their visit. As she spoke, a look passed over Laura's face that could only be described as apprehensive.

"And this woman you saw," Laura said, her teeth worrying her bottom lip, "you say she had dark hair?"

Cheryl motioned just below her chin. "Shoulder length. Neat. Kind of a modern cut, if you know what I mean."

"And she was thin?" Laura held up her hand. "About so tall and wearing glasses?"

Both she and Naomi nodded. On Naomi's face, Cheryl saw reflected the same excitement that she felt.

"Not sure about the glasses, but I guess she could have put them on later. So?" Naomi prompted. "Have you seen her?"

Laura looked from one to the other and then gave a slow nod. "I believe so." She lifted her palm before Cheryl could speak. "I believe I've seen the woman you're looking for, but I'm very sorry, ladies. I'm afraid you're too late."

"Too late!" Cheryl sucked in a breath. "What do you mean?"

Laura's gaze passed between Naomi and Cheryl. "That woman checked out several hours ago. I'm sorry, ladies. She's gone."

CHAPTER FOUR

Cheryl's stomach settled to the very bottom of her shoes. Though she'd heard the words correctly, a futile mixture of hope and disbelief bade her repeat them. "Gone? Are you certain? When?"

Laura nodded and pushed a lock of hair behind her ear. "The woman you're looking for is named Theresa Cox. She was a guest here, but I'm sorry, ladies. She checked out this afternoon."

A clock against the far wall ticked off the seconds. Dismay, urgent and pressing, crept over Cheryl on icy fingers. If Theresa was gone, and had been for several hours, she could be anywhere. And in any direction. Akron-Canton was the closest large airport. If she was headed there, they might never find her. Cheryl could almost feel Baby John slipping farther away.

She grasped her knees to keep her hands from trembling. Leaning forward, she fixed Laura with an earnest stare. "By any chance, do you remember if Ms. Cox was alone and about what time she checked out?"

"Yes, she was alone."

No baby. The relief she felt at hearing those words made Cheryl glad she was sitting. Her knees might have given way otherwise.

Laura motioned toward the front desk. "I wrote down the exact time. I can look if you like, but really, I'm pretty good at remembering these things. It was just after noon. Surprised me too."

"Surprised you?" Naomi's eyebrows rose. "Why? Was that too late?"

She shook her head. "Not too late. The woman paid in advance. She still had a whole day left on her tab. I normally need forty-eight hours' notice to issue a refund, but I told Ms. Cox I'd do it since we didn't lose any customers. We've got several empty rooms. Business won't start picking up again until right before Christmas." She shrugged. "She didn't seem to care either way. People with money don't, I suppose."

Curiosity piqued in Cheryl's mind. That was odd. Maybe, if she proved to be the kidnapper, she had actually planned to take Baby John tomorrow and something had changed her strategy— like the distraction provided by an unexpected visitor.

She swallowed the knot that rose in her throat. "Uh...did she say *why* she was leaving early?"

Laura's lips pinched into a thin line. "I assumed it was business that called her away, but now I'm not so sure."

"What about her car? Did you happen to see what she was driving?" Cheryl pressed.

"I could check. We write it on the guest receipt so we know which vehicles are in the parking lot."

She rose, riffled through the receipts until she found the one she wanted, then carried it back to where Cheryl and Naomi waited. "Here it is. Says she drove a gray panel van, like the ones florists use for making deliveries." Her eyes widened. "You don't think she had anything to do with John Swartzentruber's disappearance, do you?"

"Let's just say we're not ruling anyone out," Cheryl replied carefully. "Anyway, thank you very much for your time. And if Ms. Cox should happen to reappear, would you mind calling?"

She pulled a business card from her purse and handed it to her. Laura examined the number on the front and then shuddered.

"I'll definitely give you a call. I sure hope they find that little boy. I would just hate to think that all this time I was harboring a fugitive!"

"Now, now," Naomi soothed, "we did not say she was a fugitive. In fact, we are only hoping to locate this woman so we can ask her a few questions."

"Of course." Laura's fingers shook as she slid the card into her pocket and rose with them. "Thank you for coming by, ladies. I'll keep my eyes and ears open and let you know first thing if I learn anything."

Cheryl thanked her again, and then she and Naomi returned to the car.

"I should be getting on home," Naomi said, hurrying around to the passenger side. "Seth will be wondering where I have been."

"Home?" Cheryl stopped and turned to stare at her friend. "But...shouldn't we tell Chief Twitchell? Maybe he can put out an APB on Ms. Cox or something."

Naomi shot her a quizzical glance. "For what? Checking out too early?"

"Of course not. But her actions are definitely suspicious." Cheryl reached for her door handle. "It may be just a hunch, but I really think we need to find this woman. In fact, I'm sure of it." She slid onto the seat and waited while Naomi joined her. "My gut tells me she's our gal."

Naomi did not look convinced as she snugged her seat belt around her hips. Her gaze was troubled as she measured Cheryl from across the car. "What is going on, Cheryl? Something is bothering you."

Cheryl jammed the keys into the ignition. "What do you mean? I'm trusting my instincts, that's all."

Naomi shook her head. "I do not think so. I think it is something more troubling you. Do you want to talk about it?"

Cheryl flopped back against the seat. "Naomi, there is nothing to talk about. Besides, I don't think we can afford to waste any time. This woman may have taken John Swartzentruber. If she did, we need to figure out why and where she may be going with him. That means checking airports, car-rental companies, bus lines, maybe even trains. And we need to act fast, before she gets too far, or we might never find him."

The more she talked, the faster the words came. Finally Naomi grasped her hand, the warmth of her fingers dragging Cheryl to a shaky halt.

"Those are all goot ideas, ones I am sure the chief has already considered." She paused, and her face became solemn. "Cheryl, this was not your fault. You know this, ja?"

Beneath her understanding gaze, Cheryl felt exposed and vulnerable. She squeezed Naomi's hand rather than respond. She was a loyal friend, and as such, she would always believe the best of people, but the truth was, Cheryl did feel responsible, and the only thing that would change that would be finding Baby John and returning him to his family.

"You're probably right," she said carefully. "We should get back. I wouldn't want Seth to worry. He has enough on his plate."

With that, Cheryl reached for the keys and started the car, glad for the burst of warm air that wafted from the vents. It wouldn't drive away the chill surrounding her heart, but it would at least force the ache from her fingers.

Cheryl hurried back through Sugarcreek toward the store. She hadn't stopped to consider it before, but she really was concerned about causing Seth undue worry, and with no way to reach him, she didn't dare dally. It was a different way of life the Amish led, one not dependent on voice mails and text messages, but it was freeing too, in that she never saw Naomi checking a phone periodically the way others did. Nor was she tethered to a computer, worried about missing e-mails.

A few blocks from town, Cheryl cranked the heat a little higher then turned onto Main Street. "Is Levi meeting you at the store?"

"Ja, I think so. Seth will have sent him to meet me seeing as the hour has grown late. He does not like me traveling alone this time of year, especially with the weather getting colder." She made a *tsk* sound, but her lips curved in a smile. "That man. I keep reminding him that I know how to take care of myself, but still, he worries like a mother hen."

Indeed, a familiar figure waited in the lamplight outside the Swiss Miss as Cheryl pulled to a stop. The wide-brimmed hat and blue-collared shirt beneath a plain black jacket were recognizable anywhere in Sugarcreek, but it was the broad shoulders and casual posture that made Cheryl's breath hitch. Her hand went to her unruly hair in a vain attempt to coerce it into order before she scrambled from the driver's side to join Naomi on the sidewalk.

Levi greeted Naomi and then turned and jerked the hat from his head, exposing blond, ruffled curls. "Good evening, Cheryl."

Cheryl swallowed against a suddenly raw throat. "Hi, Levi."

The look he directed at her was fleeting, but it warmed her to the core. She wrapped her arms around herself and consciously worked to keep her feet from fidgeting.

Naomi jabbed her thumb over her shoulder in the direction of the Swartzentrubers' farm. "Has there been any word from Samuel or Rachel?"

Cheryl had been wondering the same thing. Her gaze flew to Levi.

With a shake of his head, his attention returned to his stepmother, and Cheryl's breathing returned to normal.

"Nothing." He jammed both hands into his pockets, the muscles along his jaw tensing. "*Daed* is with them still. He plans to stay a couple of hours while Samuel works out a map for the search party so that we don't waste time crossing lines. He asked that I let you know so you would not be worried when you returned home."

She nodded.

Levi replaced the hat on his head and then gestured toward the waiting buggy. "I thought I would see you home before heading back to their place. There is not much more we can do tonight, but I'd still like to stop one last time. I think it will help Samuel."

"Of course. Thank you, Levi. That is very kind," Naomi said quietly then turned to give Cheryl a hug. "We will talk more in the morning, ja?"

Something about the way she said it let Cheryl know Naomi suspected what she was feeling inside, something only her mother had ever been able to do. A sudden swell of emotion clogged her throat. "I'll look for you here first thing tomorrow. We have a lot we need to discuss."

"I agree." Naomi looked from her to Levi, but she said nothing more as she moved toward the buggy.

Levi stepped forward. His rugged features shone in the glow of the lamplight, and his blue eyes blazed like bits of cobalt. "I was hoping I would see you. I...wanted to..."

What? The possibilities buzzed inside Cheryl's head like bees.

He shoved his hands into his pockets, his breath puffing from his lungs in fluffy white wisps. "I cannot stay long," he continued. "I need to get Naomi home."

She nodded, afraid to hope that it was more than just casual interest adding warmth to his tone.

"I was concerned when I heard you were at the house when John Swartzentruber disappeared."

The tense lines around his mouth returned, and his brow furrowed. Cheryl's pulse leaped. She wasn't wrong. The affection and tenderness in his voice matched the emotion reflected in his eyes. It made her want to cry. How long had it been since she'd seen concern for her welfare in a man's eyes?

She blinked, fighting the burning gathering behind her eyelids, and then fumbled in her coat pocket for a tissue. "I just hope they find him soon."

"They will." She looked up in time to see Levi's jaw tighten. He eased closer, not touching but within reach. "He'll be all right, Cheryl. Gott is watching over him."

She knew without a doubt the words were true. What was it her father always said?

"His eye is on the sparrow, Cheryl. I know He's watching you."

That meant Baby John too. So why was she so afraid?

"Are you sure you are all right?"

Levi's gentle whisper made her weak in the knees. She closed her hands into fists and sucked in a deep breath for strength. "I'll be fine, just as soon as we can bring Baby John home."

His head dipped in an understanding nod. "*Maam* and Daed would welcome you tonight if you would rather not be alone. I can always sleep in the barn."

She rubbed her hands over her arms, wishing she could brush away the strange longing in her heart as easily. "I'll be fine. Besides, I wouldn't want to impose."

"It is no imposition, Cheryl."

The brief, urgent words hit her like a blow to the chest. Levi was a strong, handsome man, and she was attracted to him. Suddenly her mouth went dry.

"I will follow you home,"—his voice lowered—"make sure you arrive safely."

"But Naomi is probably tired..."

"It is only four blocks. With a kidnapper running loose, she will want to see you secure before we return to the farm."

The air whooshed from her lungs. So he was thinking of Naomi, not her. Chiding herself for the ridiculous disappointment she felt, Cheryl dropped her gaze and fished her keys from her pocket.

"Thank you, Levi."

He didn't move away as she expected. Instead when she looked up, he still watched her, a strange look of disquiet twisting his handsome face.

"I am praying for you, Cheryl. I have not stopped since I heard the news."

He said it so earnestly, she almost believed there was more to his words than he allowed himself to speak.

If she spoke now, or tried to around the lump in her throat, she'd burst into tears. She spun toward her car. Levi was there before her, opening the door and holding it while she swept inside. Only after she'd snapped her seat belt in place did he push the door shut and step back.

As promised, he followed her the short distance to Aunt Mitzi's cottage. She let herself in then dropped her keys on the hall table, jumping over Beau in her hurry to reach the living room window. Parting the curtains an inch, she watched as he wheeled the buggy around and headed in the opposite direction out of town toward the Millers' farm.

Drawing back, she let the curtain fall into place and paced slowly toward the kitchen. Aunt Mitzi's cheerful collection of pottery normally brought a smile to her face, but tonight she barely glanced at them. She put a kettle on to boil, then sank into a chair at the table to wait. And think. Several times she tried to reason through the day's events, but with every instance, thoughts of Levi interfered.

What troubled her most about her conversation with him? Was it that she'd not allowed herself to consider the danger Baby John might be in or what might be happening to him, or was it something more deeply personal? Something she'd dared not face, but that crept closer every time she was confronted by Levi and her growing feelings for him?

Cheryl pushed up from her chair and stormed to the cabinet above the sink. She jerked her favorite cup from the shelf, gasping when it slipped from her fingers and clattered onto the countertop.

"Oh no!"

Scrambling, she managed to right it before it dropped to the floor. Careful examination revealed no cracks or chips in the pale pink glaze. Relieved to find it no worse for wear, she set the cup down and covered her face with her hands. Would this day never end?

A warm, furry body rubbed gently against her legs. Cheryl peeked through her fingers and watched Beau circle around her left leg and repeat the motion against her right. It was more than just the anxious prodding he did when he was hungry. Beau seemed to sense her overwrought emotions and appeared to want to offer comfort.

Scooping him up, Cheryl pressed her cheek into his furry side. "Thanks, Beau. You're a very good boy. I'm sorry I ignored you earlier."

He purred in response to her apology. She set him on the counter, something she did not often allow, and pulled a canister of treats from the cupboard and offered him one. He eyed it critically, rubbing his mouth against her fingers and thumb before relenting and plucking the treat from her hand. Dropping gracefully to the floor, he scooted out of the kitchen, the black tip of his tail the last thing she saw before he disappeared out of sight.

Cats. One could always depend on them—sometimes affectionate, fiercely independent, but always reliably enigmatic. At least they didn't pretend to be something else.

The kettle whistled. She removed it from the stove, poured a cup, and then added a chamomile tea bag.

Not like people, she realized, her thoughts winging to Baby John's kidnapper.

Or more specifically, men.

This time, instead of picturing Levi's face, her rebellious brain conjured Lance, and a weight she thought she'd discarded long ago settled heavily against her chest.

"Why now, Lord?" she whispered, wiping a sudden swell of moisture from her lashes. "Why think of him when I have so much on my mind already?"

The hum of the kitchen lights filled the silence following her question. Most nights, she didn't mind the quiet. It was so different from the rush and bustle she'd known in the city. Sometimes it even felt good to unwind, to let go of the clamor that once occupied her days and let herself truly be still. Tonight, however, she wished for something—

No, it wasn't some*thing* she wished for, she realized with a start. It was some*one*. She wanted someone to share the burden weighing on her shoulders. Someone strong and steady, with a faith that pulled her closer to God when she was weak. Someone like Levi.

Sighing, Cheryl picked up her tea and carried it from the room. It would be many long hours before her restless thoughts gave way to sleep. And it would be even longer before her heart found peace.

CHAPTER FIVE

Cheryl set out eagerly for the Swiss Miss the next morning. Despite her fears, she'd fallen into a sweet and dreamless sleep after finishing her tea, a fact she could only attribute to a peace that surpassed understanding, given the state she'd been in when she climbed into bed. Perhaps it had been Levi's prayers, or her own, that had finally settled her spirit.

Thinking of Levi brought a smile to her lips as she swung past Aunt Mitzi's gate and onto the sidewalk. His kindness wasn't unexpected—the Amish were renowned for their generosity toward others—but his concern had seeped into the hidden places of her heart, and it lightened her steps as she passed Hoffman's store and the Sugarcreek Sisters Quilt Shoppe.

A breeze riffled the treetops, loosening the few remaining leaves. Cheryl loved this time of year. The scents, the sound of the season crunching underfoot, even the nip pinching her lungs as she walked made her grateful.

She lifted her chin and snugged the edges of her coat tightly together. Today would be a good day. She intended to contact all of the municipal agencies to see if there had been any single women traveling with an infant. With her help, the police would find

Baby John and put his kidnapper behind bars, and then things in Sugarcreek would return to normal.

Overhead, the sun shone in happy agreement—a rare thing for early November in Ohio. Gentle rays warmed the top of her head and tickled her cheeks. She quickened her pace, drawing in another lungful of sweet, country air. Yes, today would be a good day.

"Cheryl!"

She slowed at the sound of her name. Across the street, Naomi waved, the sleeves of her cape dress fluttering like wings. With her other hand, she clutched the bonnet to her head to keep the wind from snatching it off her head.

"Cheryl, over here."

Cheryl looked both ways and then hurried to join her friend on the sidewalk. "What's going on? I thought we agreed to meet at the Swiss Miss?"

"We did." Naomi's cheeks puffed like a chipmunk with each rapid breath, and she rubbed her hands briskly over her reddened knuckles. "I thought you should hear this. Come."

Grasping Cheryl's hand, she pulled her up the street.

Cheryl huffed to keep up. "Wait, what's going on? Where are we going?"

"The Old Amish Store. I came into town early and had time before the Swiss Miss opened, so I stopped to purchase a few supplies."

Skirting barrels stuffed with colorful fall flowers, she led Cheryl along the sidewalk until they arrived at the store. She pushed open the door and gestured toward the store's proprietor, Ezra Wittmer.

Several years older than Cheryl or Naomi, Ezra sported a full white beard and hair that grayed at the temples, but his back was strong and straight and his blue eyes normally sparkled with humor. Not today.

Today, concern troubled his gaze and his bushy gray brows were lowered in a frown. Setting aside his apron, he greeted Cheryl with a nod and then turned his attention to Naomi. "This scurrying about is most unusual, Naomi Miller. Won't you tell me what it is that has your feathers in such a ruffle?"

Pressing her palm to her flushed cheek, Naomi paused to gather her breath. "Forgive me, Ezra. I did not mean to hurry out of here so abruptly. It is just that, something you said..."

His frown deepened. "About the *Englisch* woman?"

She nodded.

"What Englisch woman?" Struggling to catch her breath, Cheryl's gaze bounced from Ezra to Naomi. She pressed her hand to her chest. "What are you talking about?"

Naomi motioned toward the proprietor. "Tell her, Ezra."

"I don't understand...," Cheryl began.

Though she prompted him, Naomi did not wait for Ezra to explain. "Ezra said an Englisch woman was in here buying Amish-made baby things," she blurted hastily.

"Okay. And?"

"And when I asked him about her, he described someone who sounds very much like Theresa Cox."

Momentarily silenced, Cheryl blinked several times and then looked at Ezra. "Is this true?"

"A woman was here, ja, but about this Theresa Cox?" He shrugged. "Of that, I am not so certain."

Cheryl repeated the description she'd given to Laura Early at the Little Switzerland Bed-and-Breakfast. Ezra's head bobbed at intervals, and he tugged at the tips of his gray beard. "She definitely sounds like the woman I saw."

"And you're sure this is the same woman who was buying baby things from your shop?" Cheryl asked, her excitement building.

Ezra scratched his head. "It could be her, I suppose. But I do not understand why you two are so curious about her. What has she done?" His gaze shifted. "Naomi?"

Naomi bit her lip, and an embarrassed flush crept over her cheeks. "Well, to be honest, Ezra, we cannot be sure she has done anything." She glanced at Cheryl. "Perhaps we ought not be stirring up rumors where there is no proof..."

"Wait...how did you even know she'd been by?" Cheryl interrupted. "Did you see her?"

Naomi shook her head. "No. Ezra and I were chatting. He mentioned what had happened, and it sounded so similar to the incident at the Swiss Miss yesterday that I got excited and started asking questions."

Naomi's bonnet strings fluttered like kite tails as she fidgeted from foot to foot, and contrition painted bright spots on her cheeks. "Perhaps I was wrong to assume so much. After all, the woman has as much right to purchase baby toys and such in Sugarcreek as anyone else."

True, but not everyone else bothered to shop for them the same day a baby was kidnapped. Perhaps living outside the gentle community of Sugarcreek had colored Cheryl's thinking, made her suspicious and cynical. Or maybe it was the experience with Lance that forced her to look beyond face value. Regardless, she wasn't taking chances. She directed her attention to Ezra. "Do you know what time you saw Ms. Cox?"

Clasping her hands tightly to her chest, Naomi turned earnest eyes to the proprietor. Cheryl's heart rate sped as the details of her conversation with Laura Early raced through her mind.

Laura said Theresa checked out just yesterday afternoon. If Ezra spotted her after that, it meant...

"She came by first thing this morning, before I had even opened the doors." Ezra pulled several folded bills from a pocket of his overalls. "I had just flipped the sign and was getting ready to sweep the walk when she blew in as flustered as a wet hen and asked if she could see our handmade toys and baby items." He held up the bills. "Paid with cash too. Would not even wait for me to give her change. She said she was in a hurry and left."

Naomi's eyes widened. *See?* she mouthed to Cheryl.

He jammed the money back into his pocket. "I was glad I'd let her in until Naomi started asking all kinds of strange questions." Worry twisted his wrinkled face. "This Englischer... I hope she is not bringing trouble to our community. That is the last thing we need after the strange things that happened a few weeks ago."

Whether Theresa Cox brought trouble to Sugarcreek remained to be seen. Her thoughts in a whirl, Cheryl thanked Ezra and then she and Naomi left the store and headed across the street toward the Swiss Miss.

"So what do you think?" Cheryl said while she and Naomi went about the business of readying the shop for customers. Naomi had brought several rounds of fresh cheese along with a few tins of homemade fudge. Plus, she still had the new set of Bible covers Levi had fashioned from leather. All of it would need to be stocked before they opened. She arranged the last tin of fudge on the shelf before moving toward the cash register.

Naomi stacked several homemade aprons on a shelf, her brow furrowed and her lips pressed firmly. "I admit, I am very curious about this woman, but we will have to be careful. It would not be right to defame her character. It is possible she has a very good reason for being in Sugarcreek."

Bracing her elbows on the counter, Cheryl drummed her fingertips against her lips. Naomi was right, rumors could be damaging…and hurtful. She'd learned that firsthand after her breakup with Lance, and she never wanted to be guilty of causing similar pain.

"All right then, I suppose the best thing would be to see if we can find this person so we can ask her some questions."

Naomi left the half-stocked apron shelf and approached the back counter. "Find her? How? We do not even know where to look."

Cheryl straightened. "Maybe I can visit the local hotels, see if she's checked in somewhere besides the Little Switzerland?"

Naomi nodded. "I could get Esther or Lydia to mind the shop while you look."

Cheryl's pacing matched the frantic buzzing in her head. "That would be good."

"And perhaps I could pay a visit to the Swartzentrubers? See if there has been any news?"

Cheryl rocked to a stop. "Wait...if you're going out to check on Rachel, I'd like to go with you."

Naomi's brows rose. "But I thought you said..."

"I have to, Naomi," Cheryl interrupted, pressing one hand to her stomach where a familiar tension had begun winding up. "I need to make sure she's okay, see if there's anything she needs."

Naomi crossed to her, the sorrow in her gaze matching what Cheryl felt. "I understand. I will wait until you have finished checking the hotels. Then we will head out to the farm together."

"Thank you," Cheryl breathed, glad for the insight that Naomi always seemed to possess at just the right moments. She reminded her so much of her mother and Aunt Mitzi. Maybe that's what she liked so much.

"Shall we meet back here around four?"

Cheryl did a quick calculation. She'd have to search the names and addresses of every hotel and inn in town, but if she called the ones farthest from town and visited the rest, she should have plenty of time to meet Naomi by four. And she still wanted to call the airports and car-rental places to see what information, if any, they could give.

She grabbed her keys off the counter. "That works. Swing by your farm and send Esther this way. While I'm waiting for her to get here, I'll log on and see what I can dig up."

Naomi nodded and scurried out the door before Cheryl had even reached her office. Once again, she was grateful for her friend's calm, sensible ways. Maybe some of that would rub off while she was in Sugarcreek.

She paused, her finger hovering over the power button on Aunt Mitzi's ancient desktop computer. Aunt Mitzi hadn't given a time frame for when she would be returning from Papua New Guinea, but it hadn't really occurred to Cheryl to think about what she might do once her aunt returned and Cheryl's services were no longer needed at the Swiss Miss.

Could she leave the friends she'd made here?

The question made her squirm, and she jabbed the power button with more force than necessary. She didn't want to think about leaving Sugarcreek, especially because it wasn't Naomi's face she imagined when she pictured the people she'd be leaving behind. It was Levi's.

Anger flared in her chest as she pondered the events that had driven her to Sugarcreek in the first place.

She went through the motions of booting up her computer. She had no business thinking about Levi in that way.

No business at all.

CHAPTER SIX

Cheryl rubbed a bit of the frustration from her temples and then crossed another hotel off her list. Slumping against the seat of her car, she expelled a weary sigh. Sugarcreek was not a large town, but it brimmed with quaint inns and bed-and-breakfasts run by elderly proprietors or young, energetic couples looking for an escape from the city. Of the four places she had called, no one claimed to have seen the mysterious Theresa Cox. The three she visited garnered similar results. She could only hope the next stop would be different.

Dropping the gear lever into drive, she eased out on to traffic and turned for the Maple Leaf, a small inn located on the very outskirts of Sugarcreek. If this stop proved futile, she would have to widen her circle to include the larger hotels located closer to the highways. Not only would that take time, it would add distance to a trip that already had her questioning the logic of the endeavor.

Her car pinged, and Cheryl dropped her gaze to the light flashing on her display. Low fuel. She'd have to fill up soon. Spying a combination gift shop/convenience store, she pulled in and rolled to a stop in front of the pumps. Gassing up took only a few minutes with her little economy car, but a sign in the window touting ice cold drinks beckoned her. She hadn't stopped for lunch. She grabbed her purse, slung the strap over her shoulder, and headed for the entrance.

Inside, the usual non-Amish tourist trinkets lined the shelves—mugs; magnets; and several colored, plastic knick-knacks. Cheryl bypassed them and made for a cooler near the rear of the store bulging with an impressive array of drinks and colas. Selecting one, she veered right toward a quiet aisle, avoiding the people clustered around the cheap souvenirs, and wove through an aisle packed with more respectable wooden keepsakes. Amish keepsakes, she realized, drawing to a halt. And many of them were items for babies and toddlers.

An idea sparking in her brain, Cheryl made a beeline for the counter, paid for her drink and a candy bar, then pointed toward the souvenirs. "Can you tell me who makes those?"

The young man standing behind the cash register gave a one-shouldered shrug. "They're Amish, I think. The owner gets them from one of the local craftsmen."

She fingered through a display of chips on the counter. "Do you always keep them in stock?"

He shrugged and held up a plastic sack. Cheryl shook her head, indicating no need, and he pushed her purchases toward her. "They sell pretty well, so the boss makes a point of keeping them handy." One eyebrow rose. "You're the second person to ask about them today."

She licked her lips and leaned slightly over the counter. "Oh yeah?"

He nodded. "Earlier this morning. A lady came in and bought a couple. Cute girl, but she was in a big hurry. Too bad. I wouldn't have minded talking with her."

Excitement bubbled up from Cheryl's middle, but appearing overeager might scare the young man, and he'd close up faster than her old bank at quitting time. She lifted one eyebrow and pretended to be only mildly interested. "It may have been a friend of mine. Young lady about so tall?" She held her hand a touch above shoulder height. "Brown hair and glasses?"

The glasses she added from Laura Early's description of Theresa Cox.

The young man nodded. "That's her. Kinda pretty." He pointed at his left hand, and one corner of his mouth lifted in an impish grin. "No ring, you know what I mean?"

So he'd found her attractive. And apparently, she was single. Cheryl smiled back. "Yeah, I get it." She jerked her thumb toward the door. "She didn't tell you where she was going, did she?"

"Not that I remember." He braced both elbows on the counter and gave Cheryl a saucy wink. "This 'she' you are talking about, does she have a name?"

Cheryl wagged her finger in the young man's grinning face and then glanced at his name badge. "Ron, is it?"

He chuckled. "That's me."

"She's too old for you, Ron."

At least, that was her guess based on the brief glimpse she'd gotten yesterday morning. Regardless, she had no desire to serve as a matchmaker for a suspected kidnapper.

She motioned toward the baby aisle. "You wouldn't happen to know who else sells that kind of stuff, would you?"

"The baby stuff?" He straightened and gave an indifferent toss of his head, making his chunky bangs flop into his eyes. He brushed them aside with a casual swipe. "Pretty much everybody in Sugarcreek. The Old Amish Store has them." He scratched his temple, thinking. "Oh, and I think the Gas-n-Go on the other side of town."

Her thoughts winging in a new direction, Cheryl thanked the young man, took her drink and snack, and left. Maybe she shouldn't be working so hard to try and find out where Theresa Cox might be staying. Maybe she'd stumble on the answer if she focused her attention on all the stores that sold Amish-made baby toys.

Beginning at one end of town, Cheryl worked her way south, stopping at every gas station, gift shop, and general store along the way. At several of the businesses, the owners thought they remembered a woman fitting Theresa Cox's description. Always, it was baby things she bought, and always, she paid with cash. Though none of the owners claimed knowledge of the woman's current whereabouts, Cheryl was satisfied enough with the information she'd gathered by day's end to head for the Sugarcreek Police Department and Chief Twitchell's office.

Rather than looking pleased to see her, he rolled his eyes when she entered and sat back in his leather chair with a sigh. "Miss Cooper. I thought I might be seein' you today. To what do I owe the pleasure?"

Great. She'd have a hard time getting him to believe her theory if he wasn't even prepared to listen. Playing a hunch, Cheryl plopped into a chair opposite his desk and gestured toward a pen and pad of paper he kept in the bin near the corner. "Nice to see you too, Chief. May I?"

His brow wrinkled, but he leaned forward and handed her the items then watched while she scribbled a hasty description of Theresa Cox. When she finished, she pushed the pad back to him and sat with her hands clenched in her lap while he read the list.

He held up the paper by one corner and eyed her skeptically. "All right, I'll bite. What is this?"

Cheryl jabbed her index finger toward the list. "That, I believe, is a description of our kidnapper."

Frowning, he replaced the list on his desk and folded his arms. "Perhaps you should start at the beginning."

At least he was listening. Gulping a hasty breath, Cheryl relayed the details of Theresa's visit and everything she had learned since the woman hurried from her store. As she'd feared, the chief seemed only mildly intrigued and gave a slow shake of his head when she finished.

"Miss Cooper…"

"Chief, I know it's not much to go on," Cheryl interrupted, fighting the urge to sound desperate, "but you have to admit, this woman's actions are a bit suspicious, given the circumstances."

He swallowed what he'd been about to say and agreed with a grudging nod. "Okay, it is a little strange. But that doesn't mean I think this information is incriminating enough to start dragging in suspects. Please understand, Miss Cooper, I need to be very careful. The last thing this town needs is a lot of false rumors circulating, especially after what happened last month."

Cheryl's optimism lagged with his last words. Abby Harper. Right. Ezra had reminded her of the same thing when they'd asked him about Theresa. The town was still reeling from discovering they'd had an abusive husband in their midst. Adding a kidnapper was beyond what their small town could handle.

Tapping her finger to her chin, she ran through her options and settled on one. "Okay, but what about tracking this woman down for questioning? That's reasonable, right?"

"Now *that*, I can do." Chief Twitchell shoved back from his desk and lifted the note pad. "You say her name is Theresa Cox?"

Her spirits reviving, she pushed to the edge of her chair. "Yes, or at least that's the name she gave when she checked into the Little Switzerland." Excitement flared inside her chest. "I could do some more checking for you if you'd like..."

"*More* checking?" He peered sternly at her from beneath lowered brows.

Cheryl felt like she'd been caught sneaking home after curfew. "Well...I...uh..." She cleared her throat. "I *have* done a little investigating on the side."

He laid his pencil down carefully and laced his fingers. "I thought you said you merely asked the business owners around town if this Theresa Cox bought any baby items?"

"That's true, I did"—her cheeks warmed—"later...after I called around to see if she had checked into any hotels."

Exasperation colored Chief Twitchell's face as he held up his hand. "Miss Cooper, I'm going to have to insist that you allow me and my officers to do our jobs."

"But Chief Twitchell..."

He shook his head, cutting her off before she could protest. "Do you believe this department is doing everything it can to try and locate that missing baby?"

A weight settled on Cheryl's chest, and she lowered her head glumly.

"What about my expertise and that of my officers?" he persisted, his tone curt. "Do you believe we have the knowledge and experience it takes to check every lead that comes across my desk?"

"Of course," she whispered.

He relented of his piercing stare and settled back against his chair. "Good, then I hope you'll believe me when I say that interferin' in this investigation will only hinder our efforts."

Cheryl knew enough to realize that everything Chief Twitchell said was true. Still, the kidnapper had used *her* as the distraction he or she needed to steal John from his crib, and that meant she *had* to help, no matter what the chief said.

The chief's eyebrows rose. "Miss Cooper?"

She lifted her chin and stood. Offering her hand, she gave Chief Twitchell's a firm shake before moving toward the door.

"Thank you for your time, Chief. Good luck with the investigation. I hope the information I shared with you helps." One hand on the knob, she paused and turned back to look him in the eyes. "You will let me know if you find out anything?"

His head swung slowly, side to side. "Now, now, you know I can't do that. Not until this thing is fully concluded and our kidnapper is in custody."

"Right," Cheryl said, adding a halfhearted shrug. "You know me, Chief. Just thought I'd ask."

Chief Twitchell didn't know it, but she had no intention of staying out of his way. Closing the door behind her, she made a beeline for the Swiss Miss. Maybe after she and Naomi had a chance to compare notes, she'd have a better plan for how to proceed. Maybe she'd even find a way to convince the chief to track down Theresa Cox. Her steps quickened.

So intent was she on her meeting with Naomi, she stepped off the sidewalk and straight into a man's broad chest, and only his viselike grip kept her from tumbling headlong into the street. Startled, she stared up, wide-eyed, into the glowering, bearded face of Jeremiah Zook.

CHAPTER SEVEN

The frown cleared from Jeremiah's face as he set Cheryl back on her feet. "I am so sorry. Are you all right? Forgive me, please. I did not see you there."

Cheryl struggled for breath, too stunned for a moment to do more than blink. Finally, she regained her balance as well as her composure. Stepping back, she tugged her shirt and coat into place and then ran her hand over her unruly hair.

"No, it was my fault. I should've watched where I was going. I was in a hurry, and I..." She motioned helplessly toward the police station. "I just wasn't paying attention."

Jeremiah's gaze followed the direction of her shaking finger. "You are leaving the police station? I hope everything is all right at your aunt Mitzi's store? After what happened last month..."

"Oh, no, it's nothing like that. Thank you, Jeremiah, everything is fine. I was just..." She dropped her hand. How to explain to a grieving father the business that had brought her to see the chief? She looked past him toward the buggy. "Never mind. It's not important."

She sucked in a breath and forced a wan smile. "So how are you and Rebecca? I've been thinking of you a lot lately. You've been in my prayers, both of you."

Suddenly, his expression closed, and the muscles in his jaw, already clenched tightly, began to twitch. *"Danki.* We are saddened by our loss, but Gott is goot. He will see us through this trial."

The words were almost too perfect and spoken in an emotionless way that made Cheryl uncomfortable. Pushing her hands into the pockets of her jeans, she tipped her head toward the buggy.

"So, uh, is Rebecca with you? I'd like to say hello, if you have time."

"No...uh..." He put out his arm and stepped between Cheryl and the buggy. "I'm afraid she is not with me today." Squirming as though he were uncomfortable, he dropped his gaze to a point somewhere near the top of his shoes.

Cheryl bit the inside of her lip. Jeremiah looked more than just worn out, he looked stressed—understandably, given their recent loss. Still, it was unusual to see an Amish man in rumpled clothing and with dirt clinging to the cuffs. Also, his hair looked slightly ragged and unkempt.

She swallowed nervously. "I'm so sorry I haven't been out to your farm. I've been meaning to visit." She lowered her voice. "How is Rebecca doing?"

His gaze darted nervously to the police station and back. Clutching the brim of his hat, he pulled it lower over his eyes. "My wife will be fine in time. If you will excuse me now, I have business I need to see to. I will tell Rebecca that you asked after her welfare."

"Of course. Good-bye, Jeremiah."

He spun and headed up the street. Cheryl studied his shoulders, more angular and hunched than ever beneath the cotton fabric of his blue shirt and black coat. Something about the man's behavior seemed particularly odd, and not just that he avoided looking at her. He seemed to want to avoid speaking to her as well.

Determined to figure out why, Cheryl hurried a few steps to catch up. "Jeremiah, wait."

His coat swung limply as he turned to wait for her. "Ja? You need to speak with me?"

"Yes, I…" She licked her dry lips. "I'm sorry. I don't think I ever told you how sad I was to hear about the loss of your son."

Grief shadowed his brown eyes and passed, like a cloud floating over the sun. He squared his shoulders and offered a brief nod. "Danki."

Cheryl held out her hand in a helpless gesture that echoed exactly how she felt inside. "If there is anything I can do…"

"No." He choked out the word and averted his gaze. "There is nothing anyone can do." As though sensing how his words sounded, he shifted his weight and shrugged. "But I am grateful to those who try."

"I understand."

She stepped closer but did not lay her hand on his arm in a show of comfort as she might have done with an Englischer. That was not something he would appreciate, even if the sentiment were sincere. Still, she wanted to do something.

She tapped her chin, thinking. "Perhaps I could come by later and check on Rebecca. I'm not nearly as good a cook as she is, but I would be glad to put something together…"

His head jerked up. "Rebecca has left town, Cheryl. I do not expect her back for some time."

She fell silent, then stammered, "L...Left town?"

He stared back, unblinking.

"But...where did she go?"

"I am sorry, Cheryl. That is family business."

He said it sharply, with a dark glower that brooked no further inquiry. What he really meant was that it was none of *her* business. Cheryl swallowed nervously. Granted, she hadn't known the Zooks long, but they had been one of the first families to welcome her to Sugarcreek and did not treat her as an outsider or even an Englischer.

She backed away, her cheeks warm. "Of course. Forgive me, Jeremiah. I didn't mean to pry."

At her awkward apology, he tipped his hat and moved off.

"I'll see you later," she mumbled lamely at his retreating back.

All the way to the Swiss Miss, a brisk wind swirled dust and leaves around Cheryl's feet, the pattern as chaotic and jumbled as her thoughts. She was troubled by Jeremiah Zook's odd behavior. And what about Rebecca Zook leaving town? Surely, she and her husband needed each other right now. What could possibly have driven her away?

By the time Cheryl reached the store, dark suspicion germinated in her thoughts and she struggled to get ahold of it before it took root. She looked forward to Naomi's arrival so that she could ask her opinion and kept one eye on the door while she rang up customers and stocked shelves.

At a quarter of two, her part-time helper and Esther's best friend, Lydia Troyer, waltzed in, her black curls bouncing, and waved a cheery greeting. She was good in the store, always willing to work hard, and she learned quickly. Plus, though she was obviously enjoying her rumspringa, she demonstrated an admirable sense of responsibility, and Cheryl never had to worry about her arriving on time. Cheryl put her to work sorting the new inventory of shirts she'd received and then returned to stocking while she thought about Jeremiah and his wife's strange departure.

A child disappeared and then a woman did the same shortly after? Why would she do that? The implication was terrible to contemplate, but what else could she infer?

Finally, the bell chimed and Naomi stepped in. She brushed a few leaves from her heavy wool shawl then tugged it from her shoulders and draped it over her arm.

"There you are." Cheryl dropped the potholders she had been arranging on hooks, grabbed Naomi's hand, and dragged her toward the office.

"Cheryl, what is wrong?"

"Nothing." She closed the door and pointed toward a chair. "Or maybe something. I'm not sure." Taking the seat next to Naomi, she frowned and ran a hand through her short, spiky hair.

"What do you mean?" Naomi had obviously gotten chilled on the way over. Her words had that strange lisp that came when a person's cheeks froze over and their lips refused to move. She pulled a tissue from the box on Cheryl's desk and dabbed her nose.

"Were you able to find out anything about the mysterious Theresa Cox?"

"Now that is an interesting story."

Cheryl sat forward, a bit of the excitement she'd felt earlier returning. Not sparing the details, she went over the steps that had led her to Chief Twitchell's office and his subsequent response.

She drummed the desktop in frustration. "I don't know, Naomi. I suppose he's right about the evidence not being incriminating enough, but don't you think it's at least worth looking into?"

"Did he say he would not?"

"Well, no, but the way he acted made me think it wasn't high on his list of priorities."

Naomi watched her with a wary look in her eyes. "*Hmm.* I know that look. What are you thinking?"

"What look? What makes you think I'm thinking something?"

She chuckled and pointed an accusing finger at her. "That innocent act will not work on me, Cheryl Cooper. I know you too well. What is going on inside that head?"

Answering with a grin, she shrugged. "Just an idea, at the moment. I have something else I'd like to ask you about first."

She started to tell her about her encounter with Jeremiah. Unfortunately, at that precise moment, the bell above the door rang, and Cheryl excused herself to help her customers. When at last the woman and her young daughter left, a bag full of Naomi's jams and fresh cheese clutched in their arms, the hour for closing neared. Cheryl said good-bye to Lydia then flipped the sign and locked the door before seeking Naomi once more.

Naomi met her at the office door. "I'll help you close up." She motioned toward the cash register. "You get started on the receipts, and I will tidy up. Then we can head out to the Swartzentrubers' farm. We will talk in the car."

Nodding, Cheryl hurried to bundle everything from the cash drawer and slip it into a bank bag. Business must have been good while she was out. She'd have a healthy deposit in the morning. When she finished, she grabbed her purse and joined Naomi on the sidewalk.

"Ready?"

Naomi nodded, and the two of them walked quickly back to the cottage to fetch Cheryl's car for the ride out to see Rachel. Along the way, Naomi filled her in on the talk filtering among the Amish.

"The elders are concerned it was not a random kidnapping, but one specifically targeting an Amish child." Her face paled with worry.

"Why would they think that?"

Naomi shrugged. "There have been crimes against the Amish before, and for no more reason than that."

True. Cheryl pondered this new angle as they drove the rest of the way to the farm. Ohio was a big state, and known for its large Amish populations. If someone wanted to target an Amish family, Sugarcreek would have been an obvious choice. She shuddered. Could she have been wrong about the kidnapping all along? And if so, what did that do to their list of suspects? Suddenly, any number of people could be guilty, and the odds of finding Baby John seemed considerably smaller.

When they pulled into the drive, where a number of buggies parked, Naomi grabbed Cheryl's hand and they bowed their heads for silent prayer before trudging up the path toward Rachel and Samuel Swartzentruber's door. Even the house looked sad—the eaves and gutters drooping beneath the weight of sodden leaves. Naomi noticed too.

"Tomorrow I will send Eli or Caleb to clean them," she said, tipping her head in the direction of Cheryl's stare.

Her thinking shifted to the Swartzentrubers. What would she say? What words could she utter that might possibly offer even the smallest measure of comfort? Her gaze drifted to the porch and the several bundles of cards and flowers that the people of Sugarcreek had placed there. One of them read, *Our thoughts and prayers for our Amish friends.*

Cheryl blew out a sigh. *Why, God? Why would anyone do such a terrible thing to such a sweet family?*

Their booted feet scraped on the cement pavers, shushing out any answer that might have come. Blowing out a sigh, Cheryl drew her shoulders back and raised her hand to knock. Rachel would need a strong shoulder to cry on, not a frightened woman as desperate for answers as she.

The door opened a crack on the second knock, and Rachel peered out, her eyes reddened and swollen from crying. Catching sight of them, she pushed open the door and burst into a fresh round of weeping, both hands covering her face and her thin shoulders shaking beneath the folds of her dark blue cape dress.

Grasping her elbow, Naomi steered her past the living room where the hum of many voices drowned out thought. Cheryl followed close on their heels. A small den opened off of the kitchen, and Naomi directed them there, no doubt to hide them from curious stares. In one corner, a wooden rocker hunched next to a large field stone fireplace. Naomi helped Rachel to sit then gave her hand a pat.

"Rest a moment and catch your breath. I will make us a pot of *kaffee*." She directed a look to Cheryl. With just the slightest inclination of her head, she indicated that she should keep an eye on Rachel.

Obediently, Cheryl sat down next to Rachel and then pulled a tissue from her purse and pressed it into her shaking fingers. "There, there now," she cooed in a voice that never failed to comfort when her mother used it. "It'll be all right."

After a moment, Rachel sniffed and then blew noisily into the tissue. "Thank you."

Cheryl sat helplessly by, unsure what to do now that she'd stemmed Rachel's bout of weeping. She used the arms of her chair to push to her feet. "I think I'll go help Naomi with that coffee."

Rachel nodded, and Cheryl scurried to the kitchen where a wealth of food and dishes waited, including a plate loaded with Greta Yoder's cinnamon rolls. Farther down the counter, the warm, spicy scent of Mary Mueller's apple pie wafted temptingly.

For a moment, sorrow dragged Cheryl's steps. So the Amish were prone to the same outpouring of culinary care that was often witnessed at Englisch funerals. Weddings too. Today was neither. She plucked at the cellophane cover on a dish of baked pasta.

"How is she?" Naomi had pulled a tin of coffee from the cupboard and was setting a pot of water to boil.

Cheryl shrugged and crossed to the cupboard to fetch the cups. "She's distraught. I...didn't know what to say, so..."

She trailed into dismal silence. Naomi set down the tin and squeezed Cheryl's shoulder.

"You were with her the day our Baby John disappeared. I have the feeling she wants to speak to you. Why don't you go back in and just say what is in your heart? I am certain she would like to hear it."

What was in her heart was fear. And guilt. Cheryl blew out a breath and forced herself to return to the den. Rachel sat rocking, her arms pulled tightly around herself, her gaze fixed on the hills outside her window.

Cheryl grabbed a chair and dragged it over to sit next to her. "The coffee will be ready soon."

"That's nice," Rachel said, though really, Cheryl wondered if she'd even heard.

For several seconds, they sat in silence, the rumble of the rocker against the wood floor the only sound. Naomi had urged Cheryl to say what was in her heart, but how exactly did she do that? She lowered her head.

Help me, Lord.

The weak prayer rattled in her thoughts. She licked her lips and dragged her eyes to Rachel's waxen face. "I've, uh, been praying for you, Rachel. How are you doing?"

She shrugged.

It was a silly question. She cleared her throat and tried again. "I understand the police…"

Rachel turned her eyes to meet Cheryl's. There was agony in their depths, and pleading. Cheryl grasped her hand, hot tears burning her eyelids.

"I am so sorry, Rachel."

Her brow wrinkled with confusion. "You have nothing to be sorry for, Cheryl."

Maybe not, but then why did she feel such guilt? "Thank you for saying that, but to be honest, I'm not so sure."

The rocking slowed, and Rachel eyed her with confusion.

Cheryl swallowed a sudden knot in her throat. "See, I can't help thinking that maybe if I hadn't stopped by that morning…if I hadn't kept you talking so long…well, maybe you wouldn't have been distracted. Maybe you would have heard a noise or something, or gone to check on the boys sooner."

The words came faster, and with them a pain in her chest that grew sharper the more she spoke.

Rachel reached out and clasped her hand. "I do not blame you, Cheryl. I blame whoever did this. Whoever took my boy…" She choked on a sob.

Unable to say more, they waited in silence until Naomi joined them bearing a tray and three cups of steaming coffee. She passed one to each of them and took the third for herself before sitting opposite them on the couch.

Naomi took a sip from her cup. "Where is our Baby Joseph?"

In the somber stillness, even a whisper sounded harsh. Rachel's chair creaked as she stiffened, and panic flitted across her face. Naomi reached over to grasp her hand.

"Is he with Samuel's mother?"

The lines of fear melted from Rachel's face, replaced by a dazed, vacant stare that filled Cheryl's heart with worry.

"Yes, that's right. Samuel's mother has him."

"He is in good hands then."

Rachel collapsed against the back of the rocker as though the very last bit of strength had suddenly seeped from her bones. She wrung her hands nervously in her lap. "I should be doing something."

"You have done all you can," Naomi assured her.

Then, because the silence called for more, Cheryl added, "I take it there hasn't been any word from Chief Twitchell?"

"Nothing." Her voice splintered into a thousand tiny slivers. "The police . . . have put out . . . an APB but . . . they don't even have a possible suspect yet. How in the world are they gonna find my baby if they don't even know where to look?"

For a moment, Rachel's speech slipped from the precise way of speaking she had adopted when she joined the Amish to the clipped slang she'd used growing up. Cheryl thought she had forgotten her Englisch ways, so hard did she try to fit in. Cheryl took Rachel's hand and gave it a firm squeeze.

Naomi leaned forward. "Rachel..."

Fresh tears brimmed in the young woman's eyes. Naomi hesitated and lines of worry creased her face. "Rachel, have you contacted your maam and daed?"

Rachel dropped her gaze and a stray lock of limp, brown hair slipped from the bonnet slapped haphazardly on her head.

"My parents have not been informed," she said. Just that quickly, she switched back into her careful, measured speech. Her fingers trembled as she shoved the hair into place. "They would not want to know. It will make no difference to them that John is missing."

"How can you say that? Of course they'd want to know," Cheryl insisted and then regretted her hasty speech when Rachel's gaze skipped from Naomi to her, the hurt and regret swimming in her eyes agonizing to see.

"You are wrong, Cheryl. I know because they were not happy when they heard that I was pregnant. They thought I had ruined my chances of ever coming home. I guess, in their minds, there was always hope that I would come to my senses."

She snorted wryly. "John is named after my father, you know, and Joseph after Samuel's father. We thought it might soften my parents' resolve to have one of the boys be his namesake. Instead, they pushed us further away. They have not come to see the boys since they were born. Not once."

Sorrow knifed across Naomi's face. Their gazes locked, and Cheryl knew that she was thinking of Seth and the pain he'd suffered after losing his daughter, Sarah, when she eloped following her rumspringa. Cheryl nodded silent encouragement.

Naomi smoothed the wrinkles from her dress while she formed a response. Though her chin quivered, her voice remained steady and strong. "We have all made mistakes, done things we later regret. Look at my Seth. For years after he lost his first wife, he fought not to let feelings of grief and bitterness consume him. But it was difficult, Rachel. His daughter, Sarah, always feared that he blamed her for her mother's death because she died giving birth to her. Even when he tried to reassure her, she never felt accepted by him.

"Seth blamed himself when she left Sugarcreek to marry an Englischer. He thought he'd let her and Ruth down by not showing Sarah how much he loved her. He still looks for ways to make peace with her. And he will never, ever stop trying to win her back, no matter what she has done."

She laid her hand on Rachel's arm. "Your parents love you, Rachel, no matter how it seems right now. Perhaps if you told them . . ."

Rachel had always been thin, but her hand looked frailer than ever as she raised it to halt anything more Naomi might say on the subject of her parents. She rose, and Naomi and Cheryl rose with her.

"I would not add to my husband's pain by subjecting him to their rejection. Again. They did not approve of my decision to join the Amish. They said so when I married Samuel. Thank you, Naomi, for trying to help, but this changes nothing."

Her fingers shook as she swiped the tears angrily from her cheeks. "I should check on Joseph. Thank you both for stopping by." She turned her gaze to Naomi. "Perhaps, if you have time to spare, you could assist with the meal? The men will be hungry after being out all day searching."

"Of course."

Rachel gave a nod of thanks and then hurried from the room.

Cheryl raked her fingers through her hair in frustration. "Wow. That poor girl. I've never seen anyone hurting more than she is." She turned to Naomi. "So now what?"

She spread her hands in a helpless gesture. "I have no idea. I cannot imagine the pain of being forcibly separated from a child. To allow it by choice is a decision I simply cannot fathom."

Cheryl understood the look of dismay that creased her friend's features. Family was very important to the Amish people. Once, Cheryl had thought them to be cold, caring more for the exercise of their religion than the people involved in it, which was an assumption based on what she knew—or thought she knew before coming to Sugarcreek—about the practice of shunning. Now she realized the motivation behind the concept, as well as the heartbreak such a decision caused to the entire community, not just the family. It was no wonder so many districts had let the practice fade.

"It is like her parents have shunned her," Naomi concluded, echoing Cheryl's thoughts. Naomi shook her head sadly. "And I fear their rejection, especially now, will be more than that poor child can bear."

A sigh seeped through Cheryl's lips. "So what can we do?"

"Nothing, I'm afraid. With Rachel adamantly refusing to contact her parents, our hands are bound. Still..."

"You're not comfortable leaving her parents in the dark."

Twin splotches of red appeared on Naomi's cheeks. "It feels dishonoring to them, regardless of what Rachel says. Besides, given time and distance, she might rethink her decision, but by then the damage could be irreparable."

Sighing, Cheryl trudged toward the kitchen to help Naomi. Making sandwiches was a far cry from catching a kidnapper, but right now she could use a menial task to take her mind off of the troubling thoughts plaguing her mind.

If only cleansing her heart could be cured as easily.

Chapter Eight

The next day passed quickly, and Cheryl was thankful for Naomi's invitation to dinner. It meant she wouldn't have to spend another evening alone with her thoughts. Doubt had battered her after leaving the Swartzentrubers' house the day before and left her feeling exhausted and careworn. She locked up the store then headed eagerly home to feed Beau and fetch her car before making the drive over.

The distance to the Millers' farm was relatively short, and she looked forward to a home-cooked meal. Not that she didn't enjoy spending time in the kitchen. She'd actually dreamed about caring for a family . . . once. There simply didn't seem to be much point now, given that she cooked for herself alone. Besides, nothing she'd ever put together compared to one of Naomi's renowned roasts.

The savory scents of pepper and sage filled the air as she entered the two-story farmhouse. As usual, happy chatter floated from the family room as the Millers gathered after a hard day's work to relax and enjoy one another's company.

Elizabeth, Seth and Naomi's eighteen-year-old daughter, was the first to notice her presence, and she swept up from the sofa to hurry across the hall. Clasping Cheryl by the hands, she drew her in from the hall with a cheery smile. "Cheryl! How good to see you. Have you come for dinner?"

At Elizabeth's announcement, all heads turned, including Levi's, Cheryl noted, and she wished she had taken a moment to freshen up before leaving the store.

"Um...yes, actually, assuming you have room for one more."

"Of course we do," Esther said, giggling as she dashed off to set another plate at the long, plank-style table.

Naomi entered from the kitchen, where she'd undoubtedly been putting the finishing touches on the meal. "Hello, Cheryl. I am so glad you could join us."

One by one, the Millers crossed to say their hellos, and then Seth motioned her into the family room. Eli stood and motioned for Cheryl to take his place on a sturdy, leather-covered sofa next to Levi. Whether Levi noticed her presence or not remained a mystery, for he kept his gaze fastened to the floor, his hands, the window—everywhere except on her.

Conversation resumed after a moment, with the elder Millers teasing Esther about her rumspringa or "running around time." It amused Cheryl to watch the various interactions and made her miss her own parents at home in Seattle, where they tended a large church. She determined to call them and then felt a twinge of nostalgia thinking of her dad's voice and her mom's gentle laugh. She even missed her brother's teasing.

"Are you all right, Cheryl?"

She glanced at Levi, startled.

He inclined his head toward her, and twin creases formed on his brow. "You sighed just now, as though something were bothering you."

She let out a soft laugh and shrugged. "I was thinking of my parents, is all."

"You miss them?" Compassion darkened his eyes, and he leaned closer.

"I do."

"Then why not plan a visit to see them?"

Because I've never worked up the courage to talk to them about Lance. The answer rose to her mind unbidden. She ducked her head quickly. "I'm sure I will soon. I've just been too busy with the store. Hopefully I'll find time to go for a visit after the holiday rush."

He gave an approving grunt. "That is goot. Families should always keep in touch, even when there is distance between them. It keeps the members close."

He turned his face away, his attention drawn to something Seth was saying. Cheryl felt released to breathe freely again until something Naomi had said earlier came back to ring like a clarion in her head.

"It is like her parents have shunned her."

She gazed at her friend, sitting so contentedly at her husband's side. Cheryl had by no means been shunned by her parents, nor had she closed them out of her life, but she'd been so concerned about what they might think about her breakup with Lance that she'd diminished contact with them in recent months. She regretted that now, thinking about the division between Rachel and her parents.

Naomi rubbed her hands together. "All right then, who is hungry?"

At her signal, the family rose and shuffled single file to their places at the table. Once again, Cheryl found herself seated next to Levi, a happy coincidence that neither vexed nor worried her. Instead, she determined to enjoy the meal rather than fret over circumstances for which she had no control.

After supper, the entire family chipped in to help wash the dishes and put them away. It reminded Cheryl of a scene from a movie, with everyone laughing and working together to accomplish the job quickly. When they finished, she and Naomi escaped to the den with cups of steaming coffee in their hands while the men went outside to finish up their chores and the younger ladies set about stitching on a quilt started for Elizabeth's hope chest.

Cheryl took a sip from her cup, thoroughly content just to savor the remains of the day.

"So." Naomi gestured toward a worn leather armchair. "Now we can finish our talk."

Our talk? Cheryl lowered her cup and frowned.

Naomi waved both hands. "With all of the busyness yesterday, and then the trip to the Swartzentrubers, you never did finish telling me what happened after you left the police station."

Cheryl set her cup aside. "Of course. Where were we?"

"You had just told me about your visit with Chief Twitchell."

"Oh yes." Organizing her thoughts into stiff order, Cheryl recounted her dim view of the chief's casual response to the information she'd spent all day gathering. "And I definitely believe we ought to be spending our time finding out everything we can regarding Theresa Cox's whereabouts," she repeated, emphasizing her opinion with a sharp rap of her fist to the arm of her chair. "No matter what the chief thinks."

"I agree." Naomi pursed her lips. "It may just be that the chief has other leads he feels are more important, but regardless, it cannot hurt to help where we can."

"Which reminds me…" Cheryl tapped the rim of her cup. "Didn't you say you planned to pay a visit to Rebecca Zook?"

"I did, though I have not yet made the time. Why?"

Cheryl scooted to the edge of her chair. "Because I saw Jeremiah yesterday. He told me Rebecca has left town."

Naomi's eyes widened. "What?"

She nodded. "It was a little odd, actually. I ran into him outside of the police station. Literally. I ran into him. I was lucky I didn't end up in the street."

Naomi laughed, and Cheryl grimaced at the reminder of her clumsiness.

"Anyway, I asked him how they were doing and told him I'd been meaning to stop by."

"That was nice. What did he say?"

"Apparently he didn't think so."

Naomi's eyebrows rose. "What do you mean?"

Cheryl gripped the arms of her chair tightly. "Look, I realize there's a lot I am still learning about the Amish culture, but is it common for the men to be so secretive?"

A frown curved Naomi's mouth. "It is common for them to be reserved. Look at my Seth. But secretive? No, that is not common. Why do you ask?"

Cheryl shook her head. "This was more than just reserve."

Slowly, she reviewed her encounter with Jeremiah, including the strange way he'd refused to meet her eyes when she asked about his wife. "Am I reading too much into his behavior?" she finished.

Concern marred Naomi's face as she rose to pace, her rubber-soled shoes making soft swishing sounds against the carpet. "No, I agree…something is not right." She paused and pressed her hand to her chest. "Poor Jeremiah and Rebecca. They are both such quiet people, and they waited and prayed for that baby for so long. I can only imagine the strain their loss has placed on their marriage."

Her words startled Cheryl. She realized the past few weeks had to have been difficult for the couple, but enough to jeopardize their marriage? Weren't the Amish immune to that?

Naomi braced both hands on her hips. "What is this? You think because they are Amish, they are above strife?"

Her gentle teasing plucked a guilty string on Cheryl's conscience, and she shrugged. "You know, I guess I did think that. I'm sorry. I thought I was done expecting Amish people to be perfect, but apparently I still have a few misconceptions."

Naomi clucked her tongue and crossed to sit next to Cheryl. "Do not be too hard on yourself. You have been open to learning our ways, just as I have tried to learn yours. It will take us both time to get past what we think we know, ja? But in the end, our friendship will be worth the effort."

Cheryl nodded, but deep inside another question pushed for an answer. Could the same be said for any relationship between an Englischer and Amish?

Made uncomfortable by the idea, she cleared her throat and shifted in her chair. "So you think that's it then? The reason Jeremiah was so uneasy yesterday afternoon was because he and Rebecca may be having trouble working through their grief?"

Naomi nodded and took a sip of her coffee. "I think that could very well be a part of it. The other part could be their farm. With Rebecca gone and Jeremiah struggling to keep the place running by himself, things may have gotten behind. I will ask Seth or Levi to check in on him, see if there is anything we can do to help."

"But…" Cheryl bit off the one word and stopped. She didn't want to risk offending her friend, even if her intent was innocent.

Naomi set down her cup, her gentle gaze steady and calm. "You are wondering why Jeremiah has not come before the elders if there is trouble?"

She gave a self-conscious nod. "The Amish are known for helping one another—like with barn raisings and all that. So why wouldn't Jeremiah ask for help if he was having difficulty keeping up with his farm?"

Cupping one hand in the other, Naomi rubbed her knuckles absently while she explained. "We are Amish. We lead separate, holy lives because we desire to please Gott. But we are also human, and we suffer from all of the same temptations, insecurity, and doubt as the rest of the world. Jeremiah is faithful to Gott. I have seen his commitment to his church and to his family."

She sighed and laid her hands to rest in her lap. "But he is also just a man. Perhaps the reason he has said nothing about Rebecca's going or needing help on the farm is because he is ashamed."

"Ashamed." Suddenly understanding dawned. Cheryl frowned sadly. "He sees all of this as a failing on his part?"

Naomi shrugged. "Perhaps. Or perhaps he worries that he has not enough faith and that is why this tragedy has befallen him." She tsked softly and squeezed Cheryl's hand. "Seth will know the words to comfort and encourage him. Thank you for telling me this, Cheryl."

Yes, Seth would be the perfect person to speak to Jeremiah. He'd confessed to battling many of the same feelings of insecurity and doubt after his wife's death. Cheryl wanted to believe that was all it would take to set things to rights with the Zooks, but deep down, questions regarding Rebecca's departure still lingered. Not that she could voice those questions, however. Not without risking hurting Jeremiah—something she'd rather not do considering the heartache he'd already suffered.

Cheryl tucked her misgivings aside and determined to find out more once Seth had a chance to visit with Jeremiah.

Memory of his careworn face and rumpled appearance flashed into her mind. Maybe it *was* just that he was struggling with feelings of failure as Naomi had said, and maybe not. Maybe it was more, as his unruly hair and dirt-crusted clothing suggested. He could be hiding something, or more likely, covering for someone, namely, his wife.

She dropped her gaze before Naomi could read the inner suspicion brewing in her eyes.

One way or another, she thought, reaching for the cream pitcher and pouring a generous amount into her coffee, she would discover why Rebecca Zook had left town.

CHAPTER NINE

Evening had fallen by the time Cheryl and Naomi finished their talk. The November sky was cloudless and the air crisp, and a thousand stars twinkled overhead. It would have made a perfect night for a buggy ride—if she didn't have to get up so early, and her car weren't parked in Seth and Naomi's driveway, and her watch didn't read nearly eight thirty—

"Nice night."

Cheryl jumped and peered through the gloom for the voice's owner. Leaving the glow cast by a single lantern a few feet away in the barn, Levi materialized, hat in hand and a crooked grin on his face.

"It is just me. Levi. I am sorry if I frightened you."

She sucked in a calming breath. *Fright* was hardly the word to describe the rapid pounding of her heart. "No, I..." She shook her head. "No."

He pointed toward her car with his hat. "You are heading home?"

She threw a glance toward the house then shuffled her feet. "Yeah. It's getting late. Naomi and I got to talking, and I lost track of time, but I should be getting home soon."

Levi had moved to stand next to her car, so close that she could see the dim light of the moon glinting in his eyes. "That is too bad. A night like this, I would not have minded a ride in the buggy."

Cheryl's breath caught. It was as though he'd read her thoughts. She tamped a sudden swell of excitement and lifted her gaze to the sky. "I have to admit, I wouldn't mind that either. Not too many nights like this one left before colder weather sets in."

He grunted in agreement and then turned to look at her. "So let us go."

Had she heard right? She dragged her gaze to meet Levi's. "What?"

"I have not put the horse away for the night. We can make it a short ride."

He was serious. And he watched her with an intensity that made her pulse race. She licked her lips, afraid if she thought about her answer too long, her courage would flee and she'd change her mind.

She slid her car keys into her coat pocket and nodded. "Okay."

His eyes gleamed as he straightened. "Okay?"

"If you're sure it's not too much trouble."

Grinning, he motioned her to follow and then took off at a run. Cheryl felt like a teenager as she ran with him, laughing, toward the barn.

The scents and sounds emanating from the stalls fulfilled every fall fantasy Cheryl had ever dreamed of hayrides and harvest. She watched with almost giddy anticipation as Levi harnessed the mare to the buggy and then felt as though a weight lifted from her shoulders when at last they climbed aboard and set off down the road.

The buggy wheels rumbled beneath her, a perfect sort of song that dispelled any awkwardness. And the sides and top formed a cozy refuge that tempted her to dream of a life far different from her own.

"Ja, there is a blanket beneath the seat if you get cold," Levi said above the clopping of the horse's hooves.

With the cold breeze nipping at her nose, she was only too glad to drag out the wool throw and drape it over her knees.

"That's better," she managed between chattering teeth.

Levi laughed, his breath swirling in ghostly wisps above his head. "This traveling by buggy thing loses some of its charm when the temperature drops, ain't so?"

Cheryl leaned forward to glance at the canopy formed by the spreading maple branches passing overhead. "I don't know. It can be pretty romantic with the right man riding alongside you," she replied and then could've kicked herself when he shot her a sideways glance.

"Or the right woman."

He said it so quietly, she wondered if she'd heard correctly…then decided it didn't matter, so long as the warm, fuzzy feeling spreading out from her stomach remained.

Levi handled the reins easily. With a flick of his wrists, he altered their direction so that they followed a less traveled gravel road that wound along the Millers' pond, moonlight bathing their path. Ducks waddled in and out among the rushes lining the banks. Before too long, the pond would freeze and the ducks would have to find a new home to shelter in for the winter. For now, she enjoyed their funny little dance.

Drawing back on the reins, Levi slowed the mare to a walk then flashed Cheryl a quick glance. "So what were you and Naomi talking about so intently?"

Back to reality. She sighed and pressed against the seat cushion. "John Swartzentruber, mostly, and trying to figure out what happened to him. Naomi and I were going over everything that's happened in the last couple of days and trying to sort out anything that could be considered the least bit suspicious."

"Such as?"

Cheryl told him about Theresa and then shrugged. "I spent all morning trying to find out where she might be staying. I made phone calls, checked online, even stopped by a couple of places to see if anyone recognized the description I gave them."

He eyed her hopefully. "Any luck?"

She shook her head. "I think she's still in town, though. Ezra Wittmer sold her a few baby toys just yesterday morning. And some kid named Ron said he saw her at the convenience store where I stopped to buy gas."

Levi frowned. "You think this woman took the Swartzentrubers' baby? But how could that be if she is still in Sugarcreek?"

Cheryl clutched the edges of the blanket. "I don't know. Not everything about this woman makes sense, but like I told Chief Twitchell, she's worth looking into. Something about the way she acted when she came into the Swiss Miss made me very suspicious."

Levi stiffened and tugged back on the reins. The mare snorted and pranced to a halt in response. He relaxed his hold then turned to look at Cheryl. "You have seen this Theresa Cox? You did not tell me that."

The underlying worry in his gaze made her mouth go dry. She nodded. "The morning Baby John disappeared."

"So what happened when she came into your store?"

The bite in his tone let her know she hadn't misread his concern. She couldn't look at him, so she squinted through the gloom and studied her hands instead.

"Outwardly, I guess I would have to say nothing happened that I could really call unusual. She bought some baby things. Paid with cash, just like she did with Ezra and at the convenience store." In her excitement, she twisted so that her knee bumped his. "But, Levi, it's the timing that makes her actions so questionable, and the fact that she always seemed to be in such a hurry to leave."

Inspiration struck, and Cheryl pointed excitedly toward her eyes. "Oh, and there's the thing about the glasses too. Sometimes she wears them, sometimes she doesn't. That's odd, don't you think?"

Levi gave a slow shake of his head. "Perhaps she wears contacts?"

"Maybe. Or maybe she's trying to change her appearance. Hey, it worked for Clark Kent."

Levi looked confused, so she waved her hand like a cape flapping in the wind and added, "Superman?"

He didn't even crack a smile. Okay, so the Amish weren't fans of comic book characters. Still, she thought everyone had heard of Superman. She stifled a giggle and jammed her hands back inside her pockets.

They had circled the pond, and now the road wound gradually over a hill and back toward the farm. Levi gave the mare a slight nudge with the reins to get her moving then blew out a sigh. "I am glad you are doing what you can to help Rachel and Samuel, but I think you should be careful, Cheryl. This woman, this Theresa Cox, she is a stranger to Sugarcreek and I..."

To her shock, he hesitated and released the reins with one hand for a moment as if he'd like to reach for her hand. His gaze remained fixed to the road, however, and he quickly grasped the reins once more. "I would not care to see you hurt."

"I'll be careful," she said, wondering if she'd just imagined that he'd almost held her hand.

"Goot." Levi gave a chirp to the mare. She responded by tossing her mane and picking up the pace.

Cheryl gripped the seat edge with trembling fingers. Naomi had confided in Cheryl that Levi too had suffered a broken engagement when his childhood sweetheart decided she loved another. Had Levi ever taken his former fiancée riding like this, on a night so clear it made the landscape look as though it had been hand drawn and with the moon casting brilliant silver light overhead? It pained her to think he had, but of course, they would have done something just like this, many times over. She had been Amish, just like Levi, and they had grown up together. Cheryl had never met the girl, and still a twinge of jealousy colored the rest of the ride back to the farm. When they arrived, Levi jumped from the buggy and before Cheryl could exit, he circled to her side and held up his arms.

"It is dark and the ground is uneven here. Let me help you. I would not want you to fall."

Cheryl's thoughts immediately turned to mud. She swallowed nervously, tried very hard not to think about tumbling into a heap in the dirt, and braced her hands against Levi's strong shoulders. He lifted her out and down as though she weighed no more than a child—and he didn't even grunt—a fact she would find time to thank him for later. In fact, he set her down so gently, it took her a moment to realize that her feet had touched the ground, or that he didn't instantly step away.

"Thank you," she whispered.

He didn't answer, but watched her with that tender, measuring gaze she found so disconcerting. "You are an unusual woman, Cheryl Cooper. I never know from one moment to the next what to expect from you. It makes me...I am always off balance when I am around you."

What could she say to that? When he finally did add to the distance between them, Cheryl heard him drag in a deep breath and let it out on a sigh, something she'd likely have missed in Columbus with all the city noises blaring about. She let her hands fall to her sides, certain the sinewy feel of his muscles would be branded into her palms for months to come.

"I...I should be going," she stammered then dropped her gaze to fumble self-consciously in her pocket for her keys. She retrieved them, only to have them slip from her clumsy fingers and land with a thump in the dry, brittle grass.

"Sugar and grits," she mumbled, using a favorite expression of her very Southern momma. She frowned. With no light to see by, she'd have trouble finding them in the dark.

Levi chuckled and bent to retrieve the keys. Instead of dropping them into her palm, he unlocked the door then held it open for her with a smile. Cheryl's heart thumped as she slid past him into the driver's seat and then held out her hand.

"Thank you."

Levi dismissed her thanks with a shake of his head and laid the keys carefully in her palm. "You will remember what I said about Theresa Cox?"

She nodded and somehow managed to insert the key in the ignition while keeping her eyes locked on Levi's. "Yes, I remember. I'll be careful."

"Okay, then. I will see you tomorrow. Drive safe." He closed the door, retreated a step, then stood watching as Cheryl started the engine and flipped on the headlights.

My, but the man could mess with a girl's calm. Cheryl had to force herself to focus on the darkened road ahead rather than on the tall figure illuminated by the glow of her taillights in her rear-view mirror. It made for a long ride home, and for a muddling of her mind that not even the blaring of the radio could break.

A few minutes later, she let herself into Aunt Mitzi's cottage then locked the door behind her, comforted by the scraping of the deadbolt as she slid it into place. The clock above the hall table chimed the half hour.

Ten thirty. Late for her, but still early in Seattle. Her parents would just be finishing up the supper dishes.

Pulling her phone from a pocket in her purse, she dropped her keys on the hall table while she walked and punched the speed dial for her mother. It rang once before she picked up.

"Hello?"

"Hi, Momma. It's Cheryl."

"Hi, sweetheart. Good to hear from you. Everything okay?"

Straight to the point, as usual. Cheryl crossed to the living room sofa. Kicking off her shoes, she poked them under the coffee table with her toe and then sank onto the cushions.

"I'm fine. How are you and Daddy doing?"

"Oh, busy as usual. And tired. You know what your pawpaw used to say."

"You're wrung drier than your laundry?"

Her mother's soft chuckle tickled her ear. "That's it."

Cheryl shifted to pull her feet up on the sofa. "You still puttin' in extra hours at the mission?"

Puttin'?

She couldn't help but smile, hearing herself slip back into a bit of Southern slang. Funny how it came so easily, considering she'd never set foot in the South. She had her momma to thank for that.

"Yeah, well, your daddy's doin' most of the work. I'm just helpin' out where I can, as usual." She was silent a moment. "We sure miss you, sugar," she said, her voice softer. "I tried callin' last week just to check on you. You sure you're all right? It's been a while since we talked."

A knot rose to Cheryl's throat, and tears burned her eyes. "I know, Momma. I'm sorry about that. I've been meaning to call."

"It's all right, sugar. I know how busy you are. How are things at Aunt Mitzi's? Did you get that mess straightened out with the inventory at the store?"

The question eased a bit of the tension in Cheryl's chest. She explained how things had returned to normal after the strange events that happened a few weeks ago. "We're actually starting to pick up a little more business now that Christmas is around the corner. Naomi is talking about doubling up on her fudge orders, and I'm planning the displays of our holiday items."

"Such as?"

"I'll have a tree up with handcrafted ornaments for sale, and I want a unique display of our festive aprons and potholders. What do you think?"

"Wonderful ideas! You really are taking this job at the Swiss Miss to heart. Your aunt Mitzi would be proud." She hesitated, and Cheryl could almost hear the gears turning. "And speaking of Christmas, will you be coming to Seattle for a visit?"

"Why not plan a visit to see them?"

Levi's words whispered through Cheryl's head. She picked at the piping on the arm of the sofa. "I...uh...actually, Momma, I'm really not sure if I can get away at Christmas. It's one of our busiest times in the store, but I'll try to come for a visit soon."

"Oh, honey, really?" The disappointment in her voice was tangible. "I sure was hopin' you'd make it. Your daddy would so love to see you. So would I."

Cheryl sucked in a breath, thinking of her father. She missed him, and committing to a trip home would feel so good, even if it were just for a few days.

"I'll come as soon as I am able, Mom. Promise."

"That'll do for now," her mother said brightly, and then she paused. "So...you're sure everything's all right? You sound a little sad, sweetheart. Somethin' on your mind?"

Now. Now would be the time to talk to her about Lance and their breakup last spring. Maybe she could even ask her mother for advice on what do about her confusing feelings for Levi.

Cheryl stared at the stitching on her jeans, her eyes blurring with sudden tears. "Actually, Momma, there is something I'd like to talk to you about."

"Yes, sweetie?"

At the last moment, she changed what she'd been about to say. "There's been a kidnapping here in Sugarcreek. A baby boy named John Swartzentruber. His parents are Samuel and Rachel Swartzentruber. I told you about them, remember?"

"Oh no! Of course I remember them. I'm so sorry to hear this. Those poor parents. What happened?"

Cheryl explained the events of the last three days and her part in trying to solve the crime.

"The police don't have any leads," she finished, reaching toward the end table for a tissue, "and really, neither do I. I feel completely helpless."

"I understand, sweetheart. I'm so sorry that it happened while you were there visiting. You know it wasn't your fault, right?"

The note of urgency in her mother's voice was surprisingly comforting. Cheryl pressed the tissue to her nose. "Thanks, Momma. You're the second person to tell me that."

Her mother waited until Cheryl's sniffling calmed and then said, "I love you, sweetie. I wish I were close enough to hug your neck."

"I love you too, Momma, and I wish you were closer. I could really use a hug right about now."

She paused, and in the silence buzzing across the signal, Cheryl felt her mother gathering for a question.

"You're a special woman, sweetheart. I've always been proud of how strong you are, but I don't like that you're alone right now. Have you thought about possibly moving back to Columbus... maybe talking things over with Lance? I never have understood what happened between the two of you."

There it was—the question she'd spent months avoiding. Not that she blamed her mother for asking. She had every right to wonder about her daughter's happiness, and Cheryl had never really been honest with her about why she refused to speak of Lance.

She bit her lip and pressed the phone tighter to her ear. "No, I haven't thought about moving back. Things were pretty clear when Lance and I broke up. He decided he wasn't the marrying kind. I don't know that he ever will be."

Her mother's soft sigh spoke volumes. "I'm sorry, sweetheart. Your daddy warned me about being a busybody. I shouldn't have brought it up."

Though her mother couldn't see it, Cheryl shrugged. "It's all right, Momma. Besides, I'm not really alone. Naomi and Seth have been so sweet. Actually, their whole family has taken me in. I just love them, and Levi..."

She broke off, afraid her mother would read too much into it if she said more.

"Levi? I don't believe you've mentioned him before. Who is he?"

Too late. Cheryl shifted the phone to her other ear. "He's Naomi's stepson. Her oldest. Did I forget to mention him? He's been a big help around the store. I've actually started stocking a few of his homemade Bible covers. You should see them. They're really beautiful."

"Next time we come," her mother promised. "So? Everything else okay? What about your aunt Mitzi? Have you heard from her?"

"Not since her last letter," Cheryl said. "I should be receiving another one soon, though. I'll call and let you know how she's doing."

"Thanks, sweetie. I know she appreciates you looking after things while she's gone, and so do I."

"I don't mind. Running the Swiss Miss has actually helped take my mind off of my troubles."

"That's good...so long as you don't let things simmer too long before you check the pot."

Which was her mother's way of saying she needed to clear things up with Lance.

"I hear you, Momma," Cheryl said, smiling into the phone.

Across the line, she felt her mother smile back. "All right, dear. I love you."

"Love you too. Will you tell daddy hello for me?"

"Of course. I'll fill him in on the baby who was kidnapped too. We'll get the church praying for him and his family."

"Thanks, Momma."

"No problem. Keep me informed if anything changes."

"I will."

They said their good-byes and hung up, Cheryl's heart lighter than it had been before she called despite the awkwardness when the conversation turned to Lance. That would pass eventually. Besides, it was good to know there were more prayers going up for Baby John. On the other hand, she still had not been completely honest with her parents about her feelings toward Lance...and now Levi.

Turning her phone to silent, Cheryl dragged off of the sofa toward her bedroom. It was highly unlikely she'd get much sleep, but at least she could go to bed knowing she had her mother's prayers.

Right now, she could feel her mother's love all the way from Seattle to Sugarcreek, Ohio.

Chapter Ten

Cheryl stared at the gleaming black and silver clock quietly ticking away the time above the display case. Only five minutes had gone by since she last checked it. Not that she could afford to stand still and watch the hours drag by, with Thanksgiving around the corner and the Christmas holiday fast approaching. It was just that with each second that passed since Baby John's disappearance, hope of finding him decreased.

She sighed and watched as the clock ticked off another minute. Hard to believe they still had no solid leads. And she was pretty certain that if she called one more time to ask about the case, Chief Twitchell would have her arrested for harassment.

"Excuse me, how much are these?"

Cheryl jerked and propped the broom she'd been using to sweep the store up in a corner. A woman of somewhat middle age stood near the entrance holding a tin of Naomi's homemade fudge in each hand.

Cheryl named the prices while the woman eyed both of the tins, moved them up and down as though weighing her options, then replaced the smaller tin on the shelf and added the larger one to her basket.

Good choice. She'd be glad she'd opted for the larger container once she sampled the chocolate.

Just then, the bell above the door jingled. Expecting Naomi, Cheryl glanced up and was pleasantly surprised when she saw Levi hurrying over. A flush colored his cheeks, and his eyes were unusually bright with excitement.

Self-consciously, Cheryl smoothed her hand over her hair. "Good morning, Levi. I didn't expect you today."

"Guder mariye." Levi gestured toward the back of the store. "Do you have a minute? I must speak with you."

Cheryl's heart gave a painful thump. Was this about last night? Untying the ruffled apron from around her waist, she laid it on the counter and nodded. "Sure. Let's go to my office."

At the counter where the cash register sat, Levi stopped her from entering the office.

"Uh..." He glanced at the woman with the fudge, who watched them with unabashed interest. "This will do."

Cheryl wanted to smack herself on the forehead. Of course. Levi would never risk the slightest appearance of impropriety. Certain her face had become as red as her hair, she cleared her throat and crossed her arms. "So what's up?"

Levi angled himself so that his back was to the curious customer. He bent forward slightly and lowered his voice. "The woman you spoke to me about last night...what was her name?"

"Theresa Cox?" Cheryl uncrossed her arms and straightened. "What about her?"

He gave a rapid wave. "Tell me again what she looks like."

She rattled off a brief description, her own excitement growing. "Why? What's going on, Levi?"

Cheryl had always thought Levi handsome, but never more than when he looked at her with startling intensity in his cobalt blue eyes—like he did at that moment.

"Is Esther here?"

She nodded.

He tipped his head toward the exit. "Do you think she can handle the store for a minute? There's something I want you to see."

"I'm sure she can." Cheryl hurried to the stockroom, told Esther where she was heading, then shrugged into her coat and met Levi at the door.

"What is going on?" she huffed as they hurried up the street toward the Old Amish Store.

Levi motioned her to a halt and then directed her under the green and white awning stretching out above the entrance to the Sugarcreek Sisters Quilt Shoppe.

"Wait," he said, his gaze fixed on the stores on the other side of the street.

Cheryl pressed deeper into the shade provided by the awning. What exactly were they waiting for? Finally, he pointed toward By His Grace Christian Books. Sunlight glinted off the glass as the door swung open and a woman stepped out.

"There. Is that the woman who came into the Swiss Miss the day John Swartzentruber was kidnapped?"

Cheryl's breath caught. A young woman of medium height and build stood on the sidewalk fumbling through her purse for her keys. She wore dark sunglasses and a bright red scarf covered her head, but even from this distance, she walked with the harried steps Cheryl recognized.

She leaned out from the awning and pointed. "That's her!"

She said it loud enough that the woman's head lifted and turned in their direction. Cheryl froze, afraid that if she so much as twitched, the woman would disappear again. She stared at them a moment and then spun on her heel and strode away.

"Levi, we have to stop her," Cheryl exclaimed, grasping his arm.

"Cheryl, wait."

But she was already moving. If she let the woman out of her sight, she might never find her again. She checked for traffic then raced across the street, one hand raised above her head.

"Excuse me, ma'am?"

Was it her imagination, or did the woman speed up? Cheryl quickened her steps.

"Ma'am, can you wait a minute? Miss Cox?"

Surely she'd heard her call out. Determined now, Cheryl broke into a jog.

"Theresa Cox!"

The woman stopped so abruptly, Cheryl almost crashed into her. Out of breath and more than a little aggravated, she jabbed a finger toward the woman's chest.

"Are you Theresa Cox?"

Behind the sunglasses, Cheryl saw the woman blink. Then, reaching up below the scarf, she tugged a Bluetooth headset from her ear and held it to her mouth.

"Hold on a second." Her gaze flitted toward Cheryl. "I'm sorry, were you talking to me?"

She nodded and struggled to catch her breath. Levi had joined them on the sidewalk, but he was nowhere near as winded as she. He motioned toward the woman.

"We are sorry to bother you, but we are looking for someone. By chance, is your name Theresa Cox?"

The woman pulled off the sunglasses and eyed them critically. "It is. Who are you?" Her gaze bounced between Levi and Cheryl. "Do I know you?"

Cheryl pointed toward the headset. "Do you have a minute? We'd like to talk to you."

She eyed them warily then lifted the headset and spoke. "I'll have to call you back." She tapped a button on the piece and slid it into her pocket. "So? How can I help you?"

Now that they'd finally found the woman, Cheryl felt at a loss for words. She glanced at Levi, who encouraged her with a tip of his head.

"Well, you see...," she stammered, lifting the edge of her coat to let a bit of cool air trickle in, "we...uh...that is, I was wondering..."

Theresa Cox was staring at her with a glare that could melt icebergs, and why not? What exactly did Cheryl think was going to happen? She'd ask if she was responsible for taking John

Swartzentruber and the woman would simply blurt out a confession? Suddenly, Cheryl felt very inadequate. And foolish.

Lord, please help me.

The faint prayer had only half formed when Cheryl felt peace wash over her like a gentle wave. She lifted her chin and looked Theresa in the eyes. "I run the Swiss Miss. I believe you came into my store the other day?" She pointed down the street in the direction of the store.

She blinked and averted her gaze. "Did I?"

"You bought a crib mobile."

Theresa tilted her head as if thinking. "Yes, well, I've purchased several things over the last couple of days. I can't remember if any were from your store."

Catching sight of the small head shake Levi directed at her, Cheryl smoothed the scowl from her face and tried again. "I remember specifically because you seemed to be in a bit of a hurry, and you paid with cash."

"So much easier than credit." Theresa gave a wave of her hand, as though dismissing her concern. "Besides, what of it? What exactly is this about?"

John's fate rested squarely on Cheryl's shoulders. Hard as it was to muster the words, she took a deep breath and forced herself to speak calmly through tight lips. "Ms. Cox, are you aware that a child was kidnapped recently from one of the local farms?"

Shock widened her eyes, and the air of nonchalance fell from her like a stone. "What?"

"It's been all over the local news. I'm surprised you haven't heard."

"I...haven't been watching the news."

Cheryl licked her lips in a gesture that could be construed as nervousness or sympathy, depending on the onlooker's bent. Right now Cheryl was leaning toward nerves, despite the fact the woman looked genuinely distressed.

"I'm staying at the Sleepy Dutchman Inn. There aren't any TVs there."

Cheryl glanced at Levi. "That's an Amish bed-and-breakfast, isn't it?"

He nodded. "The Bowmans run it."

"I wanted to get a feel for the authentic Amish lifestyle," Theresa explained, almost defensively. She crossed both arms over her chest and lowered her brows. "It's a touristy thing, I know, but I'm interested in the work of local artisans, which is why I bought the baby toys." She glanced at Levi and then back at Cheryl. "You say a kid was stolen from one of the farms?"

"A baby," Levi said, his voice quiet and low. "Stolen from his crib three days ago."

Theresa's face paled, and she pressed her fingers to her mouth. "Oh my. I'm so sorry to hear that."

"May we buy you a cup of kaffee?"

Both women turned startled gazes toward Levi. He gestured toward Yoder's Corner. "They have the best cinnamon rolls in town."

Twin lines furrowed Theresa Cox's brow. "I don't know..."

"It is the least we can do in exchange for your time."

"It won't take long," Cheryl added, holding her breath while Theresa checked her watch.

To Cheryl's surprise, it was Levi that Theresa examined before finally giving a nod. "All right then." Hitching her purse higher on her shoulder, she added, "I'd sure like to know what all this is about."

She certainly didn't act like a person worried about being accused of kidnapping. In fact, she looked genuinely confused as they entered the restaurant and selected a table near the window but away from the other patrons. Levi took care of ordering their coffee. Theresa turned down the offer of a cinnamon roll, and Cheryl did likewise.

While they waited for their drinks to be delivered, Theresa removed her sunglasses and tucked them into a pocket of her purse. "I'm afraid I didn't catch your name"—she gestured through the glass—"out there."

"It's Cheryl Cooper," she replied. "Like I told you outside, I run the Swiss Miss. And this is my...friend...Levi Miller."

Why she should stumble on the word was a dilemma she'd have to ponder later, when she found a quiet moment alone. Cheryl swallowed hard and forged on.

"I'm sorry we pounced on you unexpectedly like we did, it's just, with Baby John still missing, pretty much the whole town is on high alert."

"John? That's the baby's name?"

Cheryl nodded and looked to Levi for support.

He pressed his palms to the table, his hands large against the checkered cloth. "The family is, of course, desperate to find him. When Cheryl—Miss Cooper—and I heard about a woman purchasing baby toys and paying for them with cash and rushing out without even getting change..."

"You thought I took the baby?" Theresa's scarf had slipped from her head. She yanked it off of her neck and jammed it into her lap.

"To be honest, we can't be sure of anything right now," Cheryl replied quickly. "We're basically just trying to keep our eyes open and report any unusual happenings that we see around town." She steadied herself against the table. "I realize this is very untoward. I hope you understand, all we're trying to do here is help this family find their son."

Theresa hesitated a moment and then nodded. "Yes, I guess I can understand that, though I'm not sure what I can do to help."

Cheryl swallowed nervously. "Perhaps if you wouldn't mind telling us who the baby things are for?"

Their coffee arrived. Theresa stiffened while the waitress set the drinks in front of them then took her time stirring half a packet of sugar into her cup.

"Look, Miss Cooper, I truly do appreciate what you're trying to do, and I am sorry for that family who lost their son, I really am." She drew a breath and blew it out. "But I've already told you, I'm just a tourist interested in the work of local craftsmen. That's it. And this"—she motioned to her and Levi—"is kinda freaking me out."

Cheryl bit her tongue. Surely she had to realize why they felt compelled to speak to her and how weak her story sounded? "Look, Ms. Cox..."

Her lips pressed into a thin line, punctuated by the pink gloss she'd applied. "I had nothing to do with that missing child. Now, if you'll excuse me?" She pushed her chair back and rose from the table, leaving her coffee sitting untouched and steaming. "I really need to be going. Good day to you both."

Cheryl felt as though she were a balloon and someone had punched a hole in her and let all the air squeak out. She started to go after her and was drawn back into her seat by Levi's firm grasp.

"No, Cheryl. You have to let her go."

She glanced at the door and back. "But she hasn't told us anything."

He shook his head. "She did. She told us everything. It is we who expected something more."

Was he right? Had she assumed too much? Hoped too much? Her knees suddenly weak, she sank into her chair, hot tears burning her eyelids.

"I don't understand. I was so sure that when we found her, she'd be able to provide us with some answers."

"I'm sorry, Cheryl. I know you hoped that finding this woman would be the key to solving the mystery behind John's disappearance."

It was petty and selfish, yet more than solving the mystery, Cheryl had hoped finding John would absolve her of the guilt that had clung to her like a cocklebur since his disappearance. Misery settled like heavy mist on her heart.

"Cheryl, look at me."

She couldn't. If she did, he'd see how disappointed she was and know the truth behind her desperate desire to have Baby John returned.

"Cheryl, what happened to Samuel and Rachel was not your fault."

She jerked her head up. Sure enough, Levi was looking at her with enough warmth and compassion to make her eyes flood with tears.

"How...how did you know?" she whispered past a raw throat.

He shrugged and dropped his gaze. "We all tend to blame ourselves when things go wrong, ain't so?"

He wasn't talking about her anymore, or not *just* her. Empathy melted her heart as she thought back to the woman he'd once loved and who'd in turn broken his heart. She sniffed and wiped the tears from her cheeks with her free hand. "Yeah, I guess that's true."

"So it is possible that this guilt you are feeling now, it may not be something you truly deserve. In that case, perhaps it is something you would do well to seek Gott about, ja?"

"Ja."

She replied without thinking and then burst into a giggle at the realization that she'd mimicked his speech and the lift of his eyebrows at the same time. Levi too chuckled.

"Thanks for talking me back from the ledge, Levi. I was really bummed there for a minute."

He didn't respond immediately, but the way his face softened into a gentle smile, accentuated by the sweet crinkles around his gorgeous blue eyes, made her want to melt into a puddle.

Finally he blew out a sigh and pushed back in his chair. "I am glad we found this woman you were looking for so we can put any suspicion of her to rest."

Not exactly, Cheryl thought, directing her gaze to her cooling cup of coffee. She hadn't answered one question—why she'd bothered to check out of the Little Switzerland a day early.

Biting the inside of her cheek, Cheryl made a mental note of the inn where Theresa had said she was staying. She'd claimed she was only interested in exploring the Amish lifestyle, but it never hurt to ask questions or see if the innkeeper's story lined up. If not, Cheryl intended to plop Theresa Cox back on to her list of suspects—right near the top.

CHAPTER ELEVEN

Cheryl watched as Naomi scooped the last bit of cooked pumpkin from the rind and gave her spoon a hearty pat against the side of the large glass bowl she was using to make puree. Too hearty. A large glop of pumpkin flew from the spoon, missing her apron, and spattered against her brown dress. Cheryl ducked her head and stifled a laugh.

"Sugar and grits," Naomi mumbled.

Seth ambled into the kitchen and poured himself a cup of coffee, a wry grin on his bearded face. "What is this? For a moment, I thought Cheryl had stopped by."

"Cheryl did stop by," she said from her stool next to the window, "but what you heard was definitely your wife."

Surprise rounded Seth's eyes as he turned to catch sight of her. "There you are. Guder mariye, Cheryl."

"Guder mariye, Seth," Cheryl repeated, fighting back a smile as she sipped from her cup.

Naomi's cheeks reddened, and she dropped her gaze to the offending pumpkin splotch. "I wanted to have a fresh batch of pumpkin butter for the store, and since Cheryl has been asking for the recipe, I invited her over to watch."

Seth's eyes twinkled with mirth as he took a seat at the table. "And you thought you would sweeten it first by spreading it on your dress?" He winked at Cheryl. "I bet you did not know that was part of the recipe."

This time Cheryl couldn't hold back her laughter. It warmed her to see the gentle teasing passing between Seth and Naomi.

Grabbing a dishcloth, Naomi dabbed away the stain and then carried the bowl of fresh pumpkin to the counter for mashing. She inclined her head toward her husband. "So? What are your plans for today, aside from cluttering up my kitchen?"

Seth chuckled, and Cheryl jotted down the ingredients as Naomi added sugar, cinnamon, and ground cloves to the bowl then sprinkled in a dash of allspice.

"Will you be stopping by the Swartzentrubers' farm?" Naomi continued.

Seth shook his head, his fingers combing thoughtfully at his beard. "Actually, I thought I would try something else first. In keeping with our traditions, the Swartzentrubers have no photographs of Baby John to share with the police, and since the twins aren't identical, it wouldn't help to use a picture of Baby Joseph, even if they would allow a photograph to be taken. But our Elizabeth, she is quite a gifted artist, ain't so? Better than that officer Chief Twitchell brought in from the next county to try and create a sketch."

Cheryl lifted her head. What exactly was he thinking?

Naomi paused her stirring and turned to look at her husband. "Ja, she is talented. You are thinking about asking her to work with the police department?"

He shrugged. "I thought it might help if they had something to go on."

Admiration filled Cheryl's heart. It couldn't be easy for him to consider allowing Elizabeth to work so closely with the Englischers after losing Sarah to one.

Setting aside the spoon, Naomi wiped her hands on her apron and went to sit beside him at the table.

"That is a wonderful idea, Seth. I am very glad you thought of it."

His shoulders straightened at her praise. Cheryl looked away. Something as small as an admiring word could mean so much. Was that what had been missing between her and Lance?

Seth braced his hands against the table and moved to rise. "Goot, then I will speak to Elizabeth."

Naomi caught his arm, and her gaze winged to Cheryl and back. "Seth, wait. There is something else we need to seek your advice on."

He settled back into his seat. "Ja? What is it?"

Naomi motioned toward Cheryl, who relayed the details of her encounter with Jeremiah Zook. When she finished, Naomi blew out a troubled sigh.

"I am worried for them, Seth," she said. "Do you think we could speak to them, perhaps offer a listening ear?"

"We?" Seth waggled his eyebrows. "I do not know. Cheryl? What does your schedule look like this afternoon?"

Naomi swatted his arm. "All right... you. Could *you* speak to Jeremiah and see if there is anything we can do to help?"

He dipped his head in agreement. "I will see to it."

"Goot. Oh, and Seth..." Naomi plucked at the hem of her apron. "About Rachel Swartzentruber's parents..."

Blowing an exaggerated sigh, Seth sank against his seat and rolled his eyes heavenward. "So today we are determined to fix all of the world's problems, ain't so?"

Naomi leaned forward and fixed her husband with a determined glare. "You do not like that Rachel is refusing to speak to the Robertsons any more than Cheryl or I do."

"No, I do not, but..."

"What is it the Bible says about honoring one's parents?" Naomi tapped her temple as though thinking. "Cheryl, do you remember?"

She had no time to answer before Seth narrowed his eyes and wagged his finger under Naomi's nose. "You know exactly what it says, Wife."

"Ja, I do, and so does our Rachel. But right now, she is not thinking clearly, and I fear she will regret having allowed so great a chasm between her and her parents, especially if..."

Cheryl flipped the page on her notepad. She was glad Naomi hadn't finished the thought. John *would* come home. In the meantime, she agreed with Naomi. Rachel needed her mother, whether she admitted it or not.

Naomi reached out to clasp her husband's hand. "Think of Sarah. Is there anything you would not do to make things right with her, were you allowed the chance?"

Seth said nothing, but on his face was written a wealth of regret.

"It is wrong to let Rachel make the same mistakes that you and Sarah made," Naomi whispered gently. "I know it here." She tapped her chest. "Besides," she continued brightly, "it is not as though we would be going behind Rachel's back. There are reports all over the televisions and radios, and her parents are not Amish. They have surely heard the news by now."

Seth rubbed one large palm over his face. "That is most likely true."

Naomi pressed both hands tightly around her husband's. "We would speak to the Robertsons as parents, encourage them to reach out to their daughter. Perhaps if they knew how desperately she needed them, their hearts might be softened."

He lowered his head. "Would that I could have seen how much my Sarah needed me when she was growing up. I was too blinded by my own grief after her mother died to realize it."

Cheryl swallowed a sudden swell of emotion. For all his gruff demeanor, Seth hid a hurt in his heart that none but the Lord could heal, and that she understood full well.

Naomi laid her hand against his cheek. "We might spare another family the same bitterness and pain. Is it not our duty to try?"

He rested his chin atop his laced fingers and then sighed. "You are right, but considering the resentment the Roberstsons feel about their daughter becoming Amish, do you think they will even speak to us?"

"I had not thought of that." Frowning, Naomi dropped back against her chair and then glanced at Cheryl. "Perhaps you could come with us? Surely the Robertsons would speak with you."

She set down her pencil and straightened. "Of course, if you think it would help."

"I believe that would be a goot idea." Seth stood and nodded toward Cheryl then pressed a kiss to Naomi's forehead. "I am grateful for such a wise and loving wife."

The words brought a wash of happy tears. Naomi smiled up at her husband.

This.

This was what Cheryl was missing and what she had mourned so deeply for after Lance left. It hit her like a blow and left her blinking back tears as Naomi said good-bye to Seth and then crossed to the counter where her unfinished batch of pumpkin butter waited.

Cheryl folded up the paper she'd been using to take notes. The work was easy, and Naomi had performed the task so many times, she obviously knew the steps by heart. Watching would afford Cheryl plenty of time to think.

And pray.

CHAPTER TWELVE

New Philadelphia was a large town in comparison to Sugarcreek, yet much smaller than Columbus. It was quaint and well kept, and the views of the Tuscarawas River made the twenty-minute drive pleasant. At least, it was until they wound through downtown, past a large brick building with a sign that read Welcome to Our City in metal letters on top.

Seeing it made the biscuit Cheryl had washed down with coffee when she, Naomi, and Seth stopped for breakfast sit like a yeasty lump in her stomach. Maybe coming along on this trip hadn't been such a good idea. She had her own family problems to deal with, after all.

Cheryl pointed as the Ferris wheel of Tuscora Park came into view. "There's the park. According to my map, the Robertsons' house should be nearby."

She glanced sidelong at Naomi. "Sure you want to do this?"

Naomi craned her neck to peer at her husband in the backseat. "Seth?"

In the rearview mirror, Seth nodded. "Ja, we're sure." He peered out the window. "How much longer to the Robertsons' home?"

Cheryl took a deep breath then checked the navigation app on her phone one last time. "About five minutes."

Three turns later, they rolled to a stop in front of a large Tudor style house. Neatly trimmed hedges lined a brick path leading up to an oak door fitted with sparkling leaded glass.

She shoved the car into park. "This is it."

A bouquet of Indian corn adorned the door. To the left of the patio had been arranged several bales of hay. Pumpkins and chrysanthemums spilled from the top, and a cheerful scarecrow bearing a Welcome sign beckoned.

"We'll see how welcome we are once they find out why we're here," Cheryl muttered as she exited the Ford.

Naomi joined her on the sidewalk. "Did you say something, Cheryl?"

She forced a smile. "I was just wondering how welcome we're going to be once the Roberstons find out we're here to talk to them about their daughter."

Naomi turned to peer at the house, an anxious frown forming wrinkles on her forehead and around her mouth. Even Seth looked somber as he gestured toward the path that led to the entrance.

"We will not find out standing here. Shall we?"

At the door, Cheryl paused before ringing the bell. "Better let me do the talking, at least until we figure out how receptive they are to our coming."

Both Seth and Naomi nodded, and then Naomi squeezed Cheryl's arm. "Danki."

"For what?"

"Coming with us"—she motioned toward the house—"and speaking with the Robertsons. You did not have to."

Cheryl covered her hand. "It's the right thing to do. We both know that. Let's hope the Robertsons do too."

Some of the worry melted from Naomi's face. Seth's too, though his features were harder to read behind the full beard. Still, Cheryl knew how much they wanted to help, despite the hard feelings that existed between Rachel and her parents. Drawing a quivering breath, she reached for the bell and pushed.

At first only the bark of a small dog emanated from inside. Cheryl waited and then pushed the bell a second time. Somewhere deep inside the house a voice called, "Coming."

"This is it," Cheryl said over her shoulder, turning just as the door opened and a stylish woman with perfect hair and makeup stood looking out. She was quite attractive, with refined features that had Cheryl guessing as to her age.

"Hello. Can I help...?"

Her gaze drifted past Cheryl to Naomi and Seth. She froze, a look that could only be described as angry recognition darkening her features.

"Who is it, dear?" a man's voice from inside asked.

"I don't know." She closed the door slightly, so that her slender body filled the entire crack then turned her face toward the hall just visible over her shoulder. "John, could you come here for a moment?"

"One second, love. I'm working on that..."

"John!" The door closed even farther, and she twisted to hiss over her shoulder. "Now."

Heavy steps sounded from within and then the man's voice again. "All right, all right, Victoria, what in the world..."

She swung the door open to expose them so that all three had a clear view of the house and hallway.

John Robertson stared silently for a second, a towel twisted in his hands. "Oh. I see."

He was a tall man, just beginning to show signs of age with gray peppering the hair at his temples. He was handsome and confident—except that at the moment, his lips had gone slack. It seemed to take some effort for him to tear his gaze from Naomi to fix on Cheryl.

"Who are you?" As he spoke, he draped the towel over his shoulder and braced his hands on his hips. At his ankles, a small Yorkie terrier yapped at them. He picked the dog up in a move so practiced, it appeared he did it without thinking. The dog quieted instantly.

Cheryl stepped forward, her mouth suddenly dry. "Hello, Mr. Robertson. My name is Cheryl Cooper. These are my friends, Seth and Naomi Miller."

His gaze darted to Seth and Naomi and then quickly returned. "Is this about my daughter?"

She had been expecting a bit of resistance, maybe some tension to start with, but his forthrightness caught her completely off guard. She barely managed a squeaky, "Yes, sir, it is."

Naomi's gentle voice filled the sudden silence. "Mr. Robertson, Mrs. Robertson, would you mind if we came in for a moment? We would like to speak with you about your daughter. It will not take long."

Mrs. Robertson pressed close to her husband's side, her fingers clutching his bicep. "What about Rachel? Is she all right?"

Naomi glanced at Seth and then at Cheryl. She didn't want to share this news on the Robertsons' front steps any more than they did.

Cheryl cleared her throat. "I'm afraid we have some bad news." She waited, searching their faces for indication that they already knew what she was about to share. They both stared back unblinking, their lips pressed into tight, unyielding lines. Even the dog watched her intently, its ears perked and twitching.

Cheryl lifted her chin and forged ahead. "Were you aware that your grandson, John Swartzentruber, has been kidnapped?"

Mrs. Robertson dropped her gaze, and Mr. Robertson slipped his free arm around his wife's waist. "We...heard. Not from Rachel. It was on the news, and we've already been questioned by police."

Cheryl nodded. "Yes, sir, and we'd like to ask a few questions." She motioned toward the door. "May we?"

Mrs. Robertson lifted her face to her husband. "John?"

He shook his head, and his jawline firmed. "Actually, this is not a good time."

"What?" Scarcely able to believe her ears, Cheryl repeated his words. "Not a good time?"

"I'm afraid not."

The dog seemed to sense the tension rippling between them because it immediately began barking.

"Muffin, hush," Mr. Robertson warned. He put the dog down and then snatched the towel from his shoulder and tossed it onto a table where several flyers and pamphlets lay stacked. The last one pictured a large cruise ship. The rest slid to the floor in an untidy mess.

"I'm sorry, Miss Cooper, my wife hasn't been feeling well. I was just fixing her something to help her headache. We've both been under a lot of strain," he added, drawing his wife closer.

Cheryl's gaze drifted to Mrs. Robertson. She did appear tense, and her lips quivered in a way that suggested she might be on the verge of tears. How terrible this rift with her daughter must be to her! Cheryl felt a wave of empathy splash over her.

"I'm sorry," she said quietly.

Mrs. Robertson's gaze slid to hers, and then she nodded. "Thank you, but I'm sure you can understand why we would rather not discuss the problems with our daughter with strangers."

"Oh, but we are not exactly strangers," Cheryl began. "The Millers, here, have known your daughter..."

"You are strangers to us," Mr. Robertson interrupted firmly.

"If I may?" For the first time, Seth spoke. He removed his hat and then crossed to stand in front of Mr. Robertson, his gaze steady and calm. "I know this separation from your daughter has caused you pain. She too has suffered, which is why we felt it necessary to come...on her behalf."

"Her behalf?" A surprising amount of bitterness sharpened Mrs. Robertson's words. She glared at Seth and then at Naomi. "So she doesn't know about your visit, is that it?"

Seth shook his head sadly. "I am afraid not."

His words seemed to invigorate the Robertsons. They both stood a little straighter, their shoulders back and their chins jutting angrily.

Seth held up his hand. "Please, if you will just hear us out. I know what you are going through, what you are *all* going through, and I might be able to help."

"Oh, *you* know what we're going through?" Mrs. Robertson said, the accusation in her tone stinging. She stepped forward, away from her husband, her lips and skin white beneath her makeup and tears wetting her eyelashes. "I suppose you know what it's like to have one of your children reject everything you believe in? To deny *everything*"—her hand slashed through the air—"you've taught them their whole life so they can turn their back on you and become someone you barely recognize?"

Mr. Robertson clasped his wife's elbow. "Victoria."

She jerked her head toward her husband. "No, John. He doesn't know what we're going through. It's not fair of him to say so."

"He does," Cheryl said, loudly and firmly enough to capture the Robertsons' attention. Both turned to look at her. She drew a breath and lowered her voice. "He does know. His eldest daughter, Sarah, left Sugarcreek to marry outside the church. He hasn't seen her or spoken to her for a very long time."

The Robertsons seemed to consider this a moment, and then Mr. Robertson sighed and ran his hand through his graying hair.

"I see." He paused, though his jaw continued working as though he were struggling for words. "We're sorry to hear that.

Unfortunately, we're not ready to talk about the problem with our daughter just yet. I hope you understand and will respect our position."

With that, he stepped back into the house, pulling his wife with him, and closed the door. Cheryl stared at the bundle of Indian corn that hung from the knocker, the dried husks rattling like paper in the stiff breeze.

"We should go," Seth said, replacing his hat on his head.

Cheryl hesitated, torn between racing for her car and storming into the house and demanding that the Robertsons hear them out. Did they have any idea what agony their child was going through? Regardless of what had passed between the members of this family, she found it difficult to believe that they could close one another out so coldly.

"They didn't even give us a chance," she muttered, disbelief and frustration making the words sharp on her tongue.

"We tried," Naomi urged, grasping Cheryl's arm. "That is all the Lord expects from us."

Still, it didn't feel right walking away with the situation between Rachel and her parents still festering. Disquiet gnawed at Cheryl's stomach all the way home...that and something else...a feeling that she'd missed something she shouldn't have. In the backseat, Seth and Naomi conversed quietly. Naomi had elected to ride there, and sensing she wanted to comfort her husband, Cheryl had not objected.

They were nearing Sugarcreek before she could no longer contain the words roiling through her brain.

"I just don't get it," she said, slapping the steering wheel. "How could anyone turn their back on their own child at a time like this?" She met Seth's gaze in the rearview mirror. "I mean, I know you and Sarah have had your differences, but were you in the Robertsons' place, I have no doubt that you would do everything you could to help your daughter, right?"

His jaw clenched, but he nodded. "I would. But perhaps we are missing the point, Cheryl. It may be that the Robertsons *are* doing all they can."

Her mouth dropped, and she jerked the wheel a little too tightly. All three of them pitched side-to-side. When she had calmed enough to speak, she said, "Are you kidding? They wouldn't even talk to us."

Naomi tsked quietly. "What Seth means, Cheryl, is that we all handle our emotions differently. Those who rely on Gott have a strength and peace that is foreign to those without Him. Now, I am not saying Rachel's parents are without Gott. We have no idea what kind of people the Robertsons are. I am merely suggesting that perhaps this is their way of dealing with a situation that appears out of their control."

Cheryl frowned doubtfully, flicking on her signal and making the turn before she spoke. "I don't know. They sure didn't seem all that concerned to me. I mean, did you see the travel agency flyers on the hall table?"

"Travel agency flyers?" Seth echoed.

Naomi nodded. "I noticed them, but I did not know what they were." She sought Cheryl's gaze in the mirror. "You are sure that is what those papers were for?"

"I think so." Her grip tightened on the wheel. "I think I recognized the logo on one of them. I could check, I suppose."

But as she drove into Sugarcreek, the question she'd asked in frustration pounded over and over in Cheryl's brain.

What kind of parents plan a vacation when their grandchild is missing?

Chapter Thirteen

Cheryl dropped Seth and Naomi off at the farm and then made a beeline for the Swiss Miss and her computer. The old thing was crankier than normal. By the time she finally got it fired up, her fingers were raw from drumming.

She wracked her brain while she waited. The last flyer on the table included a picture of a cruise ship. And palm trees. Lots of palm trees. If only she'd gotten a better look! Though she couldn't recall the name of the agency, the picture was familiar, and Googling local travel sites would be easy.

She'd only searched a few minutes before pulling up a Web site with the same ship featured in the header. And the address for the agency was in Dover, not far away.

She squinted at the screen. "TransWorld Travel," she read quietly.

Cheryl sat back in her chair. She was almost certain that was the name she'd seen on the flyer. She jotted down the number then reached for her cell phone. A couple of rings later, a perky voice answered.

"TransWorld Travel. This is Faith speaking. How can I help you?"

Cheryl licked her dry lips and tried to sound casual. "Hi, Faith. My name is Cheryl Cooper. I'd like to talk with someone about planning a vacation?"

"Great! I can help you." Cheryl heard computer keys clacking and then Faith came on the line again. "Okay, let's start with some basic information first. Do you have any idea where you'd like to go?"

"Uh...not exactly. I was thinking possibly a cruise? Or maybe a trip abroad." Cheryl tacked on the latter, thinking the Robertsons looked like a couple who would use the term *abroad*.

"All righty. And will you be traveling alone, or is someone going with you?"

"Alone. For now. Well...what I mean is...yes, I'll be traveling alone."

Ugh. *For now?* Why on earth had she added that? She resisted the urge to smack her forehead and gripped the phone tighter.

"No problem. We've got lots of packages available. Do you have a specific price point?"

"Not really." Thinking that made her sound haughty, she added, "I mean, you know, I'd like to stay within reason."

"I understand. I can add on a cruise if you'd like, although this time of year, you'll most likely want to embark from a more tropical climate."

"Right. Whatever you think looks good."

There were more keys clacking, and then Faith returned to the line. "Yes, I've got several great packages available, and most of them look very reasonable. I'd be happy to show them to you. What does your calendar look like? Would you like to set up an appointment for later this week?"

"Actually, I was hoping you might be available today."

"Today would be wonderful! Just let me check my calendar..."

Faith sounded exceptionally pleased, and Cheryl had to pull the phone away from her ear.

"Yep! All clear. I can see you this afternoon, say around three? How long will it take you to get here?"

"I live in Sugarcreek, so probably about fifteen minutes?"

"That will give me plenty of time," she said. "I'll pull some material for you and have it waiting when you get here. See you soon."

The line went dead, and Cheryl was left staring at a darkened cell phone. Okay, so the lady was perky. That fit the travel agent image she'd created in her head—one who looked like Julie McCoy from *The Love Boat* and talked faster than Kelly Ripa. Grimacing, she rose, reached for her jacket and purse, and then went out to her car.

TransWorld Travel was housed in a quaint little cottage in the very heart of Dover. Painted palms adorned the windows on either side of the entrance, and on the door was a sign that read Your Paradise Awaits.

Barely had Cheryl pushed past the threshold than a cheery voice called, "Hello there! You must be Cheryl Cooper."

A petite woman waved from behind a massive desk, her gold hoop earrings swinging against her cheeks with each swipe of her arm. Hopping from her chair, she circled the desk and gave Cheryl's hand a hearty pump.

"Faith Overstreet."

"Cheryl Cooper."

"So good to meet you. Your call came at a great time, since my afternoon was free."

Faith pranced back to her desk, her curls bouncing against her shoulders. Cheryl instantly envied the woman's gossamer locks. Her hair was exactly the right shade of red—not too bright, but still vibrant enough to be called "strawberry." The only way anyone would consider Cheryl's hair a fruit was if carrots suddenly changed food groups. She sighed and slid into the chair Faith offered.

"So you're thinking about taking a vacation?" Faith pointed to the pamphlets she'd spread across her desk. "Here are several great packages to choose from. What exactly did you have in mind?"

Cheryl picked up one of the pamphlets and fingered the edge. It featured a trip to Mexico via a cruise ship. She didn't recognize it as one of the pamphlets that the Robertsons had selected, so she set it aside. "Not Mexico, I think. Too many unhappy memories."

Which was in part, true. She and Lance had discussed the possibility of taking their honeymoon in Cabo San Lucas.

"No problem." Faith slid that pamphlet and two others out from the stack. "What about Alaska or Hawaii? Either of those interest you?"

Cheryl eyed the mountains on one packet and the tropical climes on the other. Neither looked familiar. "Um...I was thinking more like England or..."

"Spain?" Faith held up a photo of a Spanish pavilion brimming with tourists.

"Yes!" That one definitely looked familiar. And the one below it, featuring the French countryside, also caught Cheryl's eye. So the Robertsons had definitely been perusing Europe?

"What else have you got overseas?" she asked, trying to sound only mildly excited rather than elated—the way she felt inside.

Sweeping aside half of the pamphlets, Faith laid out the ones that dealt specifically with destinations across the Atlantic, most of which looked familiar.

Cheryl grabbed two. "May I?"

"Of course." Faith happily pushed several more toward her. "Feel free to take as many as you like." She paused and arched a delicate eyebrow. "Now, most of these will require passing through customs. I assume your passport is up-to-date?"

She nodded. It had been part of her wedding preparations.

"Great. Then let me get your number, and I'll put together a few more packages for you. And, if you decide you'd like to see something in particular, feel free to call. My contact information is on the back." She flipped over one of the pamphlets and pointed. "There's the agency number, and here is mine. My e-mail address is there too, in case you need it."

"Thank you," Cheryl said.

Faith scribbled Cheryl's name and phone number on to a Rolodex card and then added it to a file already bulging with contacts.

"So may I ask how you heard of us?" Faith said, a smile starting at the corners of her mouth. "Was it the new TV ad? I heard it ran this morning before the local news. I set my DVR to record before I left for work. I can't wait to see it. I have a cameo."

Cheryl started to shake her head when a flash of inspiration struck. She leaned forward to rest her elbows on the desk. "Actually, I got your name from some friends of mine. Do you remember the Robertsons?"

"John and Victoria?" Faith's smile widened. "Of course I do. They came in day before yesterday, as a matter of fact. I'm putting together a European vacation for them too. How interesting."

Cheryl fidgeted in her chair. "Yes, I know. Victoria had a bunch of your flyers at the house."

Still honest, though Cheryl's cheeks were definitely starting to warm under pressure. For the next several minutes, she listened as Faith explained how excited she was to be planning a trip for the Robertsons.

"I'm talking England, France, Spain...you name it. I believe they're looking at a more extended stay than what you want," she finished. "Victoria told me she and John had been considering a trip like this for some time. They never could take it before. John was always so busy with his job and whatnot, but lately he's been thinking of taking some time off."

"Really?"

Faith grabbed a pen from a cup on the corner of her desk and began flicking the clip with her thumb. "I'm glad, really. They've had some tough times recently. Problems with their daughter, I think. At least, that's what I gathered from my conversations with Victoria."

Cheryl swallowed nervously. "Do they only have the one child?"

"Far as I know." Faith flicked one time too many and then scowled as the clip snapped off of the pen and went scuttling under a letter tray. "Rats. I'm always doing that. Anyway, as I was saying, the Robertsons have had some trouble recently. I think I heard their daughter joined a cult or something like that."

Cheryl had to bite her tongue to keep from retorting in anger. The Amish church was definitely not a cult. "Is that right?" she said instead.

Faith nodded. "Did you see that piece that *20/20* did on religious sects in America? It aired a couple of weeks ago. Or was it last week? Oh well, I guess it doesn't matter." Her eyes rolled. "Fanatics."

As her momma would say, Cheryl got her back up. It irritated her that someone with obviously very little knowledge of the Amish would judge them so harshly. She clasped her hands in her lap and formed her words carefully. "I would hardly call the Amish people fanatics. They're more down to earth than most Englischers," she said, a tad too sharply.

Faith's eyebrows rose.

"What I mean is, I live in an Amish community. The people there are known for being kind, considerate, and peace-loving. That's hardly the picture of a fanatic, right?"

She shrugged. "I guess."

Suddenly uncomfortable, Cheryl decided to change the subject and cleared her throat. "Anyway, Ms. Overstreet..."

"Faith, please." She reached across the desk and patted Cheryl's arm.

"Yeah, okay. Faith, do you think you could get me some information on packages similar to the ones the Robertsons are planning?"

It didn't take much to redirect the chatty travel agent. She swept up from her desk to retrieve a file from the metal cabinet behind her. "Of course I can. I have their information right here. I'll look through it and give you a call. Or, if you'd prefer, I can e-mail you whatever I come up with?"

"Either one will be fine," Cheryl said, adding her e-mail address to the phone number she'd already given. Slinging her purse over her arm, she made her way to the door. "Thanks again. And if you could possibly keep me informed if John and Victoria have a change of plans? I wouldn't want to schedule a trip at the same time and have them think I'm stalking them." She laughed lightly, as though making a joke.

Faith nodded and opened her mouth, but rather than risk another detailed explanation of a possible *20/20* episode, Cheryl waved and let herself out the door.

On the sidewalk, she drew a deep breath. Naomi didn't have a phone, but what Cheryl wouldn't give to be able to call her with the news that the Robertsons were planning on leaving the country. Who abandoned their child in the midst of a tragedy?

Aside from asking the Robertsons, there was only one way to find out. Cheryl pointed her Ford toward Sugarcreek and the Swartzentrubers' farm.

Outside, the house still maintained its peaceful facade, but Cheryl knew that wasn't the case inside. Even Rufus seemed to sense the difference. Instead of greeting her with a happy bark, he only whined. She approached the door, her feet heavy on the porch steps, and knocked. Within minutes, Rachel answered, little Joseph cradled in her arms.

Weary lines creased the young mother's face, and her eyes were red-rimmed and weepy. She brightened upon seeing Cheryl, however, and beckoned her inside with a watery smile.

"Come in, come in. It's good to see you, Cheryl."

"You too, Rachel." She stepped into the hall. Though it looked exactly the same as it had a couple of days ago, the air felt heavier, and the room somehow darker. She turned to give Rachel a hug. "I haven't stopped praying for a second for you and your family."

She sniffed and thanked her with a weak shrug. "We can use all the prayers we can get, that's for sure."

Something about the way she spoke and looked were definitely Englisch. And then Cheryl realized it was the absence of a prayer cap that made her think so. She reached for Rachel's arm.

"You doing okay?"

Her gaze dropped to her sleeping baby. "We're getting through. Samuel says we must not give up hope." She looked up. "Would you like to come in for some coffee?"

"That would be nice."

As before, Rachel led her to the kitchen. It was surprisingly bare. And quiet. Cheryl looked around in confusion. Where was the food? The people? The hushed whispers of well-meaning friends?

"The men are out looking with Samuel," Rachel said, as though reading her thoughts. "The women are... well... I asked them not to come. I couldn't bear the constant assurances that everything was going to be all right when deep down..."

She trailed to silence and hugged little Joseph so tight he squirmed.

Made decidedly uncomfortable in the face of Rachel's agony, Cheryl lowered her gaze. The questions she'd intended to ask Rachel about her parents could wait.

She gestured around the house. "I'm so sorry about dropping in like this. Maybe I should come back another time."

"Actually..." Her brow furrowed and her bottom lip began to quiver. "I could really use someone to talk to right now. Someone who isn't... who's not..." Her free hand went to her hair and then settled at her neck.

"Someone who isn't Amish?" Cheryl supplied gently.

She nodded and let her hand fall to her side. "I know it isn't right, but I keep wanting to scream and rant at God, and I just can't do that with all of them watching. I'm so afraid I'll disappoint them, like I'll make them think I'm not really one of them because if I were, I wouldn't have such doubts..."

Faster and faster she spoke until she broke off on a sob that broke Cheryl's heart. She squeezed Rachel's shoulder. "They're people, Rachel, just like you and me. They have doubts and fears too. And there are moments when I'm sure even Naomi wants to rant and scream. Plus, they love you. *You.* Not someone you think you have to be, but who you are inside."

Moist tears seeped from Rachel's eyes and dampened the dark fabric of her dress. "Thanks for that," she said, sniffing. She dipped her head toward a cradle someone had tucked into a corner of the kitchen. "Let me lay Joseph down, and then I'll get that coffee."

Cheryl nodded, and then, while Rachel was filling the pot, she grabbed a couple of cups and the cream and sugar bowls and carried everything to the table. Soon they were once again sipping coffee. Hard to believe that just a few short days ago they'd been doing exactly the same thing when Baby John disappeared.

"So can I ask you something?" Cheryl began, hesitantly tracing the rim of her cup with her index finger.

Rachel nodded.

She drew a breath and pushed up in her chair. "If you need someone to talk to, why wait for me? Why not reach out to your mother?"

Rachel blew out a sigh and tucked a strand of her hair nervously behind her ear. "Naomi asked me the same thing when you were here a couple of days ago."

"And?" Cheryl prompted, a little embarrassed that she'd not told Rachel about her and the Millers' visit to New Philadelphia.

Rachel licked her lips. "My parents are good people." Her eyes were pained as she met Cheryl's gaze. "They've always tried to do the right thing, hang with the right crowd, live on the right street, you know? They took me to church, brought me up in youth group, made sure I had a nice Bible and decent clothes. I was a good little girl. Everyone thought so."

Cheryl gave a guilty nod. Similar thinking about what made a person good had consumed her in Columbus, and not that long ago.

"Even so, I always knew something was missing—something I could never put my finger on. And then I met Samuel." Her gaze grew distant and sorrowful. "His faith was so real, so deep and personal. Not like the shallow lie I had been living all my life. I got angry with my parents for never showing me the truth, for allowing me to exist in this fancied up fantasy that said as long as I was a good girl, I'd get to heaven."

She sniffed and drew her cup in to wrap her fingers around then lowered her eyes as though examining the swirling coffee for answers.

"I tried asking my parents about it. My questions always made them defensive. Their answer was always that they believed in God, and that was good enough. Months later, when I finally had the courage to tell them that Samuel and I were getting married, my mother accused me of being immature and irresponsible. My father said worse—that I was a disappointment and that I was destined for hell."

Cheryl's jaw dropped. "Because you were getting married?"

"Because I was letting go of everything they believed in." She gave a slow shake of her head. "A parent's dreams are a difficult thing, Cheryl. On the one hand, they want what's best for their children. On the other, they can be crippling when they think that their offspring will never live up to the hopes they set for them. For my parents, the day I left home is the day all the dreams they'd ever had for me died."

Instead of sounding sad at that, a bit of bitterness tinged her words.

"You're angry with them," Cheryl said, not as a question, but a gentle statement.

Rachel looked up, her brows rising in surprise. "I'm..." She ran her hand over her face. "Yeah, I guess I am. And I'm stubborn too. The last thing my father said to me was that I'd never be able to give up my car, my phone, all the nice, expensive gadgets I'd had growing up. I became so determined to prove him wrong that I..." She shook her head. "I guess I swung too far the other way."

Her hands fidgeted restlessly around her cup. Cheryl patted her wrist. "Have you thought about telling them that?"

A lock of her hair fell to cover a portion of her face. "Now? I'm afraid they would see it as me running home at the first sign of trouble. Like I couldn't hack life here or something."

"This is more than just a 'sign of trouble,' Rachel. You don't think maybe they would understand that?"

Rachel bit her lip, indecision warring on her young face.

Cheryl gave her wrist another pat. "Think about it. It may be that they are just waiting for you to make the first move."

At least, she hoped so. What she'd seen today indicated something else entirely. Fresh guilt washed over her, and unable to resist telling Rachel the truth, Cheryl leaned forward and braced both elbows on the table. "Naomi, Seth, and I went to see your parents today."

Her head jerked up. "What?"

Cheryl nodded. "I know you were worried about how they might react, but at this point we were fairly certain your parents had heard about John's kidnapping on the news. We went there to encourage them to reach out to you."

Gradually, the tension melted from Rachel's spine, and she sank back against her chair. "And? What did they say?"

"They were a little defensive, which is natural I guess. They didn't want to talk about the problems between you with strangers."

Rachel nodded as though her parents' response had been just what she'd expected. "They always were rather private."

"They asked about you," Cheryl added, glad that she could say so honestly.

Color mottled Rachel's cheeks. "What about the boys? Did they ask about them?" When Cheryl didn't answer, she raised her eyes. "That doesn't surprise me. My parents are opposed to the simple lifestyle. They call it ignorant, even foolish. I think my mother was afraid that my children would grow up to be uneducated, so rather than watch, she's closed herself off from having anything to do with them...or me."

"I'm sorry to hear that." Cheryl leaned forward, thinking. "Rachel, I don't know your parents, and I can't honestly say that their hearts will be changed, even with time and prayer. But I do know that I had a lot of misconceptions about the Amish before coming to Sugarcreek. Maybe instead of separation, what your parents need is exposure to the things you believe."

Rachel tilted her head. "But they've made it so clear that they don't want to see me."

"Have they?" Cheryl asked quietly, playing a hunch.

Rachel's gaze fell. "Well, to be honest, I've been pretty hard on them. I've sorta made it an ultimatum—like, this is who I am now, so take it or leave it kinda thing."

"What does your husband have to say?"

Sorrow darkened Rachel's eyes as she looked up at Cheryl. "He encourages me to make peace with them, which only makes me angrier because my parents have never approved of him or bothered getting to know him."

Baby Joseph made a sound in his cradle, and Rachel immediately rose and went to check on him. Once he'd settled down to sleep, she laid her hand on his back, her eyes filling with tears.

"Samuel is a good man, Cheryl, but he's hurting right now. Much as I'd like for my parents to be here, helping us through this time, I just don't believe it's going to happen."

Her chin lifted, and she straightened and crossed her arms over her chest. "I won't risk adding to Samuel's pain—or mine—by subjecting him to my parents' condescension."

Cheryl rose too, aware that Rachel had said all she would on the subject. Crossing to where she stood, Cheryl gave her a tight hug and said her good-bye. "I'll be praying for you. Let me know if you hear anything, or if there's anything I can do."

Rachel nodded, and then Cheryl let herself out, her heart heavier than it had been when she first arrived and the path ahead no more clear.

Casting her gaze heavenward, she whispered a desperate plea for help. "I'm really lost here, Lord. I'm scared and feeling totally inadequate. Please, don't be silent right now. Show me which way to go."

As if in answer, a low rumble sounded from the clouds gathering on the horizon and a streak of lightning split the sky. A small laugh puffed from Cheryl's lips at the display.

Okay. God was still God, even if she couldn't see Him or didn't understand His plan.

Rummaging in her purse for her keys, she hurried to her car, anxious to get home before the storm broke. Or maybe, she thought as she climbed into the driver's seat and slid the key into the ignition, maybe it had already hit, and the rain was just one more reminder that God was in control.

It was a comforting thought as the first drops splattered against her windshield, one she clung to as she turned the car toward home.

Chapter Fourteen

With the falling rain came plummeting temperatures. Cheryl shivered and flipped the switch for the heater as she pulled into Sugarcreek. At the entrance to Amazin' Corn, Bob Gleason, touting a colorful umbrella, hung the Closed sign then waved to Cheryl as she passed. The Gleasons wouldn't welcome the rain and cooler weather. The combination would mean an early end to their season.

Cheryl drove on, passing landmarks that she was glad to realize had already become familiar. It still surprised her how quickly she had come to think of Sugarcreek as home and the people here as friends. Surely if the Robertsons bothered to try, they'd come to realize what it was about this place that drew their daughter. But first, they'd have to get past this tragedy and figure out what had happened to Baby John.

Passing a sign bearing the name of the Sleepy Dutchman Inn with a bright red arrow painted underneath, Cheryl slowed and on impulse flicked on her turn signal. Despite what Theresa Cox had said, she still had reservations, and, determined to cross at least one person permanently off her suspect list, she drove the route to the inn and pulled into the parking lot.

Pushed by the rain and wind, a Welcome sign swung on metal hinges. Cheryl stopped the swishing of her windshield wipers and then killed the engine. She'd get wet even if she ran the short distance up the path to the front door, and there was no guarantee that Theresa would see her or even that she was still in Sugarcreek, but Cheryl had to at least try.

Ducking out her door and across the driveway, she skittered up the path, nearly slipping on the wet bricks. Inside, she took a moment to shake off a little of the moisture clinging to her coat before making her way past a rack stuffed with pamphlets touting local tourist attractions toward the reception desk.

"*Guten tag*," a pretty young woman greeted from behind the counter. She was youthful enough to still be on her rumspringa, but judging from her full Amish garb, would be making her decision to stay with the church soon. Her smile widened. "Welcome to the Sleepy Dutchman Inn. What can I do for you today?"

Cheryl tugged the gloves from her fingers and set them on the counter with her purse. "I'm looking for one of your guests, a lady by the name of Theresa Cox. Do you know if she's in?"

"Do you know what room?"

She shook her head. "Sorry, I don't."

"I can check." The girl hit a few keys on her keyboard, the bright display of her monitor mirrored on her glasses. "Here it is. Let me buzz her room for you. Your name?"

Cheryl fidgeted in her damp shoes. Chances were high that Theresa wouldn't recognize her name, or if she did, that she'd refuse to see her. "It's Cheryl Cooper, but she might not remember when we met. Would you please tell her that I run the Swiss Miss?"

The young woman jotted her name on a notepad then picked up the telephone and pressed the handset to her ear. After a moment, she said, "Hello, Ms. Cox. This is Amy at the front desk. You have a visitor here to see you, a lady by the name of Cheryl Cooper. She says she runs the Swiss Miss?"

She fell silent for a moment, the pencil she'd used to write Cheryl's name tapping quietly on the counter. "Of course. I'll let her know."

Cheryl's heart sank.

Amy replaced the receiver and pointed toward the opposite end of the lobby. "Ms. Cox said she'd meet you in the dining room in about fifteen minutes. Right through those French doors."

Cheryl lifted her brows in surprise. She'd agreed?

"Oh, okay. Thank you." She collected her things and then moved in the direction Amy pointed.

The dinner hour was long past, but a few customers still lingered at the candlelit tables scattered about the room. Cheryl was surprised to realize that she was quite hungry as she approached the hostess booth, the savory scent of grilling steaks making her mouth water. Not that a sirloin and loaded baked potato would do much for her waistline.

As she approached, the woman standing there grabbed a menu and flashed a bright smile. "Just you tonight?"

Cheryl shot a glance over her shoulder. "No, actually, there will be another lady joining me." She gestured toward a table far from the entrance in a quiet corner. "Could we have something over there? My guest and I have something we need to discuss, and we'd like a little privacy."

The woman nodded and led the way. Promising to return with water, she seated Cheryl then placed one of the menus in front of her and the other in front of the vacant chair.

When she returned, Cheryl ordered a cup of black coffee, waited for it to be delivered, and then tapped the edge of the menu impatiently. It had been fifteen minutes. Where was Theresa Cox?

A second later, she heard someone enter and turned to see Theresa weaving her way through the tables toward her. Either she'd taken time to freshen up, or she was the type of person who looked perfect every minute of the day.

Cheryl stood to greet her. "Ms. Cox. Thank you for seeing me."

Theresa shook her hand then slid into the chair opposite Cheryl's. "I thought it might be important."

Cheryl nodded then motioned toward the menus. "Have you eaten?"

"I have, but thank you."

Theresa motioned for the waitress but rather than calling her over, she simply pointed at Cheryl's cup and mouthed the word *coffee*. When it was delivered, she took a hesitant sip and then looked Cheryl in the eyes.

"I've been monitoring the news online. No sign of that child who was kidnapped?"

Cheryl shook her head, unsure how much to say, but caught off guard by the concern she read on the other woman's face. "Unfortunately, no."

Ms. Cox's eyes narrowed as she watched her, and she leaned back in her chair. "You still think I had something to do with that little boy's disappearance, don't you?"

Cheryl swallowed hard, all traces of the hunger she'd felt earlier disappearing. "Look, Ms. Cox, I'm going to be honest with you. I may be grabbing at straws here, but right now I'm desparate for any information that might help us find the kidnapper. You're still on my suspect list, so please give me a reason to take you off, and I'll leave you alone and pursue other leads. I just have a few questions."

This was it. Either Ms. Cox would get mad and storm back to her room, or she'd stay and listen to what Cheryl had to say. She waited, heart pounding.

Ms. Cox motioned her on.

Cheryl's lips parted in a relieved sigh, and she let her desperation soften her voice. "I realize that you *don't* have to explain yourself to me, but it sure would help a lot if I understood exactly what brought you to Sugarcreek."

Ms. Cox turned her face away, her lips thinning while she debated a reply. Finally, she looked back at Cheryl. The set of her chin, the tension in her eyes and mouth, all said she'd made her decision.

She leaned forward to rest her forearms on the table. "My reasons for coming are actually quite personal. And you're right, I don't have to explain"—she licked her lips—"except that I agree with you." She sighed and rubbed her hands over her face. "If I were in your position, I'd be suspicious too."

Reaching into her purse, she withdrew a sheaf of folded papers and handed them to Cheryl, who took them and then looked up in surprise. "What are these?"

Theresa slid a slender pair of reading glasses out of her pocket and put them on. Tipping her head toward the papers, she said, "Those are my list of items to look for while I'm in Sugarcreek."

Cheryl flipped open the stack and quickly scanned the list. It was quite extensive, and varied, ranging from baby toys and rattles to handmade bookcases and shelves. Her brow furrowed as she finished.

"I don't understand. Do you own a store or something?"

Theresa shrugged. "Something like that. Most of my business is done online. What there is of it lately," she added. She took the papers back and shoved them into her purse. "You see, Ms. Cooper, several years ago some investors and I started an online company called Crib and Cradle. We specialize in children's merchandise—toys, beds, children's furniture—stuff like that. It was going very well at first, and I was able to talk my investors into expanding. The first actual store opened in Cleveland about eight months ago."

The pride in her tone when she talked about expanding faded. Lines of worry etched themselves deeply on her forehead.

"The problem is, the store didn't take off as I'd expected. In fact, ever since we opened our doors, we've been steadily losing business."

And money.

Though she didn't say it, Cheryl knew what "losing business" meant and felt a sinking in the pit of her stomach. "And you came to Sugarcreek because?"

Theresa took another swallow from her cup then slid her glasses off, wiped the lenses on her napkin, and slowly replaced them in her pocket. "You want to know what I think is the number one trick to promoting a new business?"

Cheryl indicated for her to continue with a tilt of her head.

"Convince people you have something they need, and then make sure you are the *best* source for them to get it. I quickly realized I couldn't compete with the larger chain stores. They offered a price and variety I couldn't even dream of matching. So I had to come up with an idea for offering unique products—something shoppers couldn't find in every store."

She waited and watched Cheryl with a keen glimmer in her eyes.

"Amish goods," Cheryl said. A bit of the tension in her chest eased when the woman nodded.

"Rather than offering more of the plastic junk people get for cheap at every discount warehouse or club, I figured I'd go for quality wooden goods." She shrugged. "It works for the Amish, right? People travel hundreds of miles to buy stuff from local artisans here and in other places."

Cheryl frowned. "So why not contract with some of the people here? Why buy the stuff on your list, pay with cash, and then disappear? Weren't you afraid that would look suspicious?"

She tapped the rim of her cup, her gaze darting from Cheryl to her hands and back. "Remember when I said I had investors?"

Cheryl nodded.

"Well, they're already showing signs of backing out. My first and second quarter sales were not good, and when I say 'not good,' I mean dismal. I lost two right off the bat. Fortunately, they were a couple of my smaller investors, but it made the larger ones nervous. I've been putting off compiling the third quarter numbers because I was hoping to have something to show them that would boost their confidence."

Her chin quivered—a chink in the otherwise perfect, businesslike armor. Cheryl slumped back in her chair. "You were planning to use the stuff you bought as templates to design your own products."

Color darkened her cheeks, but she nodded. "It was the only solution I could come up with to keep them from jumping ship." She laced her fingers tightly on the tabletop. "I told you the truth, Ms. Cooper. I had nothing to do with that baby's disappearance. My reasons for being in Sugarcreek are strictly business related."

She punctuated each word with a steady stare that dared Cheryl to dispute what she'd said. Much as Cheryl wanted to believe otherwise, she knew deep down that the story she'd just heard was true, either that or a very elaborate cover-up. And there was still the question she hadn't asked and couldn't answer. If Theresa Cox had taken Baby John, why would she still be in Sugarcreek?

Theresa leaned forward. "Do you believe me?"

Cheryl let her shoulders sag. "I admit…I really was hoping you would have some answers regarding Baby John, but everything you've told me makes sense."

The worry eased from Theresa's face, and she offered a shy smile. "Thank you."

"I appreciate your confiding in me, Ms. Cox. You didn't have to."

"No, I didn't. But I wanted…"

She hesitated and then averted her gaze as a couple swept past their table on their way out the door.

She licked her lips and began again. "Miss Cooper, of course I didn't want people thinking I had anything to do with that baby's disappearance, but I also couldn't risk having attention drawn to myself."

Her gaze swung back, and this time Cheryl saw desperation in its depths.

"I still can't. It hasn't been easy for me, Miss Cooper. I'm a woman attempting to start my own business alone. And if my investors get wind of the straits that Crib and Cradle is in, I could lose everything—my store, the online merchandise—everything I have worked so hard to achieve."

So that was why she'd agreed to this meeting. She feared that a police investigation would expose her secret.

Though she was pretty certain she had her answer, Cheryl lifted her chin. "You do realize your story will be pretty easy to confirm. All the authorities need to do is look online, maybe make a few phone calls."

She nodded quickly. "Of course. I wish you would check it out. Let me give you my card. The Web site address is on the back." She reached for her purse, slid a card out from one of the pockets, and laid it on the table then added a couple of bills. "That's for my coffee." She draped the strap over her shoulder. "In the meantime, can I have your word that the conversation we just had goes no further?"

Though she made the request firmly, there was a pleading in her eyes that Cheryl was helpless to resist. She shrugged. "No problem. Thanks again for talking with me, Ms. Cox."

She blew out a sigh and then rose. "It's Theresa. And thank *you*."

Drawing her shoulders back, she moved briskly toward the door. It was a posture Cheryl recognized, but not one she'd used since moving to Sugarcreek. It was the harried, self-absorbed part of herself that she'd left behind in Columbus.

Gratitude for the opportunity Aunt Mitzi had given flooded her, as well as something her aunt had said in her last letter:

Living here reminds me that so much of what I once thought necessary is merely trappings meant to distract me from what is real and important. I would not trade the peace I now own for anything the world has to offer.

Cheryl felt exactly the same way. Her life in Sugarcreek had not been exactly easy, but she wasn't alone. She'd made friends whom she loved and trusted, and that was far more valuable than anything she'd left back home.

Though her conversation with Theresa had taken the edge from her appetite, she knew that would not be the case later. Giving in to the temptation wafting on the air, Cheryl ordered a steak to go and then went home to ponder what she'd learned and seen.

And to wonder where she would possibly look next, now that she was certain Theresa Cox had not kidnapped John Swartzentruber.

CHAPTER FIFTEEN

Cheryl awoke early the next morning with a more hopeful outlook than she'd had the night before—a fact she attributed to an hour spent in prayer before falling into a dreamless sleep. Near her head, Beau purred loudly and then began batting playfully at her hair, a sign that he was more than ready for his breakfast whether Cheryl wanted to climb from her warm bed or not.

Sighing, she pushed back the covers and padded toward the kitchen to fill his bowl before returning to the bathroom to wash up. By the time she'd scrubbed her face and brushed her teeth, a hundred different scenarios had passed through her brain, most of which included the kidnapper being found and Baby John returned happily to his family.

She set to work brewing a pot of coffee then pulled a notepad and pen from a drawer in Aunt Mitzi's desk and sat down to think.

Why would anyone take another person's child?

On the left side of the paper, she wrote down all of the reasons she could think of that answered that question. On the right side, she wrote general groups of people she thought might possess the motives on the left.

It was an unsavory list.

No doubt Chief Twitchell had one just like it and had probably even gone a step further by including everyone in Sugarcreek.

The two names that interested her most were the two she was convinced had the strongest motive...Jeremiah and Rebecca Zook.

Of course, to be fair, she had to consider the possibility that the kidnapper was in no way connected to Sugarcreek. If that were the case, nothing she could do would be of any help in finding them. Rather than dwell on that possibility, she went back up the list and circled the Zooks' names. They weren't by any means strong suspects, but it felt productive to have a new direction to focus her attention.

Business at the Swiss Miss was slow later that morning, so Cheryl had no qualms about leaving the store in Esther's capable hands while she drove out to the Millers' farm to touch base with Naomi. The inviting scents of cinnamon and apples greeted her as Elizabeth opened the door and waved her inside.

"Come in, Cheryl. Maam is in the kitchen. We are making pies to take to the Swartzentrubers and the Zooks."

Flashing her pretty, dimpled smile, she motioned for Cheryl to follow while she led the way.

"Look who has stopped by," she announced before Cheryl was fully in the kitchen.

Naomi looked up from the apples she was slicing to smile a greeting. "Cheryl! I was not expecting you today." She waved her paring knife in the direction of the coffeepot. "Elizabeth, please get Cheryl some kaffee."

She raised her brows at Cheryl and at her nod, motioned toward the pies cooling on the counter. "And slice her a piece of that pie while you're about it. One for yourself and me as well."

Wiping her hands on her apron, she crossed to give Cheryl a welcome hug.

"I didn't mean to interrupt your work," Cheryl said, returning Naomi's hug. "I hope you don't mind my dropping in unannounced."

"Nonsense." Naomi gave a wave of her hand and took a seat at the table. "Elizabeth and I were ready for a break, ain't so, Elizabeth? We have been up baking since early this morning."

The girl gave a wry grin, and the three of them chatted while they finished their pie. Afterward, Naomi bade her daughter pack the remainder of the pie into a basket with a pitcher of milk for the men and sent her to the barn.

"So?" Naomi said, sliding a bowl and paring knife toward Cheryl. "What happened yesterday that you could not wait to tell me about?"

Cheryl wagged the tip of the paring knife. "You know me too well, my friend."

"I should. You remind me much of your aunt Mitzi."

Smiling at the compliment, Cheryl picked up an apple and began removing the skin. Briefly, she summarized her visit to the Swartzentrubers' home.

"I don't know, Naomi. I was so sure Theresa Cox was our girl. Now I'm not so sure. I'm more inclined to think it was someone local." She passed the peeled apple to Naomi for slicing.

Naomi lifted an eyebrow. "I take it you confirmed her story?"

"The moment I got home." She sighed. "Her Web site, the store, all of it checked out."

Naomi's brow bunched in consternation. "I admit, I am as confused by this news as you. I was certain she would know something, but if what you say is true?" She shrugged. "I'm afraid you may be right about it being someone local, and *that* means we are back where we started."

Cheryl grimaced and picked up another apple. "Which if we're honest, is not really all that far. I mean, what suspects do we have, exactly? Other than Theresa, the only people I can reasonably say have been acting out of character are Rebecca and Jeremiah Zook."

Wiping her hands on a towel, she pulled the list she'd worked on that morning from her purse and showed it to Naomi.

While she perused the list, Cheryl went back to peeling fruit. When she finished, Naomi lifted her eyebrows and pursed her lips.

"What?" Cheryl lowered the apple she was paring. "Did you think of someone I left off the list?"

"Not...exactly." Naomi folded the paper and then returned it to Cheryl's purse. "You see, when you first told me about your encounter with Jeremiah, I asked my Seth to find out what he could. He sent word to some of his friends. They told him that

Rebecca Zook is staying with a sister. And she's alone, Cheryl. Several people have witnessed her around town."

Using the flat edge of the blade, she slid the apple slices into a bowl then set her knife aside and wiped her hands on her apron.

"But that doesn't make any sense." Cheryl rose to pace the length of the kitchen. "Why would she go to her sister's? Why not stay here with her husband so they can help each other through the grieving process? I mean, I can't imagine you or Seth abandoning each other in a time like this. My parents either, for that matter. They've always said..."

Naomi's lips pressed into a firm line, and Cheryl halted her pacing.

"There's more. You know why she left, don't you?" She narrowed her eyes suspiciously and propped her hands on her hips. "What haven't you told me?"

Naomi shook her head sadly. "Seth says Rebecca is grieving the loss of her son harder than what is normal because she blames Jeremiah."

Cheryl's mouth fell open. "What? How could losing their son possibly be his fault?"

"Seth says Rebecca wanted to take him to a doctor sooner, but Jeremiah kept insisting that he was fine, that what he needed was rest and prayer. By the time he was diagnosed, the leukemia was advanced."

Cheryl returned to the table, her heart aching inside her chest. "Oh no."

"And that is not all. Rebecca chose to abstain from church meetings after she lost her boy. Jeremiah was not pleased and insisted they go. When she refused to accompany him, he went by himself and she resented him for it. She left while he was gone."

The gears in Cheryl's head began turning as Naomi spoke. She sank into her seat, her fingers drumming the tabletop. So Rebecca Zook had a solid alibi, but what about Jeremiah? He'd lost his son and for all intents and purposes, his wife shortly thereafter. Granted, Cheryl didn't know the Zooks well enough to draw conclusions, but she couldn't help but wonder...could Jeremiah possibly be so desperate that he would do anything to win his wife back? Grief did terrible things to people—

"Cheryl?"

She startled and focused on her friend. "What?"

"Did you hear what I said? There is no possible way that Rebecca could have been involved in Baby John's disappearance."

"Yes, I heard you, and I agree, *Rebecca* does have a pretty solid alibi."

Naomi's eyes narrowed. "What are you saying? You think...you do not believe...you suspect Jeremiah?"

Cheryl sat forward eagerly. "Think about it, Naomi. He has motive, and with his knowledge of the community and the families around Sugarcreek, he would have had ample opportunity."

Naomi's head shook as Cheryl talked. "But to take another man's child is inconceivable! It is not our way. He would never..."

"Aren't you the one who told me that the Amish are no different than anyone else? That you suffer from the same insecurities and failures?" Cheryl shrugged and lifted her hands, palms up. "It's not that farfetched. Remember Solomon?"

Naomi's brow wrinkled and then cleared. "Two mothers—one who lost her child and the other who was willing to give hers up rather than see her son killed."

Cheryl pressed both hands to the table to keep them from trembling in her excitement. "Could it be that we have a similar scenario playing out right here in Sugarcreek?"

Though her gaze reflected incredulity, Naomi did not deny the possibility. She rose and paced the same path Cheryl had taken a moment earlier. Finally, she stopped in front of the sink with her face toward the window.

"We should speak to him. Before we make any assumptions, we should pay a visit to the Zook farm and give Jeremiah a chance to answer for himself."

She turned and looked Cheryl in the eyes. "It is only right. This is a terrible thing we are thinking."

Cheryl agreed and went to stand next to Naomi. "I'm free now." She hesitated, her teeth worrying her bottom lip. "Seth would want to go with us. Perhaps I should ask him?"

"We can't wait on him, Naomi. If what we suspect is true, Jeremiah could be planning to flee this very minute. For all we know, he may already be gone."

Naomi jerked her head up. "You think he has left Sugarcreek?"

"Have you seen him since I told you I ran into him?"

Her eyes widened.

"Neither have I," Cheryl said after a moment. She reached for her purse and dug her keys out of a pocket. "How far is it to the Zooks' farm?"

"About ten miles or so."

"Fifteen or twenty minutes by car depending on traffic. Let's go."

Naomi put up her hand. "First I must let Elizabeth know where we are going so she can tell Seth and the others. Wait for me. I will only be a moment." She scurried to the barn and returned a few minutes later, her cheeks flushed from hurrying. Crossing to a cabinet, she took one of the baskets perched on top, placed one of the fresh apple pies carefully inside, then covered it with a brightly checkered cloth. "All right. I am ready now."

Cheryl motioned toward the bowls on the table. "The pies?"

"Elizabeth will finish up. Let's go."

They hastened to the car, Naomi making it unnecessary for Cheryl to look up the address on her navigation with her detailed directions. However, though the clock on the dash said they made it under the time Cheryl had predicted, the ride to the Zooks' seemed to take interminably long. When at last they turned up the winding drive leading to the white clapboard farmhouse the Zooks called home, Cheryl was a bundle of nervous energy. Even her fingers were tired from clenching the steering wheel as the car crunched to a stop on the gravel drive.

Naomi leaned forward in the seat to peer through the windshield. "That is odd."

"What?" Cheryl shoved the car into park and then craned to see what it was that captured Naomi's attention. "What do you see?"

Naomi pointed at the buggy hunkered next to the barn. "It is not hitched, yet Jeremiah failed to put the buggy away."

On the surface, that didn't seem so odd, yet Cheryl knew the Amish were particular about their horses and buggies. Normally, horses were cared for and equipment stowed away before the men even thought about sitting down to eat.

The tension in the pit of her stomach grew as she reached for the door handle. "Should we see if anyone is home?"

"Ja." Lines of concern marred Naomi's face as she hung the basket from her arm and exited the car. "I will go first."

Cheryl circled to the front of the car, and Naomi put out her hand to grasp her arm. "Cheryl, wait. Something is not right here. Do you have your phone?"

She reached into her pocket and pulled it out. "Of course, but..."

What exactly did Naomi think was wrong? She glanced toward the house. The windows were darkened, the curtains drawn. No smoke curled from the chimney. It looked empty—no—*forlorn* was a better word. A shiver traveled her spine.

She inched closer to Naomi. "Maybe we *should* head back to the farm and wait for Seth."

Or Levi. Filled with a sudden longing for his comforting presence, Cheryl glanced over her shoulder to gauge the distance between the house and the car. "What do you think?"

Naomi hitched the basket past her wrist and squared her shoulders. "We are here. Let us at least see if he is home." She directed a firm stare at Cheryl. "But if I decide it is time to go, you must not linger."

"You're starting to scare me," Cheryl said, rubbing the goose bumps from her arms. "What exactly do you think is going on?"

Naomi gazed at the house, her fingers wrapped tightly around the handle of the basket. "I cannot say. It is just a feeling I have." Her chin lifted, and she nodded. "Come, let's see if he is home."

"Sugar and grits," Cheryl mumbled as they tread the steps leading up to the wide front porch. Leaves collected in the corners where the wind had swept them. The screen door banged on its hinges, and a potted mum begged for water.

"Look at that." She pointed toward the dying plant. "You think maybe he's been gone awhile?"

Naomi pinched one of the dead flowers from a stem. "Not necessarily. People grieve differently. Maybe he's just neglected a few chores because he was too overwhelmed to deal with the farm properly."

"Maybe." Cheryl glanced down the driveway toward the mailbox and frowned. "I wish I'd thought to check it."

Straightening, Naomi followed the direction of her gaze. "Why?"

"A stuffed mailbox means he's been away awhile."

"Or perhaps . . ."

"Overwhelmed. I know." Cheryl eased to Naomi's side and motioned toward the door. "You gonna knock, or what?"

Sucking in a breath, Naomi raised her fist and pounded once, twice, and three times. There was no answer.

"Let me try." Cheryl eased around Naomi, pulled open the screen, and knocked on the glass hard enough to rattle the window. "Hello? Anybody home?"

She glanced at Naomi. "Should we peek?"

Naomi looked aghast. "Oh, I do not know about that. It seems..."

Before she could finish, Cheryl had cupped her hands around her eyes and was squinting to see past the lace curtains hanging over the window. A living room opened off the front hall. Except for the arm of a couch, she couldn't see much. Across the hall was a dining room, tidy except for a plate still sitting on the table where Jeremiah, or someone, had left it.

Cheryl huffed as she straightened. "Well, I can't exactly say for sure. It looks to me..."

She started to turn, but froze in her tracks as she caught sight of a bearded face over Naomi's shoulder. His eyes were narrowed, his mouth an angry slash as he strode across the yard toward them, his finger shaking as he pointed at Cheryl's surprised face.

"You there! Young woman. Just what do you think you are doing?"

Chapter Sixteen

For several seconds, Cheryl was too shocked to do anything but stare. Finally, her self-preservation instinct took over. She grabbed Naomi's arm and the two of them stumbled backward, adding distance between them and the man until the door handle jabbed Cheryl in the back.

"I say again, what do you think you are doing, spying into windows?" he demanded.

Beneath a broad-brimmed hat, he mustered a glower that made Cheryl's neck tingle. Had they truly been "spying"? The way he said it made them sound like a couple of Peeping Toms.

By this point, the man had reached the bottom of the stairs and stood glaring up at them, his hands braced firmly on his hips. "Well?"

Naomi tsked softly in Cheryl's ear. "I told you it was not a good idea." Drawing her shoulders back, she stepped toward the stranger. "Guder mariye." She placed her hand on her chest and then gestured to Cheryl. "My name is Naomi Miller. This is my friend, Cheryl Cooper. We are the Zooks' neighbors." She lifted the basket and threw back the cover on the pie. "We brought them something to eat, but it appears as though no one is home. Do you by chance know where they have gone?"

The man's glare softened, but only slightly. Thankfully, his chin no longer jutted, and Cheryl took that as a sign that he didn't mean to toss them into the pasture on their ears. She eased down the steps until she stood in front of him and stuck out her hand. "Cheryl Cooper."

His brows remained bunched and angry looking as he gave her hand a shake. "Ephram Zook."

"Zook?" Naomi also descended the steps and drew to a halt at Cheryl's side. "You are related to Jeremiah Zook?"

The man nodded. "He is my cousin. I am here looking after his farm while he is gone."

"So we were right—he *is* gone." Cheryl gulped as Naomi shot her a look of warning then continued more casually. "Did he happen to say where he was going?"

Ephram's gaze narrowed as he looked from Cheryl to Naomi.

"I mean," Cheryl continued, "if he isn't going to be gone long, we could go ahead and leave the pie with you." She lifted her brows innocently at Naomi. "Right?"

Naomi's mouth resembled a fish as she gaped at Cheryl, but she recovered quickly and snapped her lips into a shaky smile. "Of course." She turned wide eyes to Ephram. "It is fresh. My daughter and I made it this afternoon with apples from our farm."

"You really should try it," Cheryl said, relieved when the scowl slowly faded from Ephram Zook's face. "Naomi is one of the best cooks in all of Sugarcreek. All of my customers rave about her baked goods."

At last, he relented and waved toward the steps. "I guess that would be all right. Please, forgive my manners. I just did not expect to see anyone. Would you like to come inside?"

Cheryl nodded eagerly, caught herself, and then shrugged. "We have time, right, Naomi?"

"Right. We have time," she echoed.

An actress, Naomi was not. Thankfully, Ephram seemed not to notice. Their shoes scuffled the steps as Cheryl and Naomi followed him inside. He led them to the dining room, picking up his plate as they passed and carrying it with him toward the kitchen. While his back was turned, Cheryl motioned to Naomi.

Do you know him? she mouthed.

Naomi lifted her hands, palms up, and quickly dropped them to her sides as Ephram returned from the kitchen wiping his hands on a dishcloth.

He slung it over his shoulder and then directed his attention to Naomi. "You say you are neighbors of Jeremiah and Rebecca?"

She smiled and set the basket on the table. "Ja, that is right. We live in the same district."

"*Ach*, then you worship together." Reaching toward the china cabinet, he removed several plates and a pie server and set them on the table. "That is goot. I have worried about them since they lost their son."

Naomi nodded in sad agreement, clearly more comfortable now as she lifted the pie from the basket. "Jeremiah and Rebecca only moved here a little over a year ago. I have not known them as long as you, but they have become dear members of our congregation."

Ephram stroked his beard and sat. "My Annie was very disappointed when they moved away from Lancaster. She and Rebecca were very close. They grew up together."

He gave an appreciative sniff as the scent of apples and cinnamon filled the air. "That pie does indeed smell goot. I miss my wife's cooking, for sure and for certain."

"I am sorry we did not come sooner. I would have cooked you a roast if I had known. How long have you been here?" Naomi asked, an admirable nonchalance to her tone.

Cheryl grabbed one of the plates and placed a healthy slice of pie on it before handing it to Ephram.

"Not quite a week." He looked uncomfortable as he accepted the pie from Cheryl, but he continued speaking anyway. "Jeremiah said he had some…chores which needed tending away from Sugarcreek. I told him I would be glad to help since my farm makes maple syrup and our busy season is still many weeks away."

"It was goot of you to offer. It has been a difficult time for them," Naomi said, as though she understood what Ephram had left unsaid. "Did he give indication how long he would be gone?"

Though they had already eaten, Cheryl sliced two more pieces of pie, these considerably smaller than the one she'd served Ephram, and set one in front of Naomi and saved the other for herself.

Ephram took a bite of his pie. His lips spread in a pleased grin, and he gave Cheryl a nod. "You were right, Miss Cooper. This is goot pie. Even my Annie would admit it is as delicious as any she makes."

Naomi smiled again and thanked him. "If you're going to be staying on awhile, I could bake you another. Or perhaps you could take one home?"

She was persistent. Cheryl hid a smile around a mouthful of pie then grimaced as she swallowed. Oh, but she would be walking off these calories later.

Ephram seemed to consider this a moment. "Well, Jeremiah did not say exactly how long he would be. I assumed a couple of weeks, seeing as he was going to Middlefield."

Cheryl paused with her fork in midair. "Middlefield? Up in Geauga County? What's he doing there?"

Ephram seemed taken aback by the question. He set aside his fork, and his brow lowered in consternation. "Why, he has gone to fetch his wife, of course."

"We heard that she had gone to see her sister," Naomi said, shooting Cheryl a sharp glance as she folded the cloth she'd used to cover the pie and tucked it inside the basket.

Ephram shrugged and grabbed his fork. "It is no secret, I suppose. Rebecca was feeling a little homesick, and she and Jeremiah agreed that she should visit family. But now it is time for her to come home. Her husband needs her, and she needs him."

Ephram seemed much less tense now that he had food in his belly. They chatted easily about his farm and the things he was doing to help Jeremiah while he finished with his pie. When he was done, he rose and patted his stomach.

"You are indeed a good cook, Mrs. Miller. Your husband is a blessed man. Danki."

She dipped her head in acknowledgement of his thanks. "It is no trouble. I will ask my Seth to bring another one by before you leave."

Saying their good-byes, they returned to the car, Naomi stowing the empty basket in the backseat before climbing in beside Cheryl.

Cheryl set the heater on high and then pulled out of the drive and swung toward the highway. "Well, that was a wasted trip. It turns out Jeremiah is simply making amends with his wife."

To her surprise, Naomi merely raised an eyebrow. "I am not so certain."

"What?" She shot her a sidelong glance. "Why not?"

Naomi twisted on the seat, rubbing her hands together with excitement. "Do you remember when I told you that Seth sent word to some friends?"

"Yeah. That's how we knew that Rebecca had gone to stay with her sister."

Naomi lifted her index finger high. "*A* sister. She has four."

"Oh." Cheryl frowned. "I just assumed . . . when Ephram said Middlefield back there . . . "

"I did the same when Seth first told me she'd gone because Middlefield is where Rebecca and Jeremiah are from and where two of her sisters still live. But her oldest sister lives in Columbus."

"Columbus!" In her surprise, Cheryl jerked the wheel and then had to correct before she looked at Naomi again. "Columbus?"

She gave a slow nod. "She is not Amish. She chose not to bend the knee after her rumspringa. Rebecca went to stay with her."

"Can she do that?" Cheryl blurted it without thinking and then backtracked when she caught sight of Naomi's raised brows. "I mean, is it allowed if she's not part of the church?"

"She never took her vows," Naomi said. "She has not been banned, so yes, it is allowed."

The countryside passed in a blur as Cheryl mulled these words. "Why would Jeremiah lie to his own cousin?"

"We do not know that he did," Naomi cautioned, but her voice lacked certainty.

"Okay," Cheryl conceded, "but are you at least willing to admit that the signs all kind of indicate that things aren't exactly on the up-and-up?"

Troubled lines formed on Naomi's face. She tapped her finger against her chin, thinking. "I admit, Jeremiah's behavior concerns me. There is much we do not know. It will be worth investigating."

Thoughts about their next move spun inside Cheryl's head. Inside her chest, her heart was thumping. They *had* to find John today. She would never be able to live with herself otherwise.

Grabbing her phone, she tapped her navigation app then flashed Naomi a glance, who pointed at the phone.

"You are turning on your map thing?"

"Yep."

"Where are we going?"

Directing her gaze to the road ahead, Cheryl clenched her teeth. "We're going to talk to Rebecca. We need to find out what she knows about Jeremiah's whereabouts. That means..."

Before she could finish, Naomi nodded and turned to stare steadily through the windshield. "We've got to find a way to go to Columbus as soon as possible."

Chapter Seventeen

The drive from Sugarcreek to Columbus was accomplished in just under two hours. Traffic was light, and Cheryl navigated the streets with an ease that was both satisfying and familiar. So perhaps she hadn't left the city girl behind completely? Unsure whether to be pleased or disappointed with the idea, she shrugged aside the thought and pulled off of the highway to gas up.

"Thirsty?" she said, pointing toward the gas station.

Naomi nodded. "Can I get you something?"

"Water," Cheryl said. She withdrew the money from her wallet for Naomi and then flipped the handle to turn the pump on.

Within minutes, the car was on full and Naomi had returned loaded with drinks for them both. Several sets of eyes watched her as she hurried back to the car. How easily Cheryl understood their curiosity. An Amish woman in Sugarcreek was not unusual. The sight was a little more rare in Columbus.

If Naomi noticed the stares, she didn't say so. She slid onto the seat and handed Cheryl one of the drinks. "Here you go."

Cheryl took a swallow and then rescrewed the cap. "Okay, so where exactly does this sister of Rebecca's live?"

Naomi gave her the address, and Cheryl drove another twenty minutes before arriving at the apartment.

"Well, there's no buggy parked outside," she said ruefully.

Naomi quirked an eyebrow and then followed her inside. "Did you expect one?"

"I was hoping," Cheryl said, running her finger down the list of tenants. "Which apartment?"

Naomi pointed to one near the middle. "That one. S. Graber."

Cheryl buzzed the apartment and then held her breath, waiting.

"Hello?"

Her heart pumped double at the voice. Surely they would learn something about Baby John's disappearance here. She licked her lips. "Hi, my name is Cheryl Cooper. I'm here to see Rebecca Zook?"

Her voice rose at the end in question, as though she really weren't certain about her reason for coming. She cleared her throat and tried again. "I need to speak with her about her husband, Jeremiah."

"Uh...what did you say your name was again?"

"It's Cheryl. Cheryl Cooper."

There was a long pause, and then the voice returned. "Come on up."

A buzzer sounded, releasing the lock. Cheryl and Naomi pushed through the glass door and then crossed to the elevator.

"So what exactly are we going to say when we get up there?" Cheryl asked as the metal doors whooshed closed.

Naomi clenched her hands tightly together. "The truth—that we are concerned for her and her husband."

The truth.

Cheryl gnawed the inside of her cheek. The *truth* was she was beginning to think more and more that Jeremiah Zook was the person responsible for Baby John's disappearance, and that undoubtedly would not play well with his wife, or Naomi and the rest of the Miller family for that matter. She could only pray that if Jeremiah did turn out to be the culprit, they would not be too hurt or disappointed by the news.

When the elevator rocked to a stop on the correct floor, Cheryl and Naomi exited and walked down a broad, carpeted hall toward a beige door with the number 4B painted on it. Cheryl knocked. It opened and Rebecca Zook peered out, though it took Cheryl a moment to realize it was her. Her hair was pulled up in a loose ponytail, and she wore a baggy sweatshirt and jeans and no shoes.

Her eyes widened as her gaze drifted past Cheryl. "Naomi Miller?" She opened the door a little wider. "Come in."

Inside, the apartment was cramped but tidy. A pizza box sat on the counter next to two empty Styrofoam plates. Apparently, they'd eaten not long ago. The aroma of garlic and sauce still hung in the air. She motioned toward the kitchen.

"Can I get you something to drink?"

Both Cheryl and Naomi declined, and Rebecca turned to a pretty woman who looked to be a slightly older version of herself, or perhaps it was the makeup and sleek hairstyle that made her look so.

"This is my sister, Susan Graber. Susan, meet Cheryl Cooper and Naomi Miller. Cheryl is the lady I told you about. Her aunt used to own the Swiss Miss."

"Still does," Cheryl corrected. "I'm just running it for her while she's in Papua New Guinea."

Susan shook both of their hands, her grip confident and strong, and then excused herself to another part of the apartment. Rebecca pointed toward a worn leather sofa. "Shall we sit down?"

They did, and Rebecca rubbed her hands nervously over her knees. She looked at Naomi. "I am surprised to see you here. Did Jeremiah send you?" she asked, her voice painfully hopeful.

That one question answered everything Cheryl had come to ask. She glanced at Naomi and saw the same concern reflected in her gaze.

Naomi shook her head. "No, I am sorry, Rebecca. He did not. We thought maybe you could tell us where he is."

Her hands stilled and confusion marred Rebecca's face. "I do not understand. Are you saying he is not tending the farm?"

As though she were explaining to a child, Naomi gently informed Rebecca of the reason for their visit, including everything they knew about John Swartzentruber's kidnapping. "So you see," she finished, "it is very, very important that we find out where Jeremiah has gone."

Rebecca listened with both hands pressed to her chest and her blue eyes wide. "There is more, isn't there? More you have not said about the baby's disappearance."

Naomi looked down at her folded hands. When she looked up, her eyes were steady, but troubled. "Ja, there is more." She nodded at Cheryl. "The two of us have been doing all we can to figure out where Baby John has gone, but we are at an impasse."

Her voice gentled, and she put out her hand to cover Rebecca's. "Jeremiah's disappearance is unfortunate and troubling. Rebecca, we are concerned that his own grief may have driven him to do something that would otherwise be unthinkable."

Her face paled. Her lips too lost their color. "You mean kidnap another man's child?"

Naomi clenched her jaw and then gave a sad, solemn nod.

Rebecca jumped to her feet and shook her head vehemently. "No, Naomi. Jeremiah would never do that, not even for me. He would never cause to another person the kind of grief we have experienced." She turned pleading eyes to Cheryl and back. "I know my husband, and this he could not do."

"All right, Rebecca," Naomi soothed. "But we must still find him. Do you have any idea where he might have gone?"

Rebecca paced the room, wringing her hands the entire time. "Perhaps he…he may have…"

She stopped, and her eyes widened. "Jeremiah always said we would adopt—back when we thought we could not have children. He said we would adopt."

Cheryl's head lifted. "You think that's where he's gone? An adoption agency? Perhaps an orphanage or an attorney? Do you have any idea where?"

Love mingled with despair washed over Rebecca's face for a second before she ducked behind her hands. Great, wrenching sobs shook her shoulders, and Naomi jumped up from the couch to envelope her in a hug.

"I don't know," Rebecca gasped between sobs. "We never talked about it. He has been so distant…so hard…and unflinching. I thought I was alone in my grief, and I couldn't bear it! Now I realize he just did not know how to deal with his feelings or help me deal with mine. Oh, Naomi, what a fool I have been. My husband would do anything for me. How can I make this up to him?"

Naomi whispered something, and Cheryl eased toward the door, certain that her friend would try and comfort Rebecca and probably offer words of advice, but Naomi would do that better without Cheryl present.

Slipping into the hall, she closed the door quietly behind her and made her way back downstairs to the car. Naomi would more than likely be tied up for an hour or more. Neither she nor Cheryl had bothered to eat before they left, and they still had a long drive ahead.

She looked up and down the busy street. If she remembered correctly, there was a small mom-and-pop place around the corner that served amazing hamburgers and crinkle-cut fries that practically melted in a person's mouth. She could grab a couple meals to go and then meet Naomi back here after she'd had a chance to talk with Rebecca.

Remembering the pie she'd eaten earlier, Cheryl decided against driving and hiked the six blocks until she found the restaurant tucked between a novelty shop and a dry cleaner's. She pushed open the door and was immediately struck by memories as the scent of grilled onions and hamburger assaulted her nose.

This was one of the places she and Lance had liked to frequent back when they were dating. She still remembered laughing over chocolate shakes and then walking through a nearby park to shed some of the calories.

"Lance always did believe in staying fit," she mumbled to herself and was immediately struck by bitterness, thinking how she'd always tried to please him by pretending the same interest.

She ambled to the counter and plucked a tattered menu from a stack next to the cash register. After placing her order, she crossed to the bathroom to freshen up while she waited for their meals to be prepared. The reflection that stared back at her from the mirror above the sink could only be described as tired. And disappointed.

Hot tears burned her eyes. Two hours they'd driven, and for what? So that Naomi could play marriage counselor and she act the *maître de*?

The thought wasn't fair, but given her ugly mood, it was all she could conjure. Tearing her gaze away, she scrubbed her hands fiercely with soap and then rubbed them dry on a paper towel and flung it into the trash can. No sense hanging around Columbus. Their best bet would be to head back to Sugarcreek on the off chance that new leads on Baby John's whereabouts had turned up.

Not that she was holding out hope. Apparently, her prayers were far less important than some. Otherwise, why would God choose to remain so silent?

At the thought, another bit of darkness crept over her heart.

It wasn't fair—the events of the past few days. And at every turn, her efforts to discover the identity of the kidnapper were thwarted. Why? Why lead her back to Columbus only to meet with another dead end? Didn't He want the kidnapper caught?

Across the restaurant, she heard her number called. She crossed to the counter, collected her order, and then turned a bit too abruptly. She crashed into someone and barely managed to keep the bag with her food from slipping to the floor when a familiar voice asked...

"Cheryl, is that you?"

Chapter Eighteen

L ance?"

Cheryl narrowed her eyes and snapped her mouth shut. Lance! It *was* him. What on earth was he doing here? And was he alone?

Her gaze flicked from the counter, to the door, and then back to Lance.

"Cheryl, it *is* you. What a surprise."

Don't say it. Don't you dare say how good it is to see me!

"It's so good to see you." Lance's gaze roamed over her from head to toe. "I thought you'd moved to Sugarcreek."

Struggling to regain her composure, Cheryl squared her shoulders and lifted her chin. "I did."

He leaned in with a grin—that devastating grin that once upon a time made her heart beat fast and her knees go weak. "Came back for the burgers, eh? I totally understand."

Seriously? He was going to pretend like nothing had happened between them? A wave of outrage flooded up from her middle until she almost couldn't see straight. She wasn't love-struck anymore. She wasn't blinded by his good looks and confidence. Her fingers tightened around the paper bag holding the food, crinkling the edge. "Sorry, Lance. I've got someplace I need to be."

She skirted around him, her teeth clenched so tightly she'd give herself a headache if she didn't leave soon. She strode for the door and was surprised and angered when a hand clasped her elbow.

"Cheryl, wait."

Lance offered a lopsided smile—one so full of boyish charm she could almost smell it. Someone should bottle it. *Boyish Charm* by Lance Wilson.

She dropped her gaze to the fingers on her elbow. He immediately released her and slid his hands into the pockets of his designer jeans.

"Sorry. It's just . . . I really was surprised to see you."

Her chin rose. "Yeah, me too."

He tipped his head to look over her shoulder. "You alone?"

Cheryl lifted the bag. "Not exactly. I'm with a friend."

She said it that way intentionally and then felt convicted for implying something that wasn't true. She sighed and lowered the bag. "Naomi Miller came with me. We're here to see someone, and then we're heading back to Sugarcreek. I just stopped in to grab us something to eat."

Was that relief on Lance's face? No! Cheryl shook the thought free and shifted her weight to one foot. She refused to be sucked into the same dead-end situation that had left her heartbroken and insecure the first time around. "So what are you doing here? Don't you still own an apartment across town?"

A large, swanky apartment that cost more than she made in a year.

He shrugged. "Can't beat the food here." He patted his trim waist. "Got in a good workout earlier today, so I thought I'd splurge."

Right. Had to keep the poster-boy image. Cheryl frowned. "Well, I'd better get going. Naomi will be wondering where I am. Nice to see you, Lance."

She didn't honestly mean the last part, but was proud of herself for saying so. She gave a pert nod. "See you around."

"I'm really glad we ran into each other," he called before she could escape. "I've been meaning to call you."

Cheryl paused mid-turn and raised an eyebrow. "Why?"

A flush crept up from Lance's neck. He motioned toward a table near the door. "Do you have a minute?"

No. Never. Not for you.

The words rattled in her head, but she didn't utter them. Instead, curiosity got the best of her and she said, "Sure," and followed him to the table.

What on earth was she doing? Hadn't she spent the last few months trying to forget all about Lance Wilson? And now she was sitting down with him for a chat? The man had ripped her heart to shreds the last time they spoke.

He motioned for a waitress then shot her a glance. "Can I get you something to drink?"

Setting the bag carefully on the table, Cheryl blew out a deep, measured breath. "I really don't have a lot of time, Lance."

"Right."

Another flush crept over his cheeks. Had he always blushed like that? Cheryl studied him from the across the table, for the first time seeing him as a casual bystander might. He was handsome in a boyish way, not rugged and strong like Levi, but cute. That at least hadn't changed. And he was neat. His fingernails, as he drummed his fingers on the table, were clipped and manicured. If she remembered correctly, his hands were soft too, from working at a computer instead of a plow all day. And his arms...

Her mind went to Levi and the sinewy feel of his shoulders beneath her palms.

No comparison there.

Afraid she'd be caught daydreaming, she snapped her gaze back to Lance's face. "So"—she licked her lips—"you said you've been meaning to call me? What about?"

"Yeah, I..." He stopped and ran his hand over his face. "You know, I really hate how things ended between us. I hope you can believe that I never intended to hurt you, Cheryl."

She drew back in her chair. This was *not* a conversation she wanted to have, especially not in public. She cast a quick glance around the room at the other curious customers then dropped her voice to a loud whisper. "You said that several months ago, remember? Right before you asked me for your ring back."

He had the grace to blush. This time she didn't mind seeing it.

"I guess I deserved that."

That, and more. She wanted to say so, but instead of giving in to the urge, she thought of Naomi and what her friend would do in the same situation.

Cheryl blew out another deep breath. "Sorry. I shouldn't have said that. Old hurts."

He shrugged. "No problem. I understand."

Something flickered in his gaze. Was it regret? Or was it only her wounded pride that wanted her to think so? She glanced at her watch. "So, anyway...what can I do for you, Lance? I assume you didn't want to chat about the food?"

A muscle in his jaw ticked. Then his Adam's apple bobbed. Was he nervous? A bit of pity rolled slowly over her, like melting chocolate, and surprisingly sweet. Could it be that leaving her busy life in Columbus behind had made room for other things? Like—she swallowed—forgiveness?

"No, I...see, the thing is...I never really..." He fumbled to a stop.

"I thought I would be angry at you forever," she said quietly, adding a crooked grin to take the sting from her words. "To be honest, there are times I still am, but seeing you today..."

Seeing him the way he really was, not the way she'd built him up in her mind to be, made her realize he was no different than she—flawed and sinful. And whether he asked it or not, she needed to let go of the past and forgive him. Completely. Not just with her lips but in her heart.

Lance's eyes widened, and a large measure of the self-assurance he wore like a mantle slipped from his shoulders. He grabbed hold of her hand and squeezed her fingers. "I really made a mess of things, huh?"

She squirmed in her chair and dropped her gaze. "Yeah, well, I guess it's best we found out how different we are before we said our vows, right?"

She surprised herself with the words. It *was* a blessing that Lance hadn't waited to call off the wedding. What would she have done if she'd found herself bound to a man who would never look at her the way Seth looked at Naomi? Or the way Levi looked at...

She pulled her hand from Lance's grasp. "You really meant to call me?"

He nodded. "I wanted to tell you that I realized after you left what a good woman you are, Cheryl. You will make someone a wonderful wife someday. I only wish I'd realized it sooner."

She couldn't help it—she peered at him suspiciously for several seconds. There was no guile in his eyes, no selfish motivation or deception that she could see.

She tipped her head. "Thank you for that, Lance. It means a lot."

He clasped his hands on the tabletop. "Are you doing well in Sugarcreek? You like it there?"

"It's a slower pace than the one I was used to, but yes, I'm learning to love it there."

His eyebrows rose. "No thoughts of moving back?"

She started to shrug and then shook her head. "No, Lance. I don't think I'll be moving back. Even if Aunt Mitzi came home tomorrow," she added softly then looked him in the eyes. "I like who I am there. I'm real. Not the plastic version of myself that I always tried to be..."

She cut off before she could say the rest.

"For me," he finished for her, his lashes sweeping down to cover his eyes.

How easy it would be to lay all her past failures at his feet, but that really wasn't where they belonged and she knew it. She smiled sadly.

"No, Lance. For myself. I had a picture in my head of who I should be and how I should look. It wasn't until I moved to Sugarcreek that I realized how exhausting it was trying to be something other than the person God created me to be."

A bit of cynicism crept back on to his face. He leaned back in the chair and folded his arms across his chest. "So you found God in Sugarcreek, eh?"

She reached for the paper bag. "I found God a long time ago. I started listening to Him in Sugarcreek."

Instead of responding, he searched her face. Unsure if he found what he looked for, she dropped her gaze and fingered the edge of the paper bag. "So? What about you? How are things at the bank?"

He offered a wry grin. "Things at the office are fine. I got that promotion I wanted."

She thought about it a moment and then nodded as memory struck. Lance had always had his eye on the president's chair. He'd get there eventually. This latest promotion was undoubtedly a step in that direction. "Congratulations."

His grin widened. "Thanks."

The confidence returned full force. His chest puffed so big she thought he'd strangle himself on his shirt and collar.

"Another couple of years and I should be running the whole thing."

He waggled his brows in a way that was at once comical and sad. Lance would always believe in one thing—Lance. Why had she never realized that before?

"Well, good luck. I hope it all works out the way you want." Rising, she tucked the bag under her arm and extended her other hand. "Good-bye, Lance. I'm glad we ran into each other. It really is good to see you again."

This time she meant it. It was good to see him and know that her chances of finding happiness had not ended with his departure before their wedding. They were different. Too different. And they wanted different things. She was actually grateful for the knowledge. It made letting him go easier somehow.

He rose and his hand closed around hers for a moment too long, but instead of bitterness or longing, Cheryl only felt relief when he finally let go.

No more dreaming about what might have been. She turned and walked past a brightly lit jukebox pumping out the latest pop song. She pushed through the door and let it swing shut behind her. No more wishing for something that would never happen and in reality, was probably never meant to be.

For the first time in many months, she knew she had finally found a way to put the past behind her.

Chapter Nineteen

The door to Susan Graber's apartment closed with a solid click. Cheryl pushed up from the hallway floor where she'd sat waiting for Naomi to finish and glanced sidelong at her.

"So? How did it go? Is she coming home soon?"

Her question met with a loud sigh.

"I hope so. Right now it is a little hard to tell. Rebecca will still have to find a way to work through her bitterness and sorrow. It will take time to heal from her wounds."

She turned, and Cheryl followed her out of the building toward her car. It wasn't late, but the air had taken on a definite sharpness and darkness had fallen. Plus they still had a lengthy drive ahead. She was glad they wouldn't have to stop again to eat.

They climbed into the car, and Cheryl motioned to the bag tucked into the console between them.

"I grabbed us a bite for the ride home. Hope you don't mind burgers."

Naomi patted her belly. "Anything sounds goot right now. I am ready for something more substantial than pie."

While they drove and ate, Cheryl told Naomi about her encounter with Lance. Her emotions were much stronger now that she could speak without her defenses being up, and she fought to keep the quiver from her voice.

"We were meant to be here, Naomi, I'm sure of it. Even though the trip didn't turn out as I'd planned—or should I say, how I'd hoped—I still feel like God wanted me to come to Columbus to see Lance, to talk with him and face my feelings."

Naomi wiped a spot of ketchup from her mouth, nodding as Cheryl talked. "It is always God's will for differences to be worked out, especially among His people—even if it is for their sakes alone. This was an important step for you, Cheryl. I'm glad you found the courage to take it. Now, if only we could convince the Zooks of this...or the Robertsons, for that matter."

The Robertsons. Cheryl hadn't given them much thought since speaking to the travel agent in Dover.

"Do you think they're still planning on taking that trip to Europe?" She plucked a french fry from the bag and popped it into her mouth then brushed the salt from her fingers.

Naomi crumpled the paper wrapper her burger had come in and stuffed it into the trash. "I imagine their intentions have not changed, though I cannot understand..."

The ringing of Cheryl's cell phone interrupted her before she could finish. Cheryl glanced at the number and then widened her eyes at Naomi.

"It's the travel agent. How's that for timing?"

She fluttered her hands at Cheryl anxiously. "Answer it."

Cheryl answered the phone using her Bluetooth headset. "Hello?"

"Miss Cooper? It's Faith Overstreet calling, from TransWorld Travel. We spoke earlier this week about a trip to Europe?"

"Yes. Hi, Faith. How are you?" Convinced she'd want to concentrate on the call, Cheryl pulled off of the highway.

"Just great! Thanks for asking. Listen, I know it's late, but I just got a notification on some really great airfares flying out of Cleveland. It's a promo, so the rates won't last long. Would you like me to shoot you over the information?"

"Uh, yeah," Cheryl said, glancing at Naomi and grimacing as she repeated the message. "I'd love some information on airfares. I'm driving though, so I won't be able to check my e-mail until tomorrow morning. Is that okay?"

"Not a problem. I really wanted you to see these, though, because I doubt we'll find a better deal. You take a look, and we'll talk soon."

Acting on a hunch, Cheryl said before Faith could disconnect, "So I guess you'll be sending this information to the Robertsons as well, huh?"

"The Robertsons?" Faith made a *tsk* sound. "No, they've actually already booked a flight."

"Really?" Cheryl lifted her brows at Naomi and then said into the phone, "They booked a flight? That was fast."

"Yeah. Turns out the trip they have in mind is more business in nature than pleasure."

Business trip, Cheryl mouthed, and Naomi frowned.

"I thought they were looking into a vacation?" Cheryl said.

Faith harrumphed. "So did I. I sent them several sightseeing packages, but Mrs. Robertson told me they weren't interested. Of course, I asked if there was something else I could gather material for, but Mrs. Robertson said they wouldn't have time because they're going to be spending most of their trip looking into foreign adoptions. Who'd have thought, at their age?"

She blew out a snooty sigh. "Anyway, I was a little disappointed, considering all the hours I'd spent preparing their travel portfolio. I guess it was to be expected, given the trouble she told me they'd been having with their daughter. Still, they're a little old to be starting over with kids, don't you think? You know them pretty well, right?"

"Ah...well, you know," Cheryl replied, deliberately vague.

Naomi spread her hands in a gesture that screamed for information, but Cheryl motioned for patience.

"Okay, well, let me know what you think on the rates I sent you. If you see something that looks appealing, just shoot me a quick e-mail or text and I'll get started booking your flights."

"Will do. Thank you, Faith."

"You bet. Good-bye."

Cheryl disconnected and then dropped the phone into her lap, shaking her head.

"What is it?" Naomi poked her arm. "Cheryl, what did she say?"

"The Robertsons are looking into foreign adoptions," she replied slowly.

Naomi's eyebrows nearly disappeared into her bonnet. "They are what?"

Cheryl nodded and repeated everything Faith had told her. "What in the world do you make of that, Naomi?"

She shook her head. "I do not know. It is strange, for sure and for certain." She swiveled on the seat so that she sat facing Cheryl. "Did the travel agent say when they are going?"

Cheryl shook her head. "I didn't ask."

Naomi pinched her bottom lip between her thumb and index finger. "Well, if the Robertsons are leaving soon, we may not have another chance to speak to them about their grandson. Do you think we should even bother giving another visit a try?"

Cheryl scratched her temple. "It may not be worth the trouble. I mean, they wouldn't even let us in the house last time, and they're looking into foreign adoptions. I'd say they've pretty much written their daughter off, wouldn't you?"

"What is 'written off'?"

"Turned their back—like shunning, because they think there is no hope of ever repairing the rift between them."

Naomi wagged her finger. "Anything is possible with Gott, Cheryl. Just imagine, a week ago you surely would not have expected to have the conversation you had with Lance tonight."

Convicted about her doubting spirit, Cheryl ducked her head, her face warming uncomfortably. "That is true." She tapped the steering wheel. "It's awfully late tonight. What do you think about heading over there first thing Monday morning?"

Naomi hesitated. "What about the store?"

Cheryl frowned. "*Hmm…*do you suppose Esther or Lydia would mind putting in a few extra hours?"

"I do not think it will be a problem, but I will ask," Naomi said, "and then I will meet you at the Swiss Miss."

Back in Sugarcreek, Cheryl dropped Naomi by the farm before turning for home. The lights on Aunt Mitzi's porch shone brightly, a welcome sight after a long and very futile day. Cheryl parked the car and then let herself inside, dropping her keys on the hall table as she passed. Remembering the mail, she went back out to the box for it and was pleased to see a letter bearing a familiar script and a stamp from Papua New Guinea.

She carried the letter inside, brewed a quick cup of tea, and then went to sit in the living room. Tearing open the envelope, she read the first few lines hastily.

My Darling Cheryl,
    I hope all is well in your part of the world. For me, it is as though time has stood still.

Aunt Mitzi always started her letters the same way, with an endearment that made Cheryl feel like someone special. Pulling her feet up onto the sofa, she slowed and went back to the beginning to reread.

My Darling Cheryl,
    I hope all is well in your part of the world. For me, it is as though time has stood still. I am busier than I have ever been, and yet I am learning daily what it means to live each hour, each minute, more fully and with more joy.

Seeing Aunt Mitzi's words, hearing her voice, made peace and comfort seep over Cheryl. She took a sip from her tea while she read the rest of the letter.

Also, an incredible thing happened. I was witness to the most amazing act of kindness! Several months ago, a young woman whose legs were crushed when she was hit by a car came to the mission in search of medical attention, food, and clothes. We were only too glad to help her, though for a while, we wondered if she would even survive.

Praise God, in time, she recovered from her injuries, but she will forever walk with a limp. She has stayed on as a volunteer. Her efforts to help others like herself have been tireless, and I have counted the terrible circumstances that brought her to us as a blessing. Isn't that how the Lord works? So often He uses the worst to bring us His best.

Anyway, just a few short weeks ago, it was discovered that the man driving the car that hit her had been found, only instead of pressing charges, the woman asked if the man would also volunteer at the mission. He was reluctant at first. Many times I saw anger in his eyes—a resentment if you will, at the hold this young woman bore over him. But not once did she falter in her insistence that he remain and work alongside the rest of us. And now...oh, my dear, I weep as I write this... the young man has repented of his sins and accepted Jesus!

What a testimony to the power of forgiveness! I am certain that if we but dared even the smallest measure of grace that this young woman showed, what a difference we would make for Christ. Please keep her and all of us here in your prayers as we strive to impact the world for Jesus.

I love you, my dearest girl. I pray this letter finds you and all of my friends in Sugarcreek well. Give my regards to Naomi.

With all of my love and affection,
Your aunt Mitzi

The paper rustled softly as Cheryl went back over the last few lines.

The power of forgiveness.

Hadn't she sampled a bit of that same ingredient just this evening? Tears gathered in her eyes as she folded the letter and slid it carefully back into the envelope. Granted, Lance had hurt her, but not in the same way that the woman Aunt Mitzi wrote about had been hurt.

Pushing aside her cooling tea, Cheryl folded her hands and bowed her head. Perhaps there was still more she needed to learn about forgiveness...something she had not thought to seek God for because she'd been so blinded by her own injury.

"Okay, Lord," she whispered, "I'm listening to You now. What is it You want me to know?"

Seek My face, a gentle voice answered from deep inside her spirit.

"I don't know how," Cheryl admitted, fresh tears gathering in her eyes and spilling down her cheeks. "I need You to show me what it means to *truly* seek You."

And again, she felt it repeated in her heart...

Seek My face.

Further back, the memory of her father's voice echoed.

"Cheryl, darling, look at me when I'm talking to you."

Startled, Cheryl opened her eyes and stared at her clasped fingers. How often had she heard those words growing up when her father wanted her to pay attention?

"Look at me when I'm talking to you, sweetheart. There now . . . that's better."

Suddenly, Cheryl understood why the Lord had found it necessary to remind her to seek Him. It was because she had been so caught up in the circumstances of this storm that she had forgotten to really *look* toward God.

Dropping her head onto her crossed arms, Cheryl gave in to the flood of emotions seeping past the hidden cracks in her heart. Her tears washed away a wealth of hurt and unforgiveness.

For months, she'd deceived herself into believing she had forgiven Lance. The truth was, she had simply refused to think of him, and that was very different. Beginning today, she would learn what it meant to forgive as God did, with no memory of the injury and no reflection of the wrong.

Reaching that decision lifted a weight from Cheryl's heart, a burden that had darkened her spirit for far too long.

It felt very, very good.

CHAPTER TWENTY

Cheryl had over an hour before Naomi arrived and they left to head for the Robertsons' home, so she made a quick pit stop at the police station before heading for the Swiss Miss. The weather had turned colder overnight. Cheryl zipped her coat and pushed her hands into a pair of warm leather gloves before exiting the car and heading up the walk toward the station.

Delores welcomed her from behind a tall stack of paper and folders, a frustrated scowl creasing her forehead. At her elbow, a mug of coffee teetered dangerously close to the edge of her desk.

"Good morning, Delores."

"Hey, Cheryl." She dropped another pile of folders on the desk with a *thwump*.

Cheryl motioned toward the folders. "Chief's got you busy, I see."

Delores shoved the stack aside and blew out a breath so forcefully, it stirred the hair resting against her forehead. "More than busy. This Swartzentruber case has us both running in circles."

"Sorry to hear that." Cheryl left the entrance and crossed to stand by Delores's desk. Using the tip of her finger, she poked the mug to safety. "So I guess it's safe to say there haven't been any new leads?"

"Not exactly," she admitted with a frown, "which is why the chief has me looking through all these old case files. He's hoping maybe we'll stumble across something—similar profile, clues to the method of operation the kidnapper used"—she shrugged and jabbed her glasses higher on her nose—"anything that might help us." Her brows rose to form skeptical peaks.

Great. Though he wouldn't admit it, the chief had to be pretty desperate if he was resorting to clues from cold case files. And that meant he was no closer to tracking down Baby John's kidnapper than she and Naomi were, a fact that did not bode well for the Swartzentrubers.

Squelching a rising swell of despair, Cheryl pointed toward the chief's office. "Is he in?"

Delores shook her head. "He's heading out to see Samuel and Rachel. Elizabeth Miller came by yesterday to help the police artist with a sketch of the missing child. He wants the parents to take a look before he posts it around town."

"Okay." Cheryl pushed her hands into the pockets of her coat. "I'll stop by later then. I just thought I'd check in, see if there was anything I could do to help."

Delores lifted one finger then riffled through the folders on her desk until she found the one she wanted and held it out to Cheryl. "By chance, does this lady look familiar to you?"

She flipped open the folder. Theresa Cox stared up at her from a black-and-white photo—the kind that might have been taken for a passport... or a mug shot. Her hair was longer and pulled back into a ponytail, but there was no doubt. Cheryl blinked, her promise to Theresa ringing in her head. She flipped the cover closed then handed the folder back to Delores. "Yes, she does. That's the lady I told the chief about a couple of days ago."

Delores nodded. "I thought so." She leaned forward to rest her elbow on the desk. "Did you know her family has ties to the Amish?"

Cheryl held her breath. "Really?"

Shoving the folder back into the stack, Delores gave a curt snort. "Turns out she has a cousin or something over in Lancaster County who married into an Amish family. It really hasn't turned into anything interesting yet, but I'm checking it out, just in case."

Her heart thrumming in her chest, Cheryl nodded. "Good thinking. Let me know what you find out, will you?"

Delores gave a pert smile. "You know how that goes."

Yes, she did—Delores would fill her in on what she could and no promises on anything else. Cheryl smiled back and gave a short wave before leaving the station.

All the way to the store, her conversation with Theresa rang through her head, and a niggle of suspicion she'd thought buried sprouted to vibrant life.

Why hadn't Theresa mentioned she had ties to the Amish when they spoke? In fact, Cheryl had gotten the opposite impression when she said she'd moved to the Sleepy Dutchman Inn.

"I wanted to get a feel for the authentic Amish lifestyle."

Cheryl had assumed when Theresa uttered those words that it had been simple curiosity that had been her reason for checking out of the Little Switzerland a day early. But what if she'd had a darker motive? And if she did, what would it take to crack that nearly impenetrable facade?

Customers waited outside the door of the Swiss Miss. Spying several of them pacing and a few even moving toward their vehicles, Cheryl hurried to park and then scrambled up the walk and unlocked the doors.

"Sorry I'm late, everyone," she said, smiling politely and nodding to her customers as they filtered by. Two in particular stopped to peer pointedly at their watches.

"Good morning, Ben," she said, speaking to the elder Vogel brother. The two of them came into the store often to play checkers.

"Good morning, Miss Cooper," he replied, one eyebrow quirked in question. "Everything all right?"

She bent forward and lowered her voice. "Everything's fine, but I wouldn't mind if you helped Esther keep an eye on the store this morning while I run an errand."

The younger Vogel brother, Rueben, leaned forward. "I will be most glad to help," he said, nudging his broad-brimmed hat off his forehead with his finger.

"You can count on me," Ben said as he removed his baseball cap and then crossed to the front of the store and took up residence next to the checkerboard.

Cheryl shook her head as she followed the last customer into the store. It was a strange ritual these two had developed—meeting to play checkers but barely speaking to one another. Still, she was glad their relationship had improved and they were working on reconciliation and forgiveness.

She paused midway to the cash register. There was that word again. *Forgiveness.* God sure had been tossing it into her path a lot lately.

The doorbell chimed cheerfully, and Cheryl turned to look. Naomi hurried toward her, her cheeks reddened from cold.

"It is all settled," she said, blowing on her hands to warm them. "Esther is here now, and Lydia will come later this afternoon." She cupped one hand to her mouth. "Just in case we are detained."

The trip would take longer than they'd planned, but not for the reason Naomi hoped. Cheryl had every intention of looking in on Theresa Cox one more time on their way to New Philadelphia.

"That was good thinking, asking Lydia to come by." She grabbed her purse and slung it over her arm. "Let's get going. I have something I want to tell you, but I'll do it along the way."

Naomi was as perplexed as Cheryl had been upon learning of Theresa's Amish ties. She agreed that the information warranted another visit with the lady in question. Unfortunately, Theresa was not at the Sleepy Dutchman when Cheryl and Naomi arrived. They stood at the check-in counter together, Cheryl certain her own frown matched Naomi's.

"We could wait around awhile," she said. "Perhaps we can catch her when she comes back from"—she hitched her thumb over her shoulder—"wherever she went."

Cheryl glanced at her watch. It was already midmorning, and they still had to drive to New Philadelphia. She shook her head and collected her purse and keys. "No, let's go ahead and get going. We'll stop by here on our way back."

Naomi agreed and soon they were humming down the highway, Cheryl's thoughts a whirling, jumbled mess.

She glanced at Naomi. "Can I ask you something?"

In answer, she peered at her expectantly.

Cheryl turned her eyes to the road ahead. "For months I have told myself that I forgave Lance for breaking off our engagement, but then after seeing him again . . ."

"All those old feelings welled up inside." She said it matter-of-factly.

Cheryl nodded and then told Naomi about the Vogels' visit earlier and Aunt Mitzi's most recent letter.

She clutched the steering wheel, wishing she could grasp the emotions battling inside her as easily. "I feel as though God is trying to make me understand the difference between real, heavenly forgiveness and the shallow, superficial kind human beings extend." She shrugged helplessly. "But I don't get it, Naomi. I know He *wants* me to move past this. I wrestled with it all night. But I'm not Him. I can't remove the memory of past hurts like He does, so how do I extend the same kind of unconditional, no-holds-barred forgiveness?"

Tension built in her chest as she spoke, mingled with a feeling of utter unworthiness that made her want to cry in frustration.

Naomi was silent a moment, so Cheryl glanced her way. Naomi's teeth worked her bottom lip, and her fingers were rubbing thoughtfully at her chin. "I cannot speak for Gott," she said finally. "I can only say what I have learned from Him, and that is that sometimes His lessons are not about revealing how unfit we are, but how perfect He is. Is that not how we learn to be like Him? Not by comparing ourselves to others, but by comparing ourselves to Him."

Cheryl pondered this quietly. "So . . . you're saying that perhaps God isn't trying to show me how I've failed in forgiving Lance completely?"

"Perhaps. It could be that He wants you to understand how completely *He* has forgiven *you*."

Was that it? Was that why He kept putting reminders in her path—so that she could see and understand what kind of gift had been given to her?

"And what about the Swartzentrubers?" Cheryl asked, glancing at Naomi. "What if Baby John's kidnapper is never found? Do you think that God will expect Samuel and Rachel to find some way of making peace with that? Of forgiving the person who took him, and allowing God to somehow . . . somehow . . . work all of this for their good?"

Even in her own ears, the idea seemed impossible. Naomi's face reflected the same uncertainty.

"That will be a lesson for Samuel and Rachel—one I pray they do not have to face. In my own mind, I cannot even fathom it, but as you know, we are not Gott. We cannot know what He has planned for them, or any of us."

Though it wasn't the answer Cheryl wanted, she knew Naomi was right. God could move mountains, and if He intended for the kidnapper to be caught, there was no place that person could hide where he or she would not be found. But if—and she shuddered to think it—God allowed that person to disappear, she could only pray that Samuel and Rachel would be able to turn to Him for the strength and peace they would need to bear it.

She smudged a tear from her lashes and sniffed. "Tomorrow I'm going to write to Aunt Mitizi and let her know how much I appreciate her letters. I want her to know that even though she is in Papua New Guinea, she's still ministering to the people in Sugarcreek. Me especially."

A gentle smile smoothed the worried lines from Naomi's face. "I think that would be a very goot idea."

By the time they reached the outskirts of New Philadelphia, some of the uncertainty had filtered from Cheryl's heart. In a way, she realized she was glad she wasn't like God, able to see all of the grief and heartache that people poured on one another. That was a burden too great for her shoulders, and one she hoped never to carry. Just facing the Robertsons today would be hard enough.

When they pulled to a stop at the end of the street, close enough to see the beams marking the Tudor style house but not right in front of the driveway, she turned and clasped Naomi's hand. "Would you mind...could I possibly ask...?"

"I will wait in the car," she replied before Cheryl could finish the thought. "To the Robertsons, I am simply a reminder of a choice they did not ask for or want. Better if you go alone. They need to remember what they have lost."

She grinned and reached for Cheryl's hand. "Besides, I think that is what Gott would want." Her fingers tightened around Cheryl's, imparting courage and strength. "It is you that He has been speaking to about forgiveness. If ever there were two people more in need of that knowledge, it is John and Victoria Robertson. Just keep in mind how much they are hurting too. It will make talking with them easier."

She inclined her head in the direction of the house. "Go on now. And while you are inside, I will be seeking Gott, praying that He gives you the words to speak."

Cheryl drew in a deep breath and then nodded. "Okay. Thank you, Naomi."

She reached for the door handle, her fingers trembling. It was one thing to know that God wanted her to act, and quite another to follow through in obedience.

Her legs felt weak as she walked the same brick path she'd trod the first time she came to see the Robertsons. Once again, a scarecrow waved a cheery welcome, only this time the sign was slightly askew and it was apparent the mums spilling from atop the hay bales hadn't been watered. The leaves drooped sadly. Stirred by a gentle wind, one detached from the stem and fluttered to the ground.

You're stalling, her conscience accused. *Get moving and ring that bell.*

She glanced back toward the car. As promised, Naomi's head was bowed, what Cheryl could see of it over the car door, and her face was creased with concentration.

Bolstered by the thought of her friend's prayers, Cheryl reached for the doorbell and gave it a push. A chime sounded deep in the bowels of the house. She waited nervously, her fingers curling and uncurling at her sides. She almost hoped the Robertsons weren't home. The garage door was open, and one of the stalls was empty. Maybe they'd be gone, and Cheryl could just leave a note letting them know she'd been by and asking them to call.

She pushed the bell again. And, again, the low chimes echoed through the belly of the house. Cheryl let her shoulders relax, surprised to realize they'd been up around her ears. Releasing the breath she'd been holding, she rummaged through her purse for something to write on and was about to pencil a note when a step sounded and the front door swung back a crack.

Cheryl lifted her head. "Hello?"

The door opened the rest of the way. Once again, a dog barked.

"Sorry. One second." Victoria Robertson scooped the dog up from the floor at her feet, deposited him in a room off the hallway, then closed that door and returned to Cheryl.

"Miss Cooper. Hello." Her hair was neatly combed, and she was dressed for the day, but her face was devoid of makeup. It made her look older somehow, more haggard. She motioned toward Cheryl. "It is Cooper, isn't it?"

She nodded. "Thank you for remembering." She shoved the paper and pencil into her purse. "Listen...I know it's early, and I apologize for not calling first, but could we talk? I promise, I will only take a moment of your time."

Mrs. Robertson hesitated, her eyes reflecting worry as she glanced inside and then back at Cheryl. "My husband isn't home. He had to run a quick errand, but he'll be back shortly."

Cheryl offered a small smile. "That's okay. Like I said, it'll only take a moment."

Indecision twisted Mrs. Robertson's mouth. Her hand rose, and she absentmindedly wound a lock of her hair around her finger. "This is about my daughter, isn't it?"

Cheryl pushed her purse strap farther up her shoulder. "Yes. Yes it is."

She bit her lip, fighting the urge to say more. If Victoria Robertson wanted to know how her only daughter was faring, she'd have to ask. Cheryl wasn't going to volunteer the information, and she wasn't going to make the task of turning her away easier.

As if sensing her determination, Mrs. Robertson let her shoulders droop and motioned for Cheryl to enter. "Please, come in."

Afraid she would change her mind if she hesitated, Cheryl leaped on the invitation and stepped inside. As before, the hall was neat and perfect, but missing the travel pamphlets that had cluttered the table on her last visit. Mrs. Robertson sidestepped her and led the way toward a quaint parlor with picture-perfect furnishings that looked like they'd been lifted straight off the pages of a decorating magazine.

"Can I offer you something to drink?" Mrs. Robertson's hands were clasped tightly in front of her, and her face bore a pinched look that said she felt as uncomfortable as Cheryl did with the situation. Regardless, her manner spoke of breeding and she would play the perfect hostess no matter the cost.

Cheryl dismissed the offer with a wave. "No thank you."

Mrs. Robertson moved farther into the room. A luxurious sofa hugged one wall, and a matching chair and ottoman the other. She perched on one corner of the sofa while Cheryl took the other.

"So"—she licked her lips—"please, tell me about my daughter. Is she all right?" Her knees were locked so tightly it was a wonder she didn't topple from the sofa. Though it wasn't amusing, the picture she made somehow softened Cheryl's view of her.

She slid her purse off her shoulder and placed it on the floor. "You really love her, don't you?"

Instantly, Mrs. Robertson's eyes filled with tears, yet she managed to keep them from spilling over.

She dropped her gaze, her fingers nervously smoothing the hem of her silk blouse. "Of course I do. She's my daughter and she always will be, no matter what happens between us."

Her bare lips quivered, making her look vulnerable. "I always wanted children. When I was a girl, I couldn't wait to get married so I could have a family of my own. John and I met after college, and it seemed as though my dreams were finally coming true."

"Are you saying they didn't?" Cheryl asked softly.

"No, they did...in a way." Mrs. Robertson looked up, and Cheryl's gaze followed hers about the room—from the drapes that pooled on the floor to the intricately woven Oriental rug underfoot.

She sighed. "My husband is a wonderful provider. He's worked so hard his whole life. He was away from home a lot, but I have never begrudged him the time he spent focusing on his career. Taking care of us was his way of expressing how much he loved us."

"You and Rachel."

Sorrow soaked Mrs. Robertson's eyes as her gaze returned to Cheryl. "John and I tried for a long time to have children. Years, in fact. I went to every fertility doctor and clinic I could find—spoke to every specialist and expert. They all told me the same thing—my odds of bearing children were not good."

Her hand fluttered up and pressed against her chest, as though talking about the pain brought it back somehow.

"I had begun to despair of ever getting pregnant," she continued, "so when I learned that I was carrying Rachel..." She paused and licked her lips then sat forward, her eyes piercing. "I felt like Hannah must have in the Bible when she begged God for a son. Do you know that story, Miss Cooper?"

Cheryl nodded. She'd always been struck by the lonely woman's plight.

Mrs. Robertson rose and went to stand by the window. The sun lit her from behind, casting shadows on her thin shoulders and sharp hips. She stared out, her expression so forlorn and filled with such yearning that Cheryl wanted to wrap her arms around her and give her a hug, like her mother used to when she was a girl.

"That story always haunted me," Mrs. Robertson whispered. "I *knew* how Hannah felt."

She clutched her fist to her breast and turned to stare at Cheryl. "Can you understand why we felt so betrayed when Rachel left us to join the Amish church? After years of waiting and hoping and struggling with infertility, it didn't seem fair that God would give her to us, only to take her back."

Cheryl fidgeted on the sofa cushions. She did understand, but that didn't explain why the Robertsons chose to ignore their daughter now. "Is that what you think happened?"

Mrs. Robertson rubbed her hands over her arms briskly then crossed to pluck a tissue from an ornate silver box. She inhaled deeply and lifted her chin. "My pregnancy was not easy. We fought to have a baby, Miss Cooper. Twice, I almost lost her. When Rachel was born, we gave everything to her—anything she wanted. And because I wanted to show my gratitude and appreciation to God for blessing us with a child, I made sure we raised her up in the church. Our church."

"And then she left."

Mrs. Robertson's face twisted with pain. She quickly hid it by pressing the tissue to her nose. "I did everything I was supposed to," she whispered, "everything the church and preacher said was required. I dedicated her back to the Lord. Truly. I did not withhold my child from Him. So why then wasn't it enough?"

She broke off, and her hand went to her throat. Unable to stand idly by in the face of her grief, Cheryl crossed to her and squeezed her shoulder.

"I don't know the answer to that," she said softly. "I wish I did. I only know that your daughter still loves you, despite what you may think, and she misses you very much."

Easing to stand facing Mrs. Robertson, Cheryl looked squarely into her eyes.

"Rachel could really use her mother right now. I'm worried about her, Mrs. Robertson. John's kidnapping has just about destroyed her. You say it's been hard losing Rachel to another church...just think about what it would be like to have your child snatched from your home—to not know if he was alright or what was happening to him. If it weren't for Joseph, the fact that she has to keep going for his sake...well..." She blew out a troubled sigh. "I just don't know."

A small sound escaped from Mrs. Robertson's lips. She pressed her fingers to her mouth, her wide eyes filled with fear and dismay. "What are you saying, Miss Cooper? You think she might...?" Her mouth worked as though she couldn't force herself to speak the words.

Cheryl took her hand and clasped it between her own. "I'm saying she needs you. Not me and not Naomi. You. Her mother."

She shook her head as though disbelieving. "But she has her husband..."

"He is spending every waking moment searching for his son. He doesn't have time to take care of himself and his wife too." Reluctantly, she let Mrs. Robertson's hand fall. "I admit, I do not understand everything that has transpired between you and your daughter. I haven't been in your shoes. But right now, she is hurting, and if you *ever* want to have a relationship with her again, you need to go to her, now. Before the damage becomes irreparable."

Cheryl forced herself to stop. The passion in her heart had made her words sharper and more desperate than she'd intended. Still, she was glad she'd said them.

A wealth of conflicting emotions flitted across Mrs. Robertson's face. For a moment, she seemed as though she might crumple into a heap, but then the frown cleared and she stared with pleading in her eyes.

"Miss Cooper…Cheryl…there's something I need to tell you…"

"Victoria? Honey, where are you?"

Mr. Robertson's voice echoed through the large house. Along with panic, Cheryl thought she heard a bit of anger mixed with his tone.

The look that Mrs. Robertson sent toward Cheryl was more than desperate. She looked afraid. But when she turned to the door, her features were composed and surprisingly calm. "We're in here, John."

"I thought I heard voices…" He strode into the parlor. Upon catching sight of Cheryl, he broke off and the worried look on his face quickly became one of irritation. "Miss Cooper? What are you doing here?"

Swallowing a sudden knot in her throat, Cheryl looked from him to Mrs. Robertson. "I came by to speak with you about your daughter."

"I thought we told you last time that we would work that situation out on our own." He pulled himself up straighter and crossed his arms. He turned his scowl toward his wife. "Victoria? Is everything all right here?"

"Everything is fine." She crossed to him and laid her hands on his forearms. "But John, I think we should listen to what Miss Cooper has to say."

The scowl lines on his face deepened. "We've discussed this, remember?"

"I know we have, darling." Mrs. Robertson's voice rose to match his. "But Miss Cooper says that Rachel isn't doing well."

Her knuckles shone white against the dark fabric of his coat. She peered up at him, frantically pleading. "She's our daughter, John. She needs us."

He turned and grasped his wife by the arms. "Victoria, listen to yourself. What about what we need? Are you forgetting the hurt we've been through? What losing Rachel has done to our family? To you?" He paused, and his voice softened. "Sweetheart, I can't lose you too."

Lose her? What exactly did he mean? Cheryl stepped forward. "Mr. Robertson, if I could just…"

He whirled, putting his wife behind him in a protective motion so smooth and quick, it robbed Cheryl of speech. Just what did he think she intended to do? She stared at him, mute.

He stuck out his hand, one finger raised. "I'm afraid I'm going to have to ask you to leave and never come back, Miss Cooper. Please understand me, if I see you here again, I will call the police."

Cheryl retreated a step. "W…Wha…but…I…," she stammered.

"John, please," Mrs. Robertson begged.

He shook his head, still glaring at Cheryl. "I don't have to tell you this, probably shouldn't, but I get the feeling that if I don't, you won't let this go. So here it is—my wife is sick. Very sick. Ever since Rachel left. She's had anxiety attacks. Severe depression. Even suicidal thoughts."

"John." Mrs. Robertson stepped from behind her husband, her dark eyes wet with tears and sorrow. "It's all right." Once again, he grabbed his wife by the arms. "No, it's not, Victoria. I can't protect you if you keep allowing these people to drag up old feelings."

She shook her head. "You can't protect me anyway. You've tried." She reached up and stroked his shoulder. "You can't protect me from a broken heart."

He fell silent, and Mrs. Robertson turned to Cheryl.

"It's true, everything my husband just said. Which is partly why I haven't gone to see Rachel, why I haven't...why we haven't reached out to our daughter."

The tears that had been soaking her eyes spilled over and ran down her cheeks. She pulled from her husband's arms and turned to Cheryl. "It's not that we don't love her. It was just too difficult. Please believe that. I'm simply not...I'm not strong enough to live without her, and she's made her choice. It's not us."

"But it doesn't have to be a choice," Cheryl urged quietly. "There is room enough for all of you in Rachel's heart if you would just give her and Samuel a chance."

"I'd like to believe that," Mrs. Robertson replied, her chin quivering. "I just can't. She's changed, Miss Cooper. Not just her clothes or her hair—it's the way she talks, the things she says. I hardly recognize her anymore."

Her voice faded to a whisper, but in the suddenly silent room, it rumbled like thunder, and Cheryl knew there was no point in staying longer. As far as the Robertsons were concerned, their daughter was lost to them forever, and nothing she said would change their minds.

"I'm sorry," she said at last and realized as she said it that she truly was. This family was broken beyond repair. There was nothing sadder or more sorrowful than that.

She bent to retrieve her purse and slung the strap over her shoulder. When she straightened, Mrs. Robertson had returned to the circle of her husband's arms. Neither one looked at her as she passed them and made for the door to let herself out.

Her feet dragged as she left the path and crossed the street toward the car. Maybe Naomi would have some wisdom about how to handle the situation she'd just left. As for Cheryl, she'd never felt so completely helpless.

She approached the car, a little surprised that she couldn't see Naomi's bonneted head above the dashboard. Had she laid the seat back for a nap?

Her steps quickened. The closer the got, the more certain she was that Naomi was no longer in the car. She looked up the street and then back at the car.

"Naomi?"

"Cheryl!"

Naomi's harsh stage whisper emanated from a neatly clipped boxwood a few feet away. Cheryl moved toward it, squinting. "What on earth are you doing in the bushes?"

"Is he gone?"

She planted her hands on her hips. "Is who gone?"

"Mr. Robertson." Naomi's head poked up from the bushes. "Did you see him?"

"Of course I saw him. He came into the house."

Her eyes widened. "And?"

"And what?" Cheryl frowned. "Naomi, come out of there and tell me what's going on."

Naomi straightened, checked the street, and then hurried to Cheryl. Grabbing her by the hand, she dragged her toward the car. "It was him, Cheryl. John Robertson."

"Him, what? What did he do?"

Throwing open the door, Naomi shoved Cheryl into the driver's seat and then scurried around to climb in on the passenger side. Panting heavily, she pressed her hand to her chest.

Cheryl's own heart beat faster in response. "Naomi, what happened? What did you see?"

Naomi licked her lips, her wide eyes blinking. "It was him. The person who took Baby John. John Robertson is our kidnapper!"

CHAPTER TWENTY-ONE

Cheryl blinked and leaned forward on the seat. "Did I hear you right? You think John and Victoria Robertson..."

"Not Victoria." She grimaced and shoved the bonnet back on her head to scratch her temple. "At least, I did not think so, although now that you mention it, I suppose she would have had to know something was wrong. I mean, it would be almost impossible for him to accomplish such a thing without her knowledge, right? Even if he were to..."

She was babbling. Cheryl clasped her arm. "Naomi, out with it. What exactly did you see?"

"John Robertson definitely had something to do with Baby John's kidnapping," she replied matter-of-factly.

Cheryl frowned and pressed her fingers to her forehead to shake a bit of the confusion from her brain. "But, how do you know? What happened while I was inside?"

Naomi drew a deep breath and blew it out slowly. Her hands no longer shook, but it was apparent as she licked her lips and squirmed on the seat that she was fighting to remain calm.

"I was sitting here waiting for you," she began carefully. "I knew the conversation with Mrs. Robertson was going to be difficult, so when I saw her bring you inside, I intensified my prayers."

"Thank you," Cheryl said.

Naomi nodded. "Anyway, I was praying, and then I heard a car coming up the street from the other direction."

Cheryl's gaze followed the direction she pointed. "So?"

"So I recognized the dark blue car as being the one we saw parked in the Robertsons' garage."

"From a couple of days ago, when we stopped by."

"That is right." Naomi's head bobbed rapidly. "He pulled in and parked, and Cheryl, from where I was sitting, I could see him unloading baby supplies from his trunk!"

"What kind of supplies?"

"Diapers…large boxes." She held her hands about a foot apart. "And other things. Baby formula, I think, and baby toys. I could not tell exactly because I was too far away, but everything was very colorful and obviously for babies." She motioned toward the bushes. "That is what I was doing in the hedges. I snuck out of the car so I could get a better look."

Cheryl bit her lip, thinking. "Okay…but Faith Overstreet from the travel agency *did* tell us the Robertsons were looking into foreign adoptions."

"So…you don't think this is something we should investigate?" Naomi deflated like a balloon that someone had stuck with a pin. "I just got so excited when I saw the diapers, I did not stop to think. Still, his trunk was almost full. It is a significant amount of supplies for a couple who are only *considering* adoption, don't you think?"

True. Cheryl rolled her bottom lip between her thumb and forefinger. To what lengths did a couple go when they were considering bringing a baby into their home? How much was reasonable, and did stocking up on diapers apply?

Her gaze drifted to the house. "I don't know, Naomi. This does sound peculiar. And I can't get rid of this feeling in my gut that something is not quite right."

Naomi shifted to let her gaze follow Cheryl's. "What did Mrs. Robertson say?"

Briefly, Cheryl summed up the conversation she'd had with Victoria. She pressed into the back of the seat. "I felt so sorry for her, especially when John Robertson told me how sick she's been since losing Rachel. I mean, really sick, Naomi. John said she's even been suicidal."

"She has considered taking her own life!" Her head swung side-to-side. "That is terrible. So much grief in this family."

"Agreed." The gears in Cheryl's brain whirred busily. "I know they've been through a lot, and I guess I could understand them wanting another child. They're young enough. I mean, Victoria Robertson still looks like she could be Rachel's sister."

"Ja. And nowadays, it is not uncommon for couples to wait until they are older to begin their families."

"So then why do I have such a strange feeling right here?" Cheryl pressed her hand to her stomach.

"As do I. The minute I saw Mr. Robertson pull into his driveway, I got a sick feeling in my heart."

Cheryl grabbed the steering wheel and stuck out her chin. "I think we should take a peek inside the Robertsons' garage. What do you say?"

An impish glint sparkled in Naomi's eyes. "The door is open."

"It wouldn't be breaking and entering."

"We would just be looking…perhaps as we walked by."

Cheryl pulled one of the TransWorld pamphlets from her purse. "I could ask them about this, if they happen to catch us in the act. Well?"

Naomi reached for the door handle. "Let's go."

Cheryl needed no further prompting. She hopped out of the car and joined Naomi on the sidewalk. "Okay, I'll take the left side, closest to the house. If I see anyone coming, I'll call out. Like this." She flapped her arms and made a crowing sound. "Caw-caw."

Naomi eyed her quizzically. "What was that?"

"You know, a bird?"

Naomi frowned.

"Fine." Cheryl dropped her arms. "It was a joke anyway."

Shaking her head, Naomi gestured toward the garage. "I'll take the right side, next to where Mr. Robertson parked. There must be shelves or something inside the garage. I didn't see him carry anything into the house."

"No, he was empty-handed, at least he was by the time he joined us in the parlor."

Naomi squared her shoulders. "All right then, let's see what he has stored in there."

Though they tried to look inconspicuous, Cheryl couldn't help hunching her shoulders as they approached the house. The driveway seemed even longer than it had before, and the path leading to the front door much shorter. Her breathing quickened as they neared the garage door, but despite the barking of a dog several houses down, nothing stirred inside the Robertsons'.

She motioned toward the car. "You go first," she whispered. "I'll stand watch."

Naomi ducked inside and disappeared like a shadow. Honestly, the woman could've been a cat burglar. Cheryl waited a moment longer and then joined her next to Mr. Robertson's dark blue BMW.

Naomi motioned toward a row of cupboards mounted to the wall. "I'll check those first."

Cheryl nodded and pointed toward a metal rolling cabinet. "I'll see what's inside there."

A cursory examination revealed basic tools, wrenches, even several tubes of grease and lubricants, but no baby supplies. She moved on toward a heavy looking workbench with a removable top. Inside, Mr. Robertson had packed all of his electric and gas powered lawn equipment—a leaf blower, hedge trimmer, and the sort. She sighed and peeked over the roof of the cars to check Naomi's progress.

"Anything?"

Naomi's bonnet was slightly askew, as though she'd actually poked her head inside the cabinet to look. She frowned and pushed it back into place. "Nothing. Just a lot of bug sprays and cans of oil."

She eased the cupboard door closed then propped her hands on her hips. "Where could he have possibly put the baby supplies? I know he couldn't have taken them far."

Cheryl bit off a sigh of frustration. Just over Naomi's shoulder was a door she'd not noticed before. She pointed. "Where do you suppose that goes?"

Her eyes widened. "The house?" Her voice lowered to a whisper.

"Can't be." Cheryl jerked her thumb toward the door to her right. "The house is that way."

Inching to Naomi's side, they stared at the knob for a moment, and then Cheryl gave it a cautious turn. It wasn't locked and creaked open just enough to peek through.

"A storage room," Cheryl whispered.

"Ja," Naomi said, "and look at that."

She pointed to the far wall. Floor to ceiling shelves packed the back of the room, but more importantly, they were filled with supplies. Lots of them. Cheryl had seen Costcos that didn't stock as much inventory.

She pushed farther into the room. Along with diapers Naomi had seen Mr. Robertson unloading, boxes of powdered formula, jars of baby food, and bottles of baby lotions and soaps bulged from the shelves.

She picked up one of the jars of baby food and held it toward Naomi. "All of this for a kid they don't even have yet? And how do they even know it will be a baby? What if it's a toddler, or older? Granted, I don't know much about foreign adoptions, but it's not like going to a department store and picking out a baby."

Naomi's face bore a look of shock. Cheryl lowered the baby food. "Hey, are you all right? What is it?"

Her finger shaking, she pointed at a trash can tucked into one corner of the storage room, where cans were piled at the top of the trash—baby formula cans. And they were empty. With her thumb and index finger she gingerly tugged aside the cans. Below were white plastic garbage bags stuffed with more trash, and though the bags weren't clear, the contents were easily discernible.

Her mouth fell open. She backed up a step. "Oh my goodness."

"Cheryl, look out," Naomi whispered sharply, earnestly, but it was too late.

Cheryl's hip connected with one of the shelves. She whirled and tried to keep some of the boxes from clattering to the floor. Next to her, Naomi dove in to help.

"Quick, help me put everything back," Cheryl hissed, shoving one of the boxes into Naomi's waiting hands.

She pushed it onto the shelf and wagged her hands impatiently. "Hurry, give me the next one."

Cheryl bent to grab an armload of diapers. Before she could straighten, her breath caught and she stumbled into the trash can, nearly toppling that as well.

"Cheryl, be careful," Naomi warned.

"Uh...Naomi?" Cheryl said, loudly.

"Shh," Naomi urged, her back still turned as she tried desperately to straighten the shelves.

"Naomi, I think you'd better take a look," Cheryl ordered, chills running the length of her spine and her eyes fixed to the spot on the floor where the diapers had been.

She was staring at a pair of expensive black leather shoes.

Chapter Twenty-Two

Cheryl's gaze traveled upward from the shoes, over a pair of pleated gray pants, to the scowling, disbelieving face of John Robertson.

"What on earth are you doing?" he sputtered. "How dare you enter my garage!" He grabbed the box from Cheryl's hands and returned it to the shelf then turned to stare at them, his gaze bouncing from Cheryl to Naomi. "Well? Are one of you going to explain what is going on?"

"We...uh..." Naomi's mouth went slack, and she stared at Cheryl for help.

Eyes narrowed, Cheryl pointed accusingly at him. "We know what you're doing with all of these supplies, Mr. Robertson."

His jaw firmed, and he crossed his arms. "Really. And what is that?"

Cheryl swallowed quickly. "These are all things for a baby."

"You're right. They are."

He didn't even blink. Cheryl hesitated then lifted her chin. "So...why do you have them?"

"You mean Miss *Overstreet* didn't tell you?"

Next to her, Naomi gasped.

"Miss Overstreet?" Cheryl repeated, her chin lowering.

"The travel agent from TransWorld Travel. You did speak with her, did you not?"

Mr. Robertson wore a smug look that set Cheryl's teeth on edge. She crossed her arms. "How did you know about that?"

"The same way that *you* found out that Victoria and I were looking into foreign adoptions. Faith told us. She's a nice girl, but rather chatty, don't you think?"

Naomi tugged on Cheryl's arm. "Maybe we should go."

"Yes, I think that would be a very good idea," Mr. Robertson replied firmly. He directed a stern glare at Naomi. "I must say, I'm quite surprised. I thought you people were above trespassing."

"Now hold on," Cheryl interrupted, stepping in front of her friend.

"No, he is right." She laid her hand on Cheryl's shoulder. "We are here uninvited."

"That may be, but we need answers." Cheryl pointed a finger at Mr. Robertson. "Where are you keeping Baby John? Is there someone helping you hide him? How…"

"Cheryl, please. We should not make this any worse than it is."

"Good thinking," Mr. Robertson sneered, turning his glare on Cheryl. "At least your friend realizes how serious this is. I could call the police you know and have you arrested."

"Cheryl!" Naomi tugged on her arm desperately.

Playing a hunch, Cheryl turned and fixed her with a reassuring glance. "Don't worry, Naomi. He's not going to call the police."

John Robertson stepped forward, his mouth agape. "Seriously? You actually think I'm going to let you get away with trespassing? Not to mention harassment!"

Cheryl also took a step forward and stared at him eye to eye.

"Yes, Mr. Robertson, I do," she said, infusing the words with more confidence than she actually felt.

"And why is that?" he demanded, his gaze daring her to continue.

She pointed at the trash can. "Because I really don't think you want the police to discover what you have hidden in there."

His gaze swung to the trash can and back. In his eyes, she saw a bit of the bravado fade. His mouth worked a second, and then he looked at Naomi. "Are you leaving or not?"

Her confidence growing, Cheryl slipped her arm through Naomi's and jutted out her chin. "She's staying, and so am I. And you"—she jabbed her finger at his chest—"you are going to take us back inside that house and explain exactly what is going on or I'm going to be the one calling the police."

"Cheryl!" Naomi pulled back slightly, her mouth a shocked little O. "What are you saying?"

"I'm saying there are more than just empty formula cans in the trash, aren't there, Mr. Robertson?"

She took a step toward the trash can, hoping desperately that she'd been right about what she'd seen. If not, chances were good that she and Naomi would be spending the night in a New Philadelphia jail cell—something they'd be hard pressed to explain to their families...or the media. She held her breath and motioned toward the can.

"Well? Should we look, or are you going to bring us inside?"

"I am not going to bring you inside!" His face turned a mottled red, and he leaned toward her threateningly. "And believe me, anything you think might be in that can will be long gone before the police get here to check."

Cheryl's hand shook as she slid her phone from her pocket and held it up. "Then I guess it's a good thing I took pictures."

Her heart pounded while she waited for his reply. "Well?"

He stared at her, his face colder than marble and his eyes like slivers of gray steel. Just when she feared she'd been wrong, his shoulders slumped and he turned slowly, his feet dragging as he led the way back through the garage toward the house.

Naomi grabbed Cheryl, her fingers biting like teeth into her arm. "You don't have any pictures."

"He doesn't know that," Cheryl whispered back.

"What on earth did you see?"

"I'm really not sure...just something that looked like..." She shook her head. "Let's go."

She made for the exit, Naomi close behind at her elbow. Inside, the door from the garage opened into a rather large, gourmet kitchen which boasted the latest stainless steel appliances. Granite countertops graced sleek black cabinets, and from the ceiling an ornate chandelier gleamed.

Mr. Robertson had indeed provided well for his family.

He stopped at the threshold and held up his hand. "Wait here. I'll get my wife. We'll only be a moment." He spun on his heel and disappeared.

Naomi blew out a shuddering breath. "Well? Do we wait?"

"He's not going anywhere," Cheryl replied, jerking her thumb over her shoulder. "The garage is that way, and if my hunch is correct, they'll be too bogged down to flee on foot."

"Flee? Why would they do that? And what would bog them down?" Naomi's lips thinned. "You saw something else in that trash can. What was it?"

"Diapers," Cheryl replied. "Used ones. The Robertsons aren't planning for a baby. They already have one."

Naomi's brow furrowed in confusion. "But how can that be—?"

She got no further. At that moment, Mr. Robertson returned. On his heels was Mrs. Robertson and in her arms...

Naomi shoved past Cheryl, her mouth slack. "John?"

Her strained whisper reflected the same shock Cheryl felt. She took a step forward, staring into an angelic face, whose likeness had been plastered on newspapers and television stations across the state.

Ripping her gaze from John's face, Cheryl stared at Victoria Robertson. "You had him this whole time?"

Desperation and pleading filled her eyes. "You have to let us explain."

Cheryl drew back as though she'd seen a snake. "What is there to explain? Do you even know what you've done? Your daughter has been sick with worry..."

She broke off and fumbled in her purse for her phone.

Mr. Robertson jerked toward her. "What are you doing?"

Cheryl backed away, her hand up to stop Mr. Robertson from advancing farther. "I'm calling the police!"

"You can't do that!"

"Are you kidding me? Of course I can! You *kidnapped* a child from his home! What kind of person does that?"

Frightened by the loud voices, Baby John began to wail. Victoria too cried out and buried her face in the baby's small chest.

"Cheryl." Naomi grabbed her hand, stopping her from dialing 911. "Cheryl, wait."

"Wait for what? These t...two...they..." Cheryl stammered to a stop. Her breath came in short, sharp gasps, and her heart was slamming hard against her ribs, but Naomi appeared calm.

"Wait," she said again, quieter, and directed a pointed look at the Robertsons.

Cheryl's gaze drifted to Victoria, still sobbing, and then to John, who looked as though the last bit of strength he possessed had been sapped from his bones. Though he patted his wife's back in a vain attempt to offer comfort, his shoulders shook and silent tears streamed down his cheeks.

"Maybe we should hear them out first," Naomi said.

At her words, Mr. Robertson's head lifted and he stared at them. In his watery eyes, Cheryl glimpsed a spark of hope. Could it be? Was he the monster she thought him, or something else?

She motioned cautiously toward a tall black table at the rear of the kitchen. "Maybe we should sit down."

Mr. Robertson blew out a shuddering sigh. Grasping his wife's elbow, he led her to the table and they all sat, the Robertsons occupying the seats opposite Cheryl and Naomi.

"Thank you," he said, his voice strained.

Now that the shouting had ceased, Baby John's cries quieted. Mrs. Robertson snuggled him close. She still had not spoken, but her eyes pleaded for something Cheryl was not quite sure she could give.

"What happened?" she demanded, clasping her fingers tightly in her lap to still their trembling. "Start from the beginning."

Mr. Robertson ran his fingers through his graying hair. "The beginning?" he repeated. "If only I knew where that was. I could say this all started the night Rachel told us she was leaving, but if I'm honest, it was long before that."

His gaze shifted to his wife and the small child cradled in her arms. "I was never here for them when Rachel was growing up. If I could go back and change that, God knows, I would."

Regret and grief made his voice thick. He swallowed, his Adam's apple bobbing in his corded throat. He ran his fingers through his hair once more. There would be a lot to tell, that much was certain, but for now, Cheryl only wanted…needed…to know one thing.

"The kidnapping," she said, in a low, measured tone. "Tell us about that."

"It wasn't planned," Mrs. Robertson blurted, startling them all including Baby John. He jumped and his tiny fists flailed in the air, but he immediately soothed and settled back to sleep when

Mrs. Robertson gently ran her fingers over his cheek. Bending low, she kissed the top of his head then took a deep breath and whispered, "I only stopped by to see Rachel."

"Victoria, no." Mr. Robertson grabbed his wife's hand and held on tight then turned to glare at Cheryl. "It was me. Not her. That's all you need to know."

"No, John."

He looked at her, and she shook her head sadly. "We have to tell them the truth. All of it." Her gaze swung back to Cheryl and Naomi, and her eyes filled with tears. "I swear, I never intended to take him, but then you were there, and Rachel was busy, and I saw my opportunity."

A sob tore from her throat, and she turned her face toward her husband, who gathered both her and the baby into his arms.

"So you took him?" Naomi said quietly.

There was a moment of prolonged sniffling and then Mrs. Robertson nodded. "That's right."

"And the dog biscuit?" Cheryl asked. If it was true that the kidnapping wasn't premeditated, what had she been doing with the treat for Rufus?

"They're for our dog," John Robertson said. "She always carries one in her purse." He looked at his wife. "The moment she returned home, I knew what she'd done and why." Resolve darkened his eyes, made them strong once more. "I had to protect my wife. I had to, no matter what it cost anyone else, or what it cost our daughter."

The pain on his face stabbed Cheryl's heart like a knife. "But you had to know how devastating this would be to her, and everyone in Sugarcreek. What did you think would happen, that we would just stop looking?"

Mr. Robertson shook his head and pulled an envelope from a pocket in his shirt. Inside were two tickets to Europe. He laid them carefully on the table. "Once things settled down, Victoria and I planned to leave, disappear for a couple of years. We spread the rumors regarding foreign adoption carefully so that when we returned with a toddler, no one would ever suspect."

"And Joseph?" Naomi asked. Of them all, hers was the only voice that still sounded calm. "Why did you leave him?"

Anguish tore at Victoria Robertson's features. She pressed her nose to the top of Baby John's head and breathed deep. Finally, she said, "Despite what you may think of me, I couldn't do that to Rachel. Losing them both would have been..."

She trailed off, and Mr. Robertson clasped her hand. He turned to Naomi. "Besides, Victoria knew we couldn't take the chance. Coming back with two boys would have been impossible."

Surprised by his honesty, Cheryl could only stare. "But coming back with one of the boys was?"

Mr. Robertson gave a weak shrug. "We were desperate, Miss Cooper. Desperate and crazy with grief. For all intents and purposes, our daughter was gone, lost to us forever. Baby John was a way of getting her back."

"A piece of her anyway," Mrs. Robertson whispered, gazing at her grandson with so much love and longing it was painful to watch. Her head lifted. "But then you came. And you." Her gaze shifted to Naomi. "And you told us how much Rachel was suffering. I almost couldn't stand it. We thought about coming forward then...giving Baby John back...but I couldn't bear the thought of...losing him too..."

She broke off, silent sobs robbing her of words. Her hand fluttered to her eyes and she tried to rub away the tears, only to have them replaced by new ones. "It's no excuse. I know it's not. We were wrong."

"We admit that. We'll face the consequences," Mr. Robertson added when his wife couldn't continue. "But if there's any way...if you could possibly see a way to let us be the ones to take the baby back to his family..."

He trailed off, his face twisted and pleading.

Cheryl sucked in a breath. So that was what they wanted. Turmoil turned her insides to mush. The right thing—the correct and legal thing—would be to call the police and let them handle things. But what would Rachel and Samuel want?

She glanced at Naomi. "I don't...I just don't know," she whispered quietly.

Naomi sucked in a breath, her cheeks puffing as she blew it out. Finally, her gaze came to rest on the baby. "I do not know what the law has to say. But my heart says if this family is ever to have any hope of forgiving one another, it must be as John Robertson says."

Forgiveness? Was she serious? Cheryl's eyes rounded, and her mouth fell open. Forgiving the Robertsons would be like...like...

Like forgiving Lance.

Heat washed up from Cheryl's stomach and burned her cheeks. No, forgiving Lance was easy compared to what this family faced.

She looked at Victoria. She felt sorry for her, but this time it was because of the battle that lay ahead, not what lay behind.

"It won't be easy," she said quietly. "They may refuse to see you or speak with you once the baby is returned."

Victoria licked her lips and nodded.

Cheryl's gaze shifted to Mr. Robertson. "And the police will have to be involved eventually, no matter how Rachel and Samuel react when they find out the truth."

He reached out to clasp his wife's hand and then looked back at Cheryl, his gaze steady and calm despite the tremor that shook his chin. "We'll turn ourselves in the moment we get to Sugarcreek."

"That's good. I'm sure it will help." Cheryl turned to Naomi. "Are you ready?"

She nodded and held her hand out to Mrs. Robertson. "Come. I will help you pack some things for the baby."

Mrs. Robertson accepted her help gratefully, and the two of them exited the kitchen, leaving Cheryl to sit alone with Mr. Robertson.

He blew out a sigh then rubbed both hands against the table-top. "I know you probably won't believe this, but in a way, I'm glad it's over. The lies were tearing us both apart."

"Actually, I do believe you," Cheryl replied quietly, her thoughts winging to Lance.

Their gazes met and held, and then Mr. Robertson's mouth turned in a sad sort of smile. "I don't suppose there is any way I could convince you to let me take the fall, instead of my wife?"

"You would do that?"

He looked away, but not before Cheryl saw his eyes fill with tears. "My wife has never been a strong woman. Not like you or Mrs. Miller. I'm afraid for her, Miss Cooper. And I have never, ever felt so helpless in my entire life."

Strong? Her? Naomi, yes, but Cheryl had never thought of herself in that way. Perhaps it was because she was only just beginning to find herself.

Had found herself, she corrected as she rose to stand with John Robertson. She'd found herself in Sugarcreek, Ohio.

She liked what she saw.

CHAPTER TWENTY-THREE

The drive back to Sugarcreek was accomplished with very few words. Except for the occasional gurgle from Baby John, no one spoke. Naomi sat in the seat next to her, her lips moving in silent prayer. In the rearview, Victoria Robertson kept her gaze lowered. Every now and then she wiped away a tear. John Robertson stared out the window, the muscles in his jaw clenched and tense.

Only when the Swartzentruber farm came into view did she hear a small gasp from the backseat and knew that Victoria Robertson was preparing herself for the scene that lay ahead.

Naomi put her hand on Cheryl's arm. She slowed the car in response. Naomi twisted to look at the Robertsons.

"I think it would be best if you let me go inside first and… prepare Rachel and Samuel, ja? I will not explain. I will let the two of you do that. I will simply let them know that Baby John is back, and he is safe. Otherwise, I fear the shock might be too much."

In the rearview, Cheryl saw Mr. Robertson nod. "I agree. That's a good idea, right Victoria?"

She too nodded, but her gaze remained fixed to the child tucked into the carseat between them. Baby John's fist flailed in the air. She caught his fingers and pressed them with a kiss.

"I'll wait too," Cheryl said as she pulled into the drive.

Not that she thought the Robertsons would try to flee. Having spoken with Mr. Robertson, she felt confident that he was truly glad to see this coming to an end. Instead, she wanted to sit with them, offer silent support and comfort. Strange, considering she'd been determined to turn them over to the police just a few short hours ago.

Buggies lined both sides of the driveway. Outside the barn, several men stood talking. They looked up when they heard her car approaching and watched as Naomi climbed out alone.

She ducked to look inside the car at Cheryl. "Pray," she ordered softly and then looked at the Robertsons. "You too. Both of you. This will be difficult."

Both of the Robertsons nodded and clasped each other's hand tightly over the car seat. Cheryl waited, tense and breathless, as Naomi went inside. Her jaw ached from clenching it, and nausea rolled inside her stomach. She could only imagine how John and Victoria felt.

Finally, the front door swung open. Cheryl straightened. In the backseat, she felt the Robertsons do the same. She expected Samuel, or even Rachel, but it was Levi who approached, the set of his shoulders determined.

He circled to Cheryl's door. She rolled down the window. His gaze was somber as he looked at her and then over her shoulder at the Robertsons.

"Rachel would like to see you. Come, I will help you with the baby's things."

Victoria could not have looked more lost as she peered at her husband for help.

"It'll be all right," he soothed, unhooking the safety restraints from the baby and lifting him out.

Levi opened the door, and Mr. Robertson climbed out then held out his hand to assist his wife. They waited while Levi collected the baby's things, and then they walked slowly up the steps and entered the house, the door closing gently behind them.

In the car, Cheryl blew out a shaky sigh. One thing was certain, she'd think twice before casting judgment...or withholding forgiveness.

"I'm sorry, Lord," she whispered, slanting her gaze toward the graying sky. "I see now, even the darkest, loneliest heart deserves mercy and grace. I wish I'd realized it sooner, but I promise, from this point forward, I will try to live my life the way You would have me to live it—by granting forgiveness even when it isn't asked for, or earned."

She spent a few quiet moments thinking of the great challenge that lay ahead for Rachel and her parents, and then the front door swung open again and Levi walked out. Propping his arms in the open car window, he leaned in.

Cheryl started to squeeze his arm then stopped herself and wiped the tears from her eyes instead. "How'd it go?"

"Not good, but at least they are still talking." Levi shook his head. "Who would have thought it would be them?"

Cheryl shuddered. "Not me. I hate what all this bigotry and strife drove them to. And Rachel...how will she and Samuel ever find a way to overcome what has been done to them?"

Levi's gaze fell, and with it, a heavy sigh. "What about you? Are you all right?"

"Yes, I'm..." She looked up at him, soaking in the sight of his tanned face. Golden flecks shimmered in his deep blue eyes, adding depth...warmth. Her lips quivered and then she shook her head mutely. She wasn't all right. She was sad. Tired.

Reaching for the handle, Levi helped her out.

"Can you tell me what happened in there?"

Levi glanced toward the house. "Samuel was angry of course. Rachel wept. It was hard. I do not know what will happen now, how they will work through this, or if they even can."

Cheryl thought back over the past few days, what she'd learned about herself and what she'd discovered about forgiveness. She nodded firmly. "They can, if both parties are willing. It won't be easy, and healing may have to wait until after the courts decide what to do with the Robertsons, but I believe they will find a way with God's help."

Levi tipped his head, and his lips turned up in a grin. "You sounded like my stepmother just then."

"Thank you," Cheryl replied, answering his grin with one of her own. "I'll take that as a compliment."

He led her toward a path that ran alongside the house. "So it paid off, ja? All of the sleuthing? You put the clues together until you found the kidnapper and brought Baby John home."

"All except for the one about Theresa Cox," Cheryl said and told Levi about her ties to the Amish. "Why do you suppose she didn't tell us about her cousin when she had the chance?"

He shrugged, his stride lengthening as they left the path to veer toward an apple orchard. Pulling aside a branch, he let her through and then fell in step beside her while they walked down the rows. "Perhaps she was afraid it would make her look suspicious? It would explain why she thought to use the toys. She would have been familiar with Amish goods."

"I suppose so." Cheryl reached up to pluck a dry leaf from one of the branches. The apples had been harvested, and all but a few collected from the ground to be made into cider. It was a clear indication that times had changed, seasons given way. Remarkably, it echoed exactly how she felt inside.

She rubbed the leaf until it crumbled to dust between her fingers. "And Jeremiah Zook? Did you learn anything about him?"

Levi nodded. "He went to Middlefield, as he said to his cousin, to talk things over with his family and experience a time of healing. After that he went to fetch his wife and bring her home. Jeremiah thought that adopting a child would help to ease the pain in Rebecca's heart. They have begun the process."

That was it, the last of her suspicions laid to rest. She should feel glad, and yet she couldn't help worrying about Rachel and her parents. Cheryl jerked her thumb toward the house. "What do you suppose is going on back there?"

Levi shrugged then bent to pick up a stone. "Hard to say. I hope they are managing to talk things through. Did the Robertsons tell you why they took the baby?"

He threw the stone, and it scuttled over the grass before bouncing off a tree trunk. Cheryl had felt like that stone for so long— scuttling along, bouncing here and there, following no particular path. No more.

She explained all that had transpired in New Philadelphia, pausing when she got to the part about investigating the garage.

"I'm not even sure what made us go inside," she said, heat flushing her cheeks despite the cool temperatures. "It was like we both had a hunch and nothing was going to stop us."

Levi threw his head back and laughed—a rich sound that made her nerve ends tingle. "Now that I can believe. There are no people more stubborn or determined than the two of you."

His eyes twinkled when he spoke so that she couldn't have been irritated with him if she'd tried. She shrugged and then joined him in laughter. "I guess you're right about that."

"I can't help but feel a little sorry for them," she said when at last their chuckling quieted. She plucked another leaf and then swung her arms and let it flutter to the ground. "Even though I don't agree with what they did, I can certainly understand how it happened."

"As can I," Levi said softly. "Now will come the hard part. The Swartzentrubers consented to wait to contact the police until after they'd heard what Rachel's parents had to say."

"But will it be worth it?" Cheryl wondered out loud. "I mean, if they can somehow reconcile, will it have been worth the heartache it took to get there?"

"I think so."

Cheryl wasn't so certain, but she wanted to be.

"I think the best things in life are always the hardest to gain. That doesn't mean they aren't worth trying for."

"I agree," Cheryl said, a trifle breathlessly.

His eyes darkened. In the setting sun, they looked like pieces of the night sky. He moved a bit closer. "Do you, Cheryl? Even if it means learning to accept another person's beliefs, their way of thinking, their...faith?"

He hesitated on the last word, and the uncertainty she heard in his voice reflected in his eyes.

"This isn't just about the Swartzentrubers and Robertsons, is it?"

He looked at her silently and then shook his head.

Sorrow flooded Cheryl's heart. "You don't believe that some relationships can work."

His jaw clenched, and then he gave a curt nod. "I admit, there was a time when I did not believe that two people with such opposing views could overcome their differences. But now... seeing those two families back there and what they are fighting to achieve, I wonder."

Cheryl felt her heart catch at his words. "I wondered the same thing."

His brow furrowed. "You knew of my misgivings?"

"Only because I had them too."

His frown cleared, replaced by the beginning of a tender smile. "And now?"

She lifted her chin. "Now I am willing to believe that anything is possible, so long as hearts are open and God is in it."

His grin widened, and the hope that Cheryl felt sparkled in Levi's eyes. "Well said, Cheryl Cooper," he whispered. "Well said."

CHAPTER TWENTY-FOUR

Snow flurries greeted Cheryl the next morning. Temperatures had fallen during the night, and all over Sugarcreek a light dusting of powdery white coated everything from streetlamps and flower boxes to rooftops and awnings.

Smiling, she stepped off of her porch, her feet crunching in the snow as she turned for the Swiss Miss. At the corner, she snuggled deeper into her coat and tugged the collar higher around her ears. She liked snow and didn't mind the cold, but today the fluffy frosting blanketing the earth was even more special because the Swartzentrubers would get to witness it together. All of them.

She tipped her head back and blew out a happy sigh. It was amazing how God always managed to straighten the most twisted of circumstances. Last week she would never have believed that a family could recover from the things Rachel and her parents had suffered. Today it not only seemed possible, but probable.

Chief Twitchell had taken statements from all of the parties involved and given special consideration to Rachel's and Samuel's tear-filled requests that no charges be filed. Though their fate remained uncertain, the chief seemed confident the Robertsons would be spared prison, a thought that filled Cheryl with gladness.

As for her own parents, she'd spoken long into the wee hours with both her mother and her father and been relieved to discover that their love and support of her had only increased with her candid confession of her unforgiving spirit toward Lance. For the first time in many months, she felt free—lighter somehow, like the flakes fluttering all around her—and she realized that she'd borne a weight that had hindered her in a way she hadn't recognized until now.

Veering right, Cheryl made a beeline across the street toward Yoder's Corner. It had been a while since she'd sampled one of their famous cinnamon rolls, and if ever she'd earned the right to splurge, it was today.

Humming a tune, she pushed open the door and was welcomed by a blast of sweet, cinnamon-scented air. Several patrons looked up when she entered. A few bobbed their heads in greeting, and others offered shy hellos. Cheryl returned them all then shrugged out of her coat and claimed a table near the kitchen. She had just plucked a menu from the centerpiece when the front door swung open and Naomi bustled in on a wintry November breeze.

Cheryl put down the menu and waved. "Naomi, over here."

Naomi nodded and wound her way toward her, stopping now and then to say hello to people she knew. Finally, she reached the table and scooted out a chair to sit. Unwrapping a wide, wool scarf from around her neck, she draped it over the arm of her chair and blew on her reddened fingers.

"I believe it is safe to say that winter has officially arrived." She shuddered and rubbed her hands over her arms. "Kaffee sounds goot on such a cold morning, ja?"

"It sure does," Cheryl said, pushing the menu toward her. "I'm surprised to see you today."

Naomi shrugged and lifted an eyebrow. "Perhaps we both had the same idea?"

"Cinnamon rolls?"

Naomi laughed, and Cheryl soon joined in.

"So?" Cheryl asked. "How is Rachel this morning? Have you heard?"

Naomi unbuttoned her cape and draped it over an empty chair with her scarf. "Levi is supposed to let me know. He and Caleb were going by there today to help Samuel catch up on the chores he missed while he was out looking for John."

"Good plan." Cheryl nodded. "Maybe if I have time this afternoon, I'll drive over just to check on how everyone's doing." She quirked an eyebrow. "I'll be sure to take someone with me this time."

They both laughed, and then Naomi glanced toward the kitchen. "Have you seen August or Greta?"

Cheryl shook her head and leaned back to peer around the counter. "Not yet. I sure could use some coffee though."

Around her, several other patrons grumbled the same thing. An older man held up an empty cup.

"Anybody working today?"

Hmm... it wasn't like the Yoders to neglect their customers, but Cheryl refused to let anything dampen her mood. She propped her elbows on the table and smiled.

"Actually, I'm really glad we both had the same idea this morning. I haven't had a chance to talk with you about everything that happened with the Swartzentrubers."

Naomi gave a satisfied nod. "It truly was a miracle, ja?"

"Indeed it was," Cheryl said.

At last the door to the kitchen creaked open and a flustered August Yoder scurried out. In his hand was a pot of coffee, which he quickly dispensed to waiting customers before turning to Cheryl and Naomi.

"I'm sorry for your wait, ladies." He held up the pot. "Coffee?"

"Yes, please," Cheryl and Naomi chimed together, and then while he filled their cups, Naomi added, "And one of your largest, gooiest cinnamon rolls."

"Make that two," Cheryl said. "No sharing today. I fully intend to work off all of these extra calories with a long walk this afternoon."

August set down the pot with a heavy sigh. "Unfortunately, I'm afraid I can't do that."

"What?" Cheryl exclaimed, feigning exaggerated outrage. "No cinnamon rolls? Don't tell me you've sold out already. It's only seven thirty."

August merely grunted. "I wish that were the case. No, we didn't sell out of rolls. Somebody took them. A whole platter that Greta had cooling on the back table. It's a sad day we're living in when a man can't even cool his rolls."

He ambled away, muttering to himself as he went and shaking his shaggy head sorrowfully.

Cheryl swung her gaze to meet Naomi's. "A platter of stolen rolls? What in the world do you make of that?"

Smiling, Naomi reached for a packet of sugar and stirred it lazily into her cup. "If you ask me, it sounds like a typical day in Sugarcreek."

Typical? Cheryl laughed. If there was one thing she'd learned since coming to Sugarcreek, it was that there was no such thing as a typical day, but that didn't bother her the way it might have done once.

She picked up her coffee cup and held it toward Naomi. "To missing rolls?"

Naomi grinned and reached for her own cup. "To missing rolls."

And to nontypical days, Cheryl added silently, taking a sip of her coffee and savoring the sweet, unspoiled taste of a regular cup of joe.

It was a thought that filled her with unexpected joy.

AUTHOR LETTER

Dear Reader,

What a blessing it has been to dwell with these characters in Sugarcreek! Like so many people who enjoy Amish fiction, I have been hungry for stories of hope and healing and am honored to have partnered with such talented authors and editorial staff on this project.

Cozy mysteries are unique in Christian fiction, something I learned several years ago when I landed my first series contract! Amish mysteries are even more special. Along with the challenge of figuring out "whodunit," readers are allowed a glimpse into the day-to-day lives of the devout, humble people who inhabit this quaint town. I tried earnestly to illustrate the hard-working spirit and love, which is so typical among the Amish, but also among the people of the Midwest—many of whom I am proud to call family. I hope you will enjoy your time spent with these characters and that your life will be richer for having done so.

Peace and blessings to you,
Elizabeth Ludwig

ABOUT THE AUTHOR

Elizabeth Ludwig is the best-selling author of *Christmas Comes to Bethlehem, Maine,* and the highly successful Edge of Freedom series. Her popular literary blog the Borrowed Book enjoys a wide readership. Elizabeth is an accomplished speaker and teacher, often attending conferences and seminars where she lectures on editing for fiction writers, crafting effective novel proposals, and conducting successful editor/agent interviews. Along with her husband and children, she makes her home in the great state of Texas. To learn more, visit ElizabethLudwig.com.

Fun Fact about
the Amish or Sugarcreek, Ohio

I learned a lot about the Amish right along with Cheryl Cooper, the main character in the Sugarcreek Amish Mysteries series. One of the things that interested me most was the practice of rumspringa or the "running around" time of Amish youth. I quickly learned that there are many commonly held misconceptions about rumspringa, including the idea that it is a "time-out" from being Amish. In actuality, rumspringa is intended to be a period during which boys and girls are given greater personal freedom so that they may make the decision to either become Amish or leave the community. While it is true that some Amish youth may choose to engage in what would otherwise be considered sinful behavior, their parents do not encourage such.

Just as with all young adults, the late teen years are a confusing time in an Amish person's life. Rumspringa is intended to help these young people "find themselves" and thereby enable them to make a fully informed decision to accept the lifelong requirements of the Amish church.

Something Delicious from Our Sugarcreek Friends

Homemade Pumpkin Butter

Pumpkin Puree
1 Pumpkin (yield is usually about two or three cups of puree per six-inch diameter pumpkin)

Pumpkin Butter
7 quarts pumpkin puree
2 tablespoons ground cinnamon
1 teaspoon ground cloves
½ teaspoon allspice
4 cups sugar

Wash the exterior of the pumpkin in cool or warm water, no soap. Cut the pumpkin in half. Scoop out the seeds and scrape the insides. Be sure to get all of the stringy stuff that coats the inside surface. A heavy ice-cream scoop works great.

Remove the stem, and put the pumpkin halves into a microwaveable bowl. Put a couple of inches of water in the bowl, cover it, and put in the microwave. Cook for fifteen minutes on high. Check to see if the pumpkin is soft and then repeat in smaller increments of time until it is soft enough to separate the pumpkin meat from the exterior "shell," up to twenty or thirty minutes in total.

Place ingredients in a Crock-Pot on low or medium heat. Stir well. Cover loosely. (You don't want to seal it tightly because you want the steam to escape so it can reduce in volume and thicken.) Cook for six to eight hours. For creamier texture, blend with a hand-held drink mixer and pour into resealable jars. Store in refrigerator.

For thinner pumpkin butter, add a little bit of apple juice and blend. For thicker pumpkin butter, extend cooking time with the lid off, so the steam can escape.

Enjoy!

Read on for a sneak peek of another exciting book
in the Sugarcreek Amish Mysteries series!

The Buggy before the Horse
by Tricia Goyer

Cheryl Cooper drove her dark blue Ford Focus down the quiet country road, passing a horse and buggy. The holidays were approaching, and she looked forward to experiencing them in this quaint town of Sugarcreek. Her heart ached a bit as she realized this was the first time in five years she wouldn't be spending it with Lance. For the longest time, she'd been angry that he'd walked away from their engagement, but as that anger had subsided the familiarity of their ordinary routines created a hole inside that she hadn't expected.

Still, with managing the Swiss Miss and her new friends, she could look forward to a season filled with quietness and friendship. It was a nice change from her harried and busy life in Columbus. Maybe that's something she'd been wanting for a while but just didn't know it until she got to Sugarcreek: peace.

She ran her fingers through her spiky red hair. *Oh, bother.*

November had brought misty, cold rain to Sugarcreek, providing just enough moisture to cause her hair to frizz. She almost wished she had an Amish prayer *kapp* to hide her out-of-control hair. That would be useful on days like this. Perhaps by the time Thanksgiving rolled around in a few weeks they'd have snow.

She drove past the Millers' petting zoo and maze and along the beautiful, teal-colored creek toward the Millers' farm. She crossed a charming covered bridge that stretched over the babbling water.

A kissing bridge. That's what the locals called it. When slow-moving buggies traveled through it, courting couples sitting inside slipped from view, giving them a perfect opportunity to snatch a kiss.

Heat rose to Cheryl's cheeks as she considered whom she'd share a kiss with. *Levi Miller.* She'd told herself time and again that being enamored with an Amish bachelor wasn't acceptable. She patted her cheek, willing those thoughts to leave or she'd make a fool of herself at the Millers' farm.

When she reached the other side of the bridge, there sat the familiar huge, white farmhouse with a wrap-around porch. There were no buggies in the yard today, and it appeared the horses remained in the barn. She glanced around and didn't see Levi, but that didn't mean he wasn't nearby. Cheryl patted her hair again.

"Maybe I should ask Naomi to borrow a kapp," she mumbled with a sigh as she parked on the Millers' dirt and gravel driveway. Before exiting her car, Cheryl grabbed the handles of the paper sack on the passenger seat, feeling its weight. Since hearing that Naomi was under the weather, she'd promised her friend two things. First, that she'd come pick up the newest batch of homemade candles and preserves Naomi made for the store. Second, that she'd bring some chicken noodle soup. It was Cheryl's mother's recipe and something she always enjoyed when she was sick. The bag held a large Tupperware container of the soup, still warm.

The Millers' dog must have heard the car because a friendly bark greeted her. She stepped out of the car, shut the door, and then glanced to the field past the barn. The pup's head bobbed as he ran through the stubble of hayfields.

Cheryl's black Mary Janes crunched on the gravel, and the misty rain brushed her cheeks. She stopped on the path to give the pup time to catch up and soak in the sight of…peacefulness. She needed this. Needed to remember that even though she'd left behind a lot in Columbus, God had brought her to the perfect place where her soul—her heart—could heal.

The wide, gray sky stretched over the fields. This spot would provide a perfect star-gazing view on a cold winter's night. In addition to passing down the delicious soup recipe, her mother had taught her to spot Orion, Jupiter, and other winter stars in the eastern sky. She pictured herself sitting on the front porch next to Levi–Naomi's oldest stepson, and watching for shooting stars. He always brought a smile to her face.

Cheryl sucked in a deep breath, enjoying the moment, and then she decided to take a quick picture with her phone. She aimed the camera at the silos that stuck up in the horizon between the cornfields and stretches of woods beyond the farm.

Sometimes she wanted to pinch herself for the blessing of living in Sugarcreek. It was so different from Columbus. Her life was so different. It was like being inside a stuffy building all day and then stepping outside to clean, fresh air. She hadn't realized how stuffy her life had been for years until now. Until the fresh air had soaked into every part of her.

The dog finally reached her, bouncing with excitement. He didn't look quite a year old and had lots of energy. Forgetting his manners, his front paws tapped her tan slacks, leaving a smudge of dirt.

"Rover, down!" A man's voice split the air, and Cheryl jumped. Levi strode from the barn. A large bag of mulch was slung over his shoulder, yet he walked with ease as if he carried a feather pillow. His blond hair stuck out from under his brimmed hat.

Levi scowled at the dog. A muscle tightened in his jaw. "Sorry to startle you. My little brother is supposed to be training this guy, and the pup has no manners."

She brushed the dirt from her slacks. "No problem. My work apron will cover it. He's just a puppy after all."

Levi approached and paused then he sniffed the air and smiled. "Something smells *goot*. Got something tasty in the bag?" He looked down with those dark blue eyes, the color of the night sky, and her stomach did a small flip.

"Soup for your *maam*." She smiled back. "Esther said she has a nasty cold. I do hope your mom is staying off her feet."

Levi shook his head. "You know my stepmother. I'd need to tie her down to get her to stay off her feet." He looked toward the house. "But Maam did say you were coming. I'm thankful she didn't go into town today. I'll put this mulch by the flower beds and then get your things. Maam asked me to pull out a few dozen jars of preserves and set some cheese aside for you in the root cellar. I'll also grab the candles and other items for your store."

It wasn't her store—she was just running it for Mitzi while her aunt was in Papua New Guinea—but she didn't want to argue. Cheryl also thought about reminding Levi that the distance wasn't that far, and even quicker when one was driving in a car, but she changed her mind. Instead, she ran her fingers through her spiked hair and smiled up at him. "That's kind, Levi, thank you."

Levi moved toward the flower beds with Rover following, and Cheryl continued to the front door. Her heartbeat had quickened more than normal, and she told herself to take a deep breath. She reminded herself that he was Amish, and she was English and she needed to think long and hard before allowing their relationship to move beyond friendship.

Cheryl knocked twice and then opened the door and walked in. The Amish way was not to knock at all, but she still couldn't get used to that.

The large living room was warm and cozy. Heat radiated from the wood-burning stove. The oak floors gleamed, leading the way to the kitchen.

A loud sniffle came from the kitchen. Cheryl walked tentatively toward the open space. Naomi sat at the long dining room table with her Bible open before her. She wore a dark blue dress covered with an apron, her graying hair perfectly tucked in her prayer kapp.

"Why are you just standing there?" Naomi scooted back her chair and rose. "Cheryl, come in. Come in!"

Cheryl hustled in, waving her free hand in Naomi's direction. "Don't you dare get up. I brought you some soup like I promised." She placed the paper bag on the table near Naomi.

The kitchen smelled of wood, kerosene oil, and baking bread. Sure enough three loaves of wheat bread cooled on the counter. Leave it to Naomi to have time to bake this morning, even when she wasn't feeling well.

Naomi settled back down into the chair. "*Wunderbar.* A bowl of soup is just what I need. It's so good to see you. A bit of sunshine. Do you have time to stay for a cup of tea? Water's hot." She pointed to the teakettle on the stove.

"I'd love a cup. Since the store doesn't open for an hour, I have time." Cheryl removed her jacket and placed it over the back of the dining room chair at the head of the table. "I just hope Ben and Rueben aren't too disappointed that the front door won't be unlocked early today."

Cheryl smiled thinking of the two brothers who loved to show up in the morning and play checkers at the table set up in her store. Their relationship had been strained over the years since Ben left the Amish, but Cheryl was glad to see that time was beginning to heal old wounds.

"Oh, I'm sure the brothers will survive." Naomi closed her Bible, but not before Cheryl saw the title *Prayer List* on a sheet of paper tucked inside and the first few names. Sarah, Naomi's stepdaughter, was at the top of the list. Cheryl knew how hard it was for Amish parents to see their children leading an English lifestyle. Would reconciliation also come to the Miller family, just as it had started with Ben and Rueben?

The second name on the list was Mitzi. Thankfully, many people were praying for Cheryl's aunt. Some thought she was far too old to run off on a missionary adventure in Papua New Guinea, of all places. Cheryl prayed too. And worried. She hadn't heard from her aunt in a few weeks. Did no news really mean good news?

Cheryl also wondered if her name had made that list. Did Naomi pray for her? Warmth filled her chest at the idea.

She moved to the open cupboard and removed a plain, brown mug. A small basket of tea bags sat on the counter. She took a tea bag, placed it in the mug, and then used a potholder to grab the teakettle off the stovetop. She tipped the kettle, preparing to pour, when the front door banged open. The loud noise caused Cheryl to jump. She gasped, and her hand holding the teakettle jerked. Hot water splashed on the counter.

"Oh no!" She returned the kettle to the stove.

Naomi rose. Levi rushed in, and Naomi's gazed moved from Cheryl to Levi and back to Cheryl. "You didn't burn yourself, did you?"

"No, nothing like that." Cheryl wiped up the spilled water with a flour sack dish towel. "I'm fine, but..." Her eyes widened as she looked to Levi. His left hand held his right one, and blood dripped from his fingers. "Are you all right?"

She grabbed the damp dish towel and hurried to him. He took two steps toward her and held out his hand. "I should have known better," he mumbled. "But the root cellar..."

"Here, let's get that to the water tap," Cheryl interrupted. She dabbed at the dripping blood with the towel. He followed her to the kitchen sink. He held his hand under the water, and she saw a pretty deep gash on his palm. He wore a puzzled expression.

Naomi hurried over to view the damage. "Levi, what happened? How did you hurt your hand?"

He turned off the water and turned to his stepmother. "It's bad, Maam." At her stricken look, he shook his head. "Not my hand, but it seems someone's gotten into the root cellar. They swiped some of the homemade candles we'd set aside for Cheryl. And a few jars of peach preserves are gone too, along with some apples."

"Someone? Who?" Naomi placed her hand over her mouth. Then she lowered her hand again, eyes wide. "Someone was in our cellar? A thief?"

Levi nodded and then pulled his hand from Cheryl's grasp. "I'm afraid so." He cleared his throat. "They dropped a jar of peaches, and I was foolish enough to pick up the broken glass."

Cheryl looked from son to stepmother. Concern creased the older woman's forehead. Was it because of worry about Levi's hand or worry about the thief? She wasn't sure. Maybe both.

Cheryl's gaze turned to Levi's hand. It had started bleeding again. Naomi spotted it too. She reached into the drawer and pulled out a clean towel. Instead of turning to Levi she glanced over at Cheryl. "Press this into his hand while I get bandages."

Cheryl nodded, finding humor in her friend's response. It seemed Naomi was bent on mothering her oldest stepson, despite the fact he was a full foot taller than her. Still, Cheryl did as she was told. She pressed the clean towel onto Levi's cut palm as Naomi hurried from the room.

Levi shifted his weight from one foot to another. "Um, I can hold that if you'd like."

"And face your mother's wrath? I know better than to disobey." She chuckled and then dared to look up into his face. Levi squinted in worry. She guessed what he was thinking: *Who would break into their cellar and steal from them? And why?*

Naomi hurried back to the kitchen, and Cheryl let her take over the doctoring. The cut looked deep, and Naomi expertly applied antibiotic cream and bandages.

"Will you need stitches?" Cheryl asked Levi.

"Nah, it's just a paper cut." Levi forced a smile and winked. "Or, if I have to, I've been known to sew . . ."

The front door swung open, slamming against the woodbox. Cheryl jumped, and their attention turned to the door. Naomi's husband Seth strode in, moving with quickened steps through the living room into the kitchen.

Seth was usually a quiet and serious man, but now he seemed frazzled. He walked toward them, and his face held a puzzled expression.

"Something wrong, Seth?" Naomi asked.

"Wrong? *Ja*, I would say something is wrong." He shook his head. "It seems to me someone's sleeping in our winter buggy."

Naomi gasped. "Sleeping in the buggy?"

Levi rubbed his brow. "It must be the same person who got into the root cellar."

Naomi took a step toward her husband. "I hope they did not get too cold last night."

"Too cold?" Cheryl muttered the words under her breath. "I'd be worried more about your safety." She knew she shouldn't interfere. It wasn't really her place. Then again, she was from Columbus. She'd seen her share of crime. She read the papers. A shudder traveled down her spine. "What if they tried to come into your house? Do you even lock the front door at night?"

Their silence told her they didn't.

"We live in Sugarcreek, Cheryl." Naomi placed a hand on Cheryl's arm. "I know this may be hard for you to understand, coming from a big city and such, but if there is someone sleeping in our buggy and poking around in our cellar, then our concern isn't so much about the taken items. But rather our biggest concern will be to help... to offer what we can."

Seth stroked his long beard, and then he clucked his tongue. "I'm not sure that's the wisest thing to do this time, Naomi." His tone was serious. "Whoever is sleeping in our buggy has some farfetched ideas about our town."

"What do you mean? How do you know?" Naomi's gaze searched her husband's face. He opened one of his balled fists and revealed a piece of paper folded inside. It appeared to be a piece of crumpled up notebook paper that someone had smoothed and then refolded. Seth unfolded it and then held it out so everyone could read the words.

There was a time when communities cared for their own, but with great loss came diminished hope. And no town could live without hope. Sugarcreek was slowly dying but nobody knew it, especially not the two men who sat on Main Street playing checkers.

MEET THE REAL PEOPLE OF SUGARCREEK

Sprinkled amid our created characters in Sugarcreek Amish Mysteries, we've fictionally depicted some of the town's real-life people and businesses. Here's a glimpse into the actual story of the owner of the Honey Bee Café.

My mom, my sister Patty, the rest of my family...Why wasn't anyone listening to me? Why wasn't God listening to me? They all knew what I wanted. I'd told them. For two years, ever since my husband, Gerry, died of injuries from a car accident, I'd been running our remodeling business in the Columbus, Ohio, suburbs on my own. Successfully, but it took up so much of my time—time I would rather be spending with our two young sons. I'd always dreamed of having my own café, a place where I would serve healthy lunches and great coffee, befriending the customers. I could set my own hours and have plenty of time with the boys.

The more I thought about it, the more I was sure we needed a fresh start. Someplace different. Someplace far away, where there wouldn't be constant reminders of Gerry and how much we missed him. I sold the remodeling business. My plan was to move to a big city with a thriving coffee culture that would provide a customer base for my café.

So why were Mom and Patty trying to get me to stay in Ohio? "I know you want to move," Patty said. "How about closer to all of us? You need family around you." She kept tossing me suggestions, places she'd heard were up for sale.

Her latest? Some building in the heart of Ohio Amish country, in the town of Sugarcreek, near where we grew up. "It's right on Main Street. Used to be a hardware store, so it's roomy," she said. "Perfect for your café. Come take a look!"

I agreed mainly to get her off my back. One spring day in 2012, I drove the two hours to Sugarcreek and parked at 993 West Main Street. A three-story structure with a sagging front porch. *What a wreck!* I thought. I would've turned around and driven off if Patty and the real-estate agent hadn't been waiting with such hopeful expressions on their faces.

The place did not look much better on the inside. "This building is one hundred and fifty years old," the agent told me.

And definitely showing its age. What the place needed—new roof, new floors, new everything—went beyond an extreme makeover. "Thank you, but this isn't going to work for me," I told the agent. But the whole two hours back to Columbus, I couldn't stop thinking about that old building. Visualizing it coming to life. Neighbors having coffee on the porch. Tourists stopping by for my bacon-apple-and-cheddar grilled cheese. The boys and me living on the top floor, their after-school snacks coming from my café menu.

Thank You for Your patience, God, I prayed. *I get it now. I'm the one who wasn't listening.*

I called the real-estate agent and put in an offer. It was accepted. Construction started in February 2013. I hired a four-man Amish crew that Gerry and I had worked with. We tried to preserve the character of the building, reusing old cabinets, windows, and doors. Soon I was on a first-name basis with Marlin at the lumberyard. Folks came right over to say hello. Amish families stopped by to wish us well. A Mennonite woman brought us homemade soup. It felt healing to be in a small town where everyone knew and cared about their neighbors. And to be closer to my family. My sister was right. The best customer base I could ever hope for was right here.

My siblings and I came up with the name Honey Bee Café— in honor of our dad, who kept bees as a hobby. I put together the menu, including honey muffins, honey oatmeal cookies, and the Honeycomb, a custom coffee concoction sweetened with vanilla syrup and honey. Now to find a honey supplier. One afternoon a man I recognized from Winfield United Methodist Church, Mr. Andrews, drove up in his truck. "I run an apiary," he said. "I hear you need honey."

I wanted everything else to be locally grown and made too, to support the community that had welcomed my boys and me. Produce and cheese from Amish farms. Fresh bread from the Dutch Valley Bakery.

The Honey Bee Café opened last July. It's more than a coffee and sandwich shop. It's a gathering place for folks to listen to music (we have a piano for anyone to play) or meet up after choir practice. And of course, it's our home.

When I told Mom that the boys and I were moving to 993 West Main Street in Sugarcreek, she said, "That's the old hardware store, right? You know who used to live on the top floor?"

I had no idea.

"Your great-grandma Ida. I used to visit her there."

No wonder I felt so at home.

Recently I got a call from the editor of Sugarcreek Amish Mysteries, a series of novels featuring two women, an Englisher and her Amish friend, who work together to solve mysteries set here in town. The editor wanted to include the café and me in the books. I couldn't be more thrilled. There's a scene where one of the sleuths comes to the Honey Bee for her favorite bacon-apple-and-cheddar grilled cheese. Now that's a woman after my own heart.

A Note from the Editors

We hope you enjoyed *Sugarcreek Amish Mysteries*, published by the Books and Inspirational Media Division of Guideposts, a nonprofit organization that touches millions of lives every day through products and services that inspire, encourage, help you grow in your faith, and celebrate God's love.

Thank you for making a difference with your purchase of this book, which helps fund our many outreach programs to military personnel, prisons, hospitals, nursing homes, and educational institutions.

We also create many useful and uplifting online resources. Visit Guideposts.org to read true stories of hope and inspiration, access OurPrayer network, sign up for free newsletters, download free e-books, join our Facebook community, and follow our stimulating blogs.

To learn about other Guideposts publications, including the best-selling devotional *Daily Guideposts*, go to Guideposts.org/Shop, call (800) 932-2145, or write to Guideposts, PO Box 5815, Harlan, Iowa 51593.